Straight Fire

NEW YORK TIMES BESTSELLING AUTHOR

ABBI GLINES

Copyright © 2023 by Abbi Glines
All rights reserved.
Visit my website at
www.abbiglinesbooks.com

Cover Designer: Damonza.com
Editor: Jovana Shirley, Unforeseen Editing
www.unforeseenediting.com
Formatting: Melissa Stevens, The Illustrated Author
www.theillustratedauthor.com

No part of this book may be reproduced or transmitted in any form or by any means, electronic or mechanical, including photocopying, recording, or by any information storage and retrieval system without the written permission of the author, except for the use of brief quotations in a book review.

This book is a work of fiction. Names, characters, places, and incidents either are products of the author's imagination or are used fictitiously. Any resemblance to actual persons, living or dead, events, or locales is entirely coincidental.

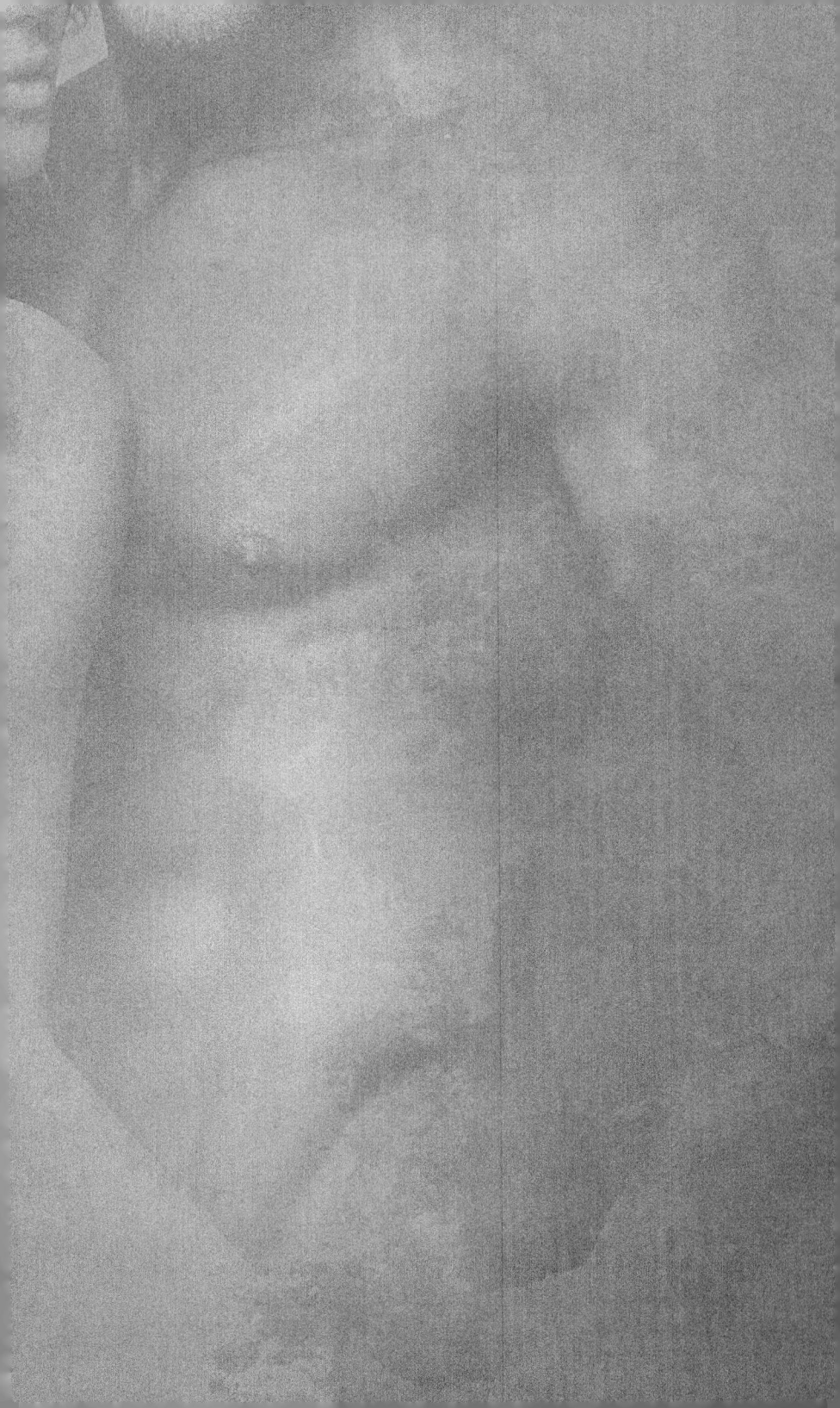

*To my husband, Britt.
Without you there wouldn't have been a Gage.*

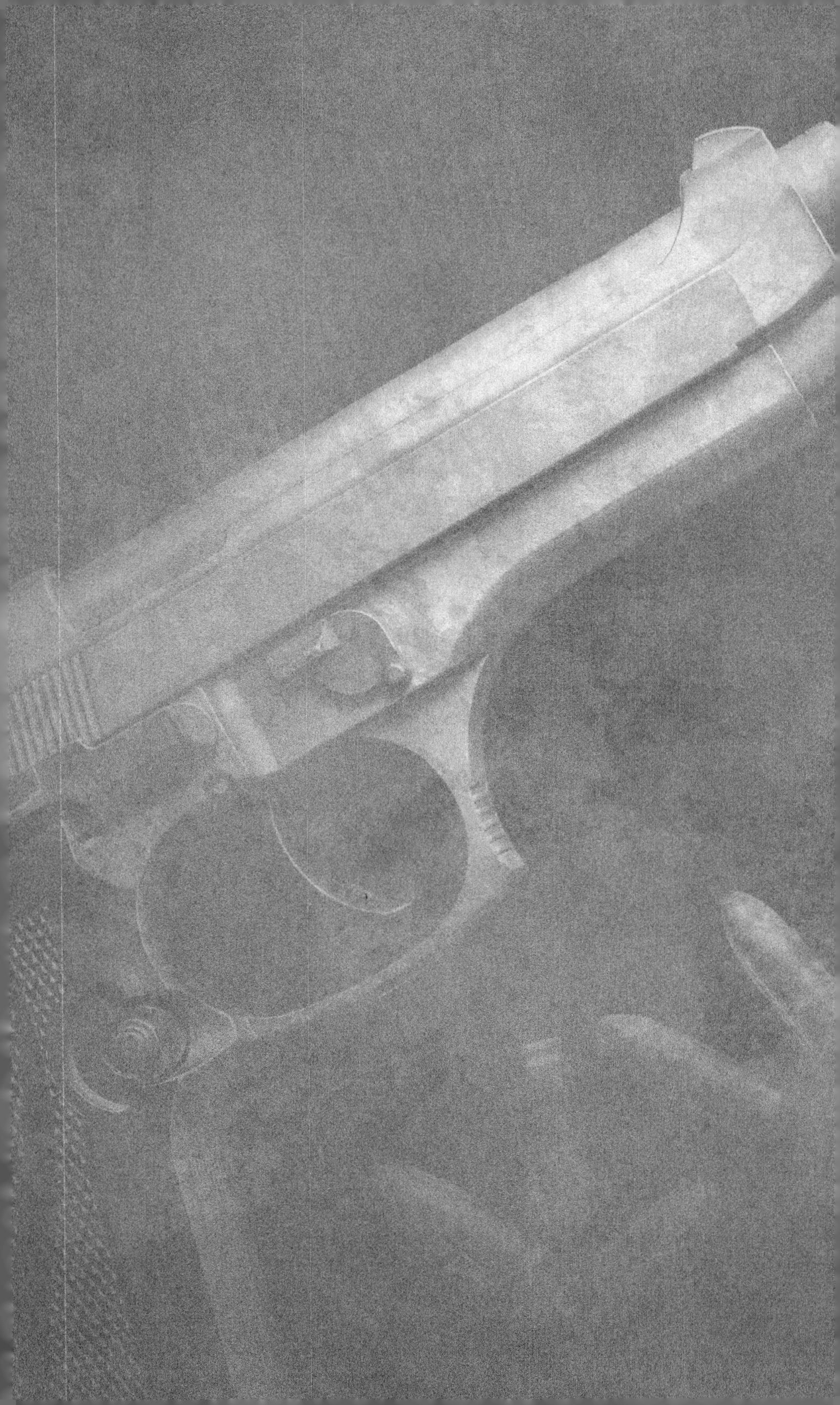

I

"What's past is prologue."
—*William Shakespeare*

to try:

Rocky Road ice cream with potato chips

~~Whoopie Pies~~ lavender? yum!!

Questions for Gage -

Chapter ONE

SHILOH

I was a list-maker. I made lists about everything. I followed the lists, and I achieved my goals. It was why I always carried a notebook and pen with me. Using technology for my list-making didn't feel the same. Physically writing on paper was the only way the system worked for me.

My uncle Neil, Mom's older brother, glanced over at the notebook in my lap as he drove his truck to our appointment. He was nervous about where we were going, which, to be honest, intrigued me.

Working for my uncle was the only job I knew. He'd hired me eighteen months ago when I left my life in Boston and came to Ocala, Florida. My parents, especially my mother, were furious. She rarely called me, and the few times we had spoken, it had been harsh. I'd let her down by choosing a life she felt was beneath me. Getting up every day and going to my uncle's private practice gave me stability and purpose.

Most of my lists consisted of things to get done in the office. It was something she would never understand.

"A few important details we need to go over," Uncle Neil said, snapping me out of my thoughts. "I have your signed NDA and the other paperwork, but I want to make sure you understand the seriousness of the situation."

I turned to give him my full attention in hopes of assuring him I would be fine. This wasn't the first house call I'd made with him. Since Lynn, his former nurse, had gotten married and moved, I had been going with him to check on patients that he made house calls to. They were all wealthy people who couldn't be bothered with going to an actual hospital or doctor's office. I had found it was for privacy purposes with most of them. This patient, however, seemed to have a new level of privacy attached to them. I had never been required to sign an NDA before.

"This isn't a normal house. There are things you will see and hear that you will question. Don't. And when I say don't, I mean, DO NOT ask any questions, do not repeat anything you hear, do not use your cell phone while on the property, do not engage with any of them unless they ask you a question. You are to simply do what you're being paid to do. Take care of the patient. He will be difficult. He will be inappropriate, and honestly, if he wasn't in such bad shape, I wouldn't let you near him. Being as it is, he can't do much. There is a woman in the house. I've met her. She's very nice and kind. But do not make friends with her. She is Huck Kingston's fiancée, and he's very protective of her."

I nodded my head. This wasn't the first time he had given me this lecture since he'd called me this morning to let me know he had a job for me. It was obvious he was nervous about my being in this house. I had asked if they were famous, not that I cared. It was rare I knew or recognized anyone famous. They weren't famous. They were just powerful.

"I'll be fine. I promise."

He reached over and squeezed my hand. "I know you will. I just don't want anything bad to happen to you. These are dangerous people, and they are connected to a very powerful family."

"Yes, the Hugheses. They own a lot of stuff. Horses and things," I replied. I wasn't sure why that made them so important, but I'd heard my uncle mention them with reverence and respect more than once since I'd been working with him.

We stopped outside a large iron gate, and Uncle Neil pressed a code, then spoke his full name into a speaker. The gate slowly swung open. It was very secure and a bit over the top, but I didn't say that. Uncle Neil might turn around and take me back to the office if I said something negative.

"The patient has a punctured lung, three broken ribs, a leg cast due to the severity of his break, and what else?" I asked, wanting to make sure I remembered everything.

I had read over his chart that Uncle Neil had given me, but I wanted to make sure I'd missed nothing. The full leg cast was temporary and would be cut down to below his knee in two weeks. However, three weeks recovery time is suggested. That had been written at the bottom in red.

"Bruised ego and an anger issue," he replied with a frown. "That is the most important thing for you to remember."

I gave him a firm nod. "He's mean and angry. Got it."

Uncle Neil gave me another stern look. "I'll do the talking. You speak when required. I've been working for this family for over twenty years. I have a good relationship with them, and for the most part, I do trust them." He paused, then sighed. "Let's go meet the patient."

3

Uncle Neil had already done the surgery. This had all happened in the middle of the night.

"He is sedated for now. That will give us enough time to introduce you to the others here and go over what you need to handle," he told me as we walked up the front steps to the house.

One of the large double doors opened when we reached the top step. A Viking-sized man filled the door with a scowl on his face. I paused because he was intimidating and slightly terrifying. That was one thing Uncle Neil hadn't mentioned.

"He's awake and bitching," the massive man said. "Can you shut him the fuck up?"

Uncle Neil chuckled and nodded his head. "I should have figured he'd be hard to sedate for long. Huck, this is my niece, Shiloh. She is my replacement for Lynn and understands the importance of your privacy."

Huck's gaze swung to me, and his scowl deepened. The way he was looking at me would make me believe he disliked me on sight. "Shiloh." He said my name as if he knew me and, again, wasn't a fan.

That caused me some concern because I knew that perhaps he did know me—or the me before. The me I didn't know myself. This had happened a few times since my return to Ocala, but not once had someone acted as if they didn't like me. I did, however, have a few reservations about the former Shiloh.

Uncle Neil cleared his throat. "Uh, yes." He glanced at me with a worried frown. It wasn't like I could answer this. "She's responsible and excellent at bedside care. Gage's personality will require someone who isn't easily upset. Shiloh works well in that department."

Huck continued to study me, as if waiting for me to say something. I smiled in return. If these people did their research, they'd find my picture and name on my uncle's website. He could have known who I was for that reason because if he knew the former me, he wasn't saying it. Finally, he stepped back to allow us to enter.

"I'll let Gage make this call," he said, still watching me with unease.

Uncle Neil went inside first, and I followed him. Curious as to why Huck didn't seem pleased with my being the nurse. I did hope Uncle Neil had noticed and would perhaps broach the subject.

"I'll take her upstairs and deal with the patient," Uncle Neil told him.

Huck was still scowling, but he simply gave a nod, then walked away.

Uncle Neil turned to me. "Ready?"

"Yep," I replied.

The tension in his shoulders and tight line of his mouth made it clear he had noticed Huck's odd behavior toward me. Why hadn't he said something? My uncle tried to shelter me from the life I used to have. It didn't bother me normally because I preferred to not have to ask questions. But if I was going to be in this house regularly, then I thought it needed to be addressed.

If they had known the Shiloh Ellis before two years ago, then they needed to know she no longer existed. I'd forgotten her life the moment I hit the black ice and crashed into the side of a mountain.

Chapter TWO

GAGE

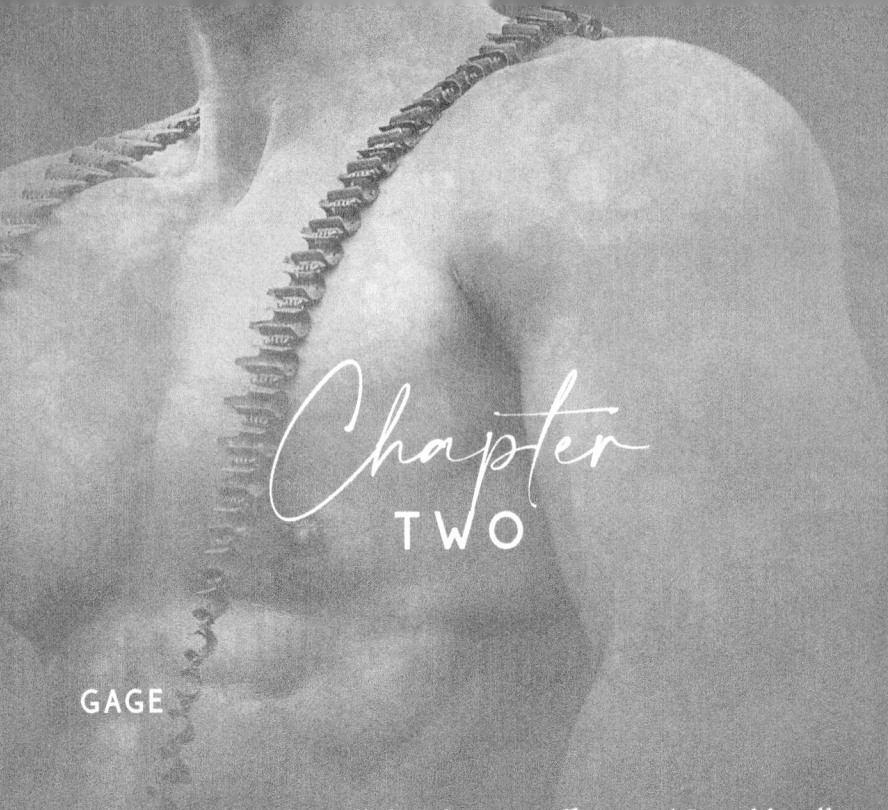

Fucking hell. When all this shit was off me and I could walk again, there were some motherfuckers who were going to die slow, brutal deaths. How the fuck was I supposed to stay in this house for a week, much less two? There was no way in hell I was going to be down for three weeks, like Carmichael had suggested.

I tried to sit up, but the pain in my chest stopped me. FUCK! That hurt like a bitch. Bastard who had stabbed me was going to be sliced to pieces while he bled to death. Dammit, why had I walked into the place like Rambo? Levi and Huck would have been there in ten minutes. I could have waited, and this shit wouldn't have happened.

The door to my bedroom opened, and Dr. Carmichael entered the room. Thank fuck. I needed some painkillers or a fifth of whiskey. I opened my mouth to tell him this when my gaze locked on the woman walking in behind him. Maybe the meds hadn't worn off after all because there was no fucking way Shiloh Ellis had walked into my room.

"Gage," Carmichael said, but I didn't look away from the raven-haired female behind him.

Why the fuck couldn't she have aged poorly? Was it not enough that the bitch had been so damn beautiful that it hurt when she was a teenager? I was high. Had to be. This was not happening. Shiloh wasn't a fucking nurse. She had never even done a chore in her life. The idea that she'd lift a perfectly manicured finger to play nurse to anyone, especially me, made me want to laugh.

"This is my niece, Shiloh. She's taking Lynn's place now that she's moved away," the good doc told me.

Taking my eyes off her was difficult, but I did.

"Am I fucking high?" I asked him. "I thought the meds had worn off because I'm hurting like a son of a bitch."

Carmichael frowned. "It's almost time for you to have more. Where is your pain scale? One to ten?"

I wanted to shout at her to get the fuck out of my sight. If this was real and she was standing in this room, then someone was going to pay. I glared at her, and I saw her smile falter. The uncertainty in her gaze was almost believable.

"Gage?" Carmichael asked again.

"Ten," I bit out.

This was a fucking dream. Drug-induced sleep. There was no way that Shiloh Ellis would be in my house. No, she would be married to her med-school boyfriend by now, living a country-club life in Boston.

"Shiloh has read your chart and is aware of your injuries. She will be here during the day to make sure you're healing properly. I have complete faith in her abilities, and she will contact me if there is any question at all."

It was her. There was no other chance in hell that her fucking doppelgänger lived in Ocala with the exact same name. Seriously, if this was real, had Huck not seen her? He wouldn't have let her in the fucking house.

"Gage?" Carmichael said my name again, and I gave her one last look before turning to him.

"Yes, Doc. Uh, pain. Yeah, it hurts like a motherfucker," I replied.

His glaze flicked to his niece for a moment, then back to me. I could see the unease in his expression. Wouldn't she have told him when she saw my chart? This was a bad idea, but then again, this couldn't be happening. She hadn't lived in Ocala in five years. She was not a damn nurse.

"Just the chest or the leg too?" he asked me.

"Both, but the chest is the worst."

Carmichael turned to look at Shiloh. "Morphine."

She nodded, then walked over to the IV drip. My eyes followed her. No acknowledgment at all. Even in my drug-or-concussion-brought-on dreams, wouldn't she recognize me? Remember me? Fuck yes, she would.

"I'm going to give Shiloh a run-through of where things are. The meds will kick in soon, so in case you're asleep when I'm done, I'll be back tomorrow morning unless I'm needed before then."

Turning my attention back to the doctor, I could see his thoughts churning. He didn't look as if he was comfortable with leaving his niece with me. *Oh no, Doc. My dream, my decision.* She was staying. I'd deal with her ass. Make her regret being a lying bitch.

"Thanks, Doc. I'm sure we will be just fine."

His gaze flicked to his niece, and he sighed, then nodded.

I listened as he told her about my medications and where they were, along with my bandages and other things. That made me fucking laugh. Yeah, tell Shiloh Ellis where to find my bandages for the gnarly knife wound on my chest. I was sure she'd happily get right on cleaning that shit up. He lowered his voice, and I couldn't hear what he said. You'd think my dreams would be more agreeable.

The door opened, then closed as their voices trailed off down the hallway. I began to feel the effects of the morphine a little and sighed in relief—or maybe my dream was shifting. I closed my eyes. This would end, and then someone else would appear. Perhaps it could be one of the strippers at Devil's who liked to eat pussy as much as she liked to suck cock. I'd prefer to have one of them taking care of me. Fuck, anyone would be better than Shiloh.

My eyes were getting fucking heavy when the door opened again. Except it wasn't a stripper or some nurse from a porn I'd watched. It was Huck.

What the hell was wrong with my head? Could I not get better dreams than this?

"What the fuck are you doing in here?" I grumbled.

"I'd think that was obvious. I'm assuming you want her out. Is that what I should tell Carmichael? I thought you'd handle it, but he's showing her around like she's staying."

I smirked, but didn't open my eyes. "Sure. Let Shiloh fucking Ellis stay. Because that makes complete sense. A fucking nurse. Yeah, right. The princess is all about getting her hands dirty."

Huck sighed. "Are you doped up on the meds?"

"Yep, and dreaming fucked up shit about Shiloh," I drawled. My tongue felt thick.

"You're not dreaming, Gage. It's her. Carmichael is her uncle. She's working as his nurse. Not a dream. Now, what the fuck do you want me to do about it?"

I chuckled. This shit was rich. My eyes felt like they had lead weights on them, and I felt pretty damn good.

"Fucking hell," I heard Huck growl.

That was the last thing I remembered him saying before he faded away.

Chapter THREE

SHILOH

Uncle Neil continued to go over things with me and make sure I knew where to locate everything that I could possibly need. When he was done, he turned and leveled his gaze on me. This was his serious look.

"I think I need to go talk to Huck," he said with a deep sigh. "Gage isn't always pleasant. He can be cruel and dangerous. The way he was looking at you makes me think he recognized you and wasn't happy with your appearance. Huck had also looked at you as if he knew you. Them knowing you, however, seems very unlikely since they are five years older than you." Uncle Neil's eyebrows were scrunched together in a frown. "I just want to talk to Huck first. Make sure he understands the situation. I can't leave you here until I know that the odd behavior from Gage was just from the pain he was in."

I wanted to argue. It was time for me to prove I could do a job this serious. I wanted to do more. Get out of the office.

However, I had noticed the disgusted look in Gage's eyes too. It was smart to discuss it and clear things up. If he hated the former me, he needn't worry. We were nothing alike. I hadn't liked her choices in life either. Which was why I was here instead of in Boston.

The other thing I was slightly concerned with was that I was attracted to Gage Presley. That was a first for me. Sure, I noticed when people were nice-looking, but I wasn't ever drawn to them. I didn't want to look at them or touch them. It was one of the many reasons my engagement had ended. The woman who had said yes to Isaac Jeffrey was not the woman I was today. That man had been intolerable.

Seeing Gage Presley shirtless, even though he was bandaged and badly bruised, had made my stomach flutter. For a moment, I had wondered what arms like that felt like. The muscle ripples on his stomach had been fascinating. Perhaps I wasn't completely broken in that area. There was definitely a strong admiration for the way that man looked stirring inside me.

I followed my uncle into the kitchen. He'd pointed it out while showing me other areas I would need to be familiar with but he hadn't taken me in there. Huck was leaning against the counter with a cigarette between his lips, scowling at his phone. There was another man at the table who looked up at us and nodded. His eyes, however, scanned over me with a look of distaste.

"Excuse me, gentlemen, but I think there might be an issue we need to discuss," my uncle began.

Huck's eyes lifted from his phone, and then he glanced back at the other man in the room before giving Uncle Neil his attention. I was thankful he kept his glacial-blue eyes off me. He made me nervous. The man was a brick wall.

Straight Fire

Uncle Neil cleared his throat, then shifted his gaze to me. "Uh, I believe—or I am concerned that Gage might have known Shiloh before. I can't see how they would have crossed paths since she is so much younger than all of you. You wouldn't have even been in high school at the same time."

Huck's glare was once again trained on me.

"You ask Shiloh about it?" Huck replied.

Uncle Neil cleared his voice again. He did that when he was uncomfortable. I had noticed it in the office when he dealt with patients.

"Yes, well, you see"—he looked at me again—"Shiloh had an accident two years ago. Her car hit black ice. She had severe head trauma and was in a coma for a few days. When she did wake up, she didn't know who she was. Shiloh has focal retrograde amnesia, which means she has the ability to form new memories and her intelligence and the ability to learn new skills are intact. She, however, remembers nothing about her life before the accident," Uncle Neil explained.

This had once bothered me. Not knowing myself or anyone in my life. I'd gone through a series of emotions, but in the end, I had come to accept that I'd been given another chance. I chose to make the best of it and build a new life. One that made me happy.

I finally met Huck's steady glare. He was studying me as if he wasn't sure he believed this or not. I'd gotten that a lot too. Especially from Isaac. It seemed hard for people to accept that I truly had no memory of them at all. Isaac had kept trying to make me that girl again by forcing things I had once enjoyed on me. When I was honest and told him that those things didn't appeal to me, he would get angry. Since leaving him and Boston, I had less migraines, dizzy spells, and seizures. The pressure he had put on me hadn't been good for me or my well-being. Something my mother refused to accept.

"Hmm," Huck replied, then took another pull from his cigarette.

"If there is an issue with her being here, I can find someone else. It might take a few days. I need to make some calls. It's the trust factor, of course. I trust Shiloh completely. Finding someone else that I trust with this situation will be a little harder."

Huck looked back at the other man for a moment. It was as if they were having a silent conversation. Finally, he turned back to Uncle Neil.

"She can stay until you find someone else," he replied.

My stomach sank. I wanted this job. The urge to argue my case was strong, but Uncle Neil would be angry if I said anything.

"Very well. I will start working on a replacement right away," he replied. Then turned to me. "I'll be back at six to check on the patient and take you home."

I felt a lump in my throat but refused to let any of them see that this affected me. "Okay."

The sympathy in his gaze didn't help the disappointment. He looked like he wanted to hug me, but he didn't. I watched him give the men a nod before he turned to leave. I started to follow him. I needed to go check on the patient, and I also wanted to get away from the other two men. At least the one upstairs, although he didn't like me either, was injured and needed my help.

"Stay." Huck's command startled me.

Slowly, I turned back around to face him.

"I need to go see if he's awake now and talk to him before you go back up there," he told me.

What I should do was say *okay* or just nod. Instead, "He knew me?" came out of my mouth.

Huck's cold glare returned. "Unfortunately," he replied, then walked away, leaving me alone with the other man.

Straight Fire

My eyes met the man sitting at the table as he studied me. He didn't appear as angry, but he wasn't giving me a welcoming feeling either.

"Since you don't remember, I'm Levi," he said, "and shit around here is about to get real fucking interesting,"

Chapter FOUR

GAGE

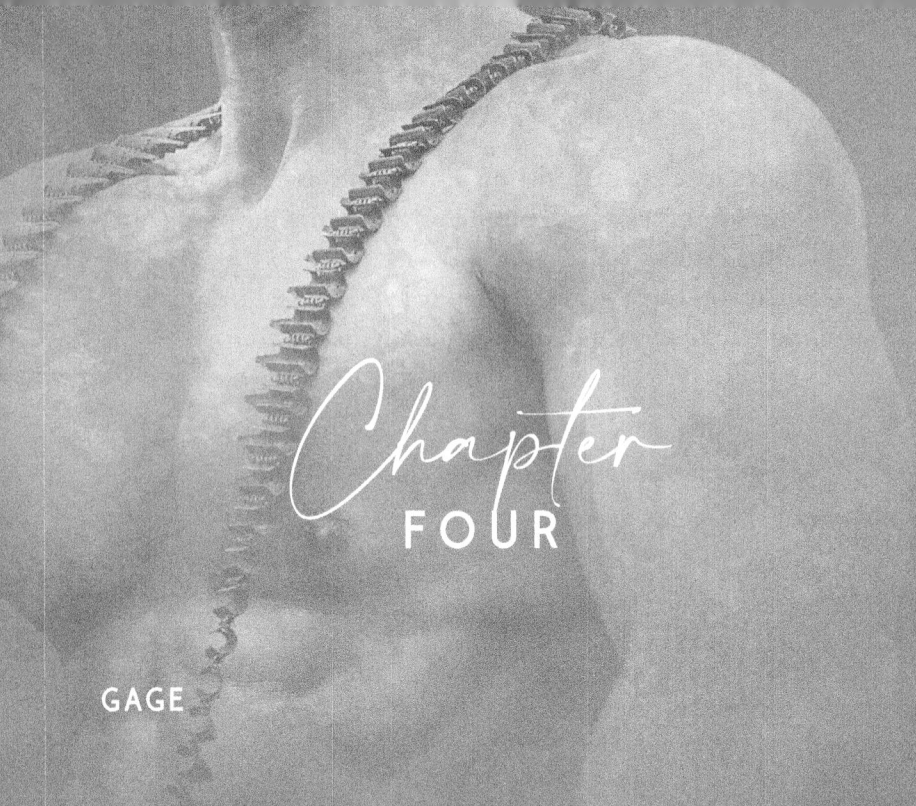

My eyes opened just as Huck walked in the room.

He closed the door, then turned to me. "You still fucking high?" he asked.

How the hell was I supposed to know? He wasn't Shiloh Ellis, so that was a good sign that I wasn't tripping anymore.

"Not sure," I muttered.

"Do you remember Shiloh Ellis coming in here with the doc?"

Fuck.

"Yeah, I'm still high," I confirmed. "Because you wouldn't be talking about fucking Shiloh."

Huck muttered a string of curse words. "You're not fucking high. Shiloh is in the damn kitchen. But I told Carmichael to get someone else. He said to give him a couple days. He needs to find someone he trusts and who's willing to come into this house and work."

I groaned. "Sure. Whatever," I mumbled and closed my eyes. Once the fucking morphine wore off, I wasn't taking any more of that shit. Hallucinating was supposed to be fun.

"Fuck, Gage. Will you listen to me? She's going to bring her ass up here to check on you in a few minutes. She was in a car accident two years ago and now has fucking amnesia and doesn't remember shit. At least nothing before the accident. Carmichael called it retro ... fuck, I can't remember."

I opened my eyes and turned my head to look at him. "What the fuck are you talking about? My fucking subconscious is not this creative."

He scowled. "Carmichael explained it in more detail. He picked up that we fucking hate her and of course had no idea we knew her. She didn't say anything because she doesn't remember shit."

Amnesia? I had to process this. That girl had fucked with my head. No, she'd fucking ripped out my heart. After her, I'd never given anyone else the chance to get close enough to matter. My life was good. I'd gotten what I'd wanted. The Hugheses trusted me and let me in the family. This was what I was meant to do, and for a moment, I had almost let that bitch take it away from me. I didn't love her—that emotion was bullshit. She had been an obsession I couldn't shake, even when she fucked me over. It had taken me too long to get her out of my head.

"Question is, can you handle her staying? You need someone who can take care of you during the day, and for now, she's all we've got."

Could I handle seeing her? She didn't mean shit to me anymore. Whatever I'd felt for her had been dead for years. If she didn't remember anything, then what the fuck did it matter if she was here?

"I don't give a fuck. I just need to get this shit healed so I can get out of this fucking bed and go kill the fuckers who put me here."

"She doesn't act like the same person," Huck pointed out. "Just want to make sure where your head is. Where Shiloh Ellis is concerned … well, she was your crazy trigger."

He paused, and I knew what he was fucking thinking. That was no longer the case. She didn't hold that power over me anymore.

"Not anymore. That shit is dead."

Huck nodded. "All right. Then, until we get a replacement, she stays."

He turned and walked out of the room, and I stared at the ceiling. She might not remember, but I did. I wasn't that stupid pussy-whipped kid anymore. Life had changed.

EIGHT YEARS AGO

"Who the fuck is she?" The beer in my hand paused as I stared at the hottest piece of ass I'd ever laid eyes on.

"Jailbait," Huck replied.

"There's no way. The one with black hair, fucking killer tits, and legs I want wrapped around my waist."

"I know who you're talking about. Jackson's girlfriend. Why the fuck he has a girlfriend, I don't know. He could have different pussy every day. He's leaving for Georgia in a week, and when he's the quarterback for an SEC team next year, he's gonna have pussy thrown at him."

I smirked. He might be a football star, but he was still a kid. The only reason he got invited to the parties we had was because of his football status and his father's connection with the Hugheses.

"Get that fucking grin off your face. She's sixteen years old. Stay the fuck away from her," Huck said before standing up.

Sixteen? Shit. Remembering Jackson had just graduated high school was hard. He was six foot four and had fucking facial hair.

I started to look away from her and go find some other bitch to suck my dick when blue eyes locked with mine. Fuck me. It felt like I'd been kicked in the chest. That was just fucking cruel. Sixteen? Fuck! I needed to look elsewhere, but damn if I could bring myself to.

Her full red lips turned up, and a dimple appeared. This might be the first time I'd gotten a hard-on over a fucking dimple. Jesus Christ, she was smoking hot. They had not made sixteen-year-old girls like that when I was in high school.

She turned her head to look up at Jackson, and I instantly tensed up. Like I had the right to be pissed she was talking to her boyfriend. But damn if my hands didn't ball up into fists and my heart didn't start hammering. Yeah, I was gonna need to go fuck someone and forget about that one. She was trouble I didn't need. My dad was already pissed off about having to get me out of jail last week for public indecency.

"You look lonely." Natalia—*or was it Talia?*—straddled me and sat down in my lap, facing me.

Distraction. She'd make a good one.

I put my hands on her waist and grinned at her. "You wanna fix that?"

She bit her bottom lip and nodded. The girl was a favorite around here. Especially since she could take on me and Levi at the same time.

I slid my hands up and cupped her tits. "My cock needs sucked," I told her before pulling down one side of her bikini top and rubbing her nipple.

She moaned and slid her hips forward until her pussy was over my hard cock.

"Talia, looks like that pregnancy didn't slow you down any."

My fucking cock jerked from the delicate, sweet sound. The girl in my arms tensed, but my attention wasn't on her anymore. My eyes locked on the owner of the voice that reminded me of fucking honey or an expensive bourbon. Those damn crystal-clear blue eyes met mine, and I could see the mischievous glint that she wasn't even trying to hide.

"What the fuck are you talking about?" Talia snapped at her.

She lifted her tanned shoulders, which I wanted to lick, and barely gave Talia a glance. "Oh, you know, word gets around almost as fast as you do."

Damn, this baby had a bite. One corner of her mouth curled as she held my gaze. I was fascinated, and this was not fucking good. I couldn't fuck her out of my system—she was too goddamn young.

"Bitch," Talia snarled at her and started to get out of my lap, but I put my hands on top of her thighs to hold her there.

"What's your name?" I asked.

"Shiloh," she replied.

There was a challenge in those blue eyes. One I wasn't going to accept.

"You always this nasty, or was this just an excuse to talk to me?"

The way her expression changed for just a moment, as if I had struck her, made my chest tighten in an uncomfortable way that I was going to ignore. For both our sakes, she needed to get away from me.

Straight Fire

"Hey, baby," Jackson's fucking voice called out. She turned to look back at him as he came up to her and slid his hand around her waist. My body went rigid as I glared at his hand on her before jerking my gaze to Jackson and forcing a smile.

"Need to keep baby on a leash," I told him, then smirked and turned my attention back to Talia. "Come on, love. You can suck my dick now," I told her, then pressed a kiss to her mouth.

Jackson chuckled. "We'll leave you to that."

I didn't look back at them as they left, but damn if it wasn't difficult.

Chapter FIVE

SHILOH
PRESENT DAY

Gage had been asleep since I had returned to the room. For that, I was grateful, but I knew it was almost time to clean his knife wound, then change his bandage. Waking him up was not something I wanted to do.

My gaze kept going from the book on my e-reader to his bare chest. I had reread the same page five times, and I still had no idea what was happening. This was my first time seeing a man shirtless with a body like that. I mean, sure, I'd seen them on television or in ads. It was different, seeing it in real life. The fact that I was going to have to touch his chest to clean his wound and change his bandages should not excite me. He was hurt and sleeping, yet here I sat, ogling him. Shaking my head, I forced my gaze back to the book.

Focus on the words, Shiloh. That man is your patient. He's dangerous, and he apparently hates you.

I shifted in my seat nervously, thinking about that issue. I wasn't sure I'd ever know what I had done to make these guys dislike me so much. Asking them seemed like a bad idea. I wasn't allowed to ask questions. Talking to them in general was probably not going to be taken well.

"Fuck," Gage groaned, his deep voice husky from sleep.

I snapped my head up to meet his gaze. He was looking at me through his long, thick eyelashes. His amber-colored eyes were disarming enough. It seemed unfair that he'd gotten those lashes to go with them.

"You weren't a drug-induced dream."

I winced. Just my luck that the first man I found attractive couldn't stand me.

"So, you don't remember shit?" he asked.

I shook my head. "Nothing past waking up in the hospital room."

"How convenient," he said, then tried to move but grunted instead.

"How is your pain?" I put my e-reader down and stood up to go help him.

"Oh, I don't know, Shiloh. I was stabbed in the fucking chest, hit with a metal pole a few times. What the fuck do you think?"

I ignored his snarly voice and tried not to show how the image he'd just put in my head bothered me. "You need to move a little. Even if it is to scoot up some on your pillow," I told him.

"I can fucking move myself."

No, he couldn't, but I wasn't about to force him to let me. I stood there and waited on him to try. The furious expression on his face as he attempted to and failed made my chest ache. He was only causing himself more pain.

"Whatever I did to you, I am sorry. I won't be here long. I'm sure my uncle will get a replacement. But please, while I am here, let me help you," I begged.

He was going to open his wound back up if he wasn't careful.

His hate-filled eyes locked on mine. "I don't fucking care that you lost your memory. Because I didn't. And if there is one thing I wish I could do, it would be to wipe you from mine." He muttered another curse, then nodded his head toward the door. "Go get Huck or Levi if I need moving."

I nodded. "Let me clean the wound, then change your bandages. Do you need me to get the urinal? Uncle Neil took the catheter out and said you didn't want to use it."

"You're not going anywhere near my fucking dick," he snapped at me.

I'd expected that. "When I go down to get one of them to move you, can I get you anything to eat? Are you hungry yet?"

This was my first experience with being spoken to like this. That had to be why I felt sick to my stomach. I was thankful that I'd be leaving soon. I no longer wanted this job. Working in the office was just fine.

"Trinity will bring me my meals. I don't want you touching my food," he replied.

Of course. He didn't want me doing anything, it would seem. He also didn't want to breathe the same air as me.

I went to get the supplies for his wound and took a moment to regroup. He was screwing with my emotions in a way I wasn't used to, but maybe that could be a good thing. It was a learning experience for me.

Look on the bright side, Shiloh.

Turning back to him, I focused on what had to be done. The least I could do was make sure he was taken care of properly while I was here. If I couldn't touch him, then it was going to be impossible to give him a sponge bath. I'd let Uncle Neil figure out how to handle that one.

Gage could despise me all he wanted. I wasn't here to make friends, and I'd never see him again once I left.

When I reached up to take the bandage off, his hand wrapped around my wrist so tightly that it was painful. I shot my eyes up to his face, afraid I'd hurt him.

"If you have to touch me, make it quick," he said through clenched teeth.

I nodded, but said nothing. My heart was in my throat, and the grip he had on my wrist was getting painful enough to make my eyes water. I let out a gasp when he let me go. My eyes did a quick glance at my wrist and saw the imprint of his fingers. I was probably going to bruise. My pale skin always bruised easily.

Staying focused and working as quickly as I could, I didn't speak or make eye contact with him. I wanted to breathe a sigh of relief when I was finished and could move away.

"I'll go get one of the other men to help you move and set out the urinal. Perhaps one of them will help you with using that too," I said before exiting the room.

I closed the door behind me and leaned back against it a moment to catch my breath and rub my sore wrist. Any harder, and he'd have broken it. I wasn't sure I could come back here tomorrow if Uncle Neil didn't have a replacement yet. The way Gage had looked at me, it'd felt like he could actually kill me and would enjoy it.

"You okay?" a female voice asked.

I turned my head toward her, quickly dropping my wrist back to my side. A beautiful brunette with a kind smile and a tray of food in her hands was walking toward me. This must be Trinity.

I nodded and forced a smile. "Yes. Fine. Just taking a minute. I was going to find one of the other men to help Gage move a little and use the urinal. He doesn't, uh, want me to help ... or touch him at all," I explained.

She set the tray down on a table beside the door, then turned back to me and held out her hand. "I'm Trinity. You met my fiancé already, Huck," she said.

I slipped my hand in hers. "Shiloh. It's nice to meet you and to see a face that isn't glaring at me like I'm the spawn of Satan."

She let out a small laugh, and her brown eyes danced with amusement. "This bunch would likely welcome the spawn of Satan."

I glanced back at the door and thought she might have a point.

"I'm sorry he's being difficult. Huck explained things to me. This has to be uncomfortable for you."

I shrugged. "Only because he hates me and I have no idea why. I won't be here long though, so hopefully, the next nurse makes him happy."

Trinity grinned again and shook her head. "Honestly, even with what I've been told, I'm struggling to believe Gage is still angry with you, but then he's a hard one to understand. I don't think anyone truly knows what goes on in his head."

That didn't ease my mind. "The sooner I'm gone, the better. I think the sight of me makes him ill. Which doesn't speed up his recovery at all. Getting me out of here will help. Not sure I'll return tomorrow. I'm going to suggest that my uncle take a day off from the office and stay here."

After he saw my wrist, he would probably do that anyway.

Trinity looked disappointed. "I understand. Gage can be scary. I've been on his shit list once. Never want to experience it again."

I frowned. I wanted to ask her how she had been on his shit list, but I didn't. Gage must have a death wish himself if he'd done something to scare Huck's fiancée. Uncle Neil had told me not to make friends with her or ask questions. So, I kept my curiosity in check.

"If you don't mind, I think he'd prefer you stay in there while he eats. I can wait out here," I told her.

She pressed her lips together and nodded. Relieved I had some time away from him, I wanted to thank her but figured I'd better just leave it at that.

"Go downstairs and get something to eat," she told me. "I made chicken salad and set out some croissants. There is also a bowl of fresh berries and some whipped topping for them."

There was no way I was going down there. Not with those two angry men in this house. I was hungry, but I could wait until I got home. "I'm fine, but thanks."

The concerned look in her eyes made me think she was going to argue, but she didn't. Instead, she picked up the tray, and I opened the door for her. She went inside, and I quickly started to close it behind her.

"What did my favorite girl bring me to eat?"

Gage's voice made me pause. It was … pleasant. My stomach did a little flip. That was the only time I'd heard that version of him. I closed the door softly, feeling slightly envious of her. I wondered what it felt like to see him look at you with something other than hate and disgust.

One more thing I would never know.

Chapter Six

GAGE

Trinity scowled as she entered the room, taking me off guard. "I saw her wrist," she bit out after she set the tray of food down on the table beside my bed.

"Fuck, I don't want to talk about her. Let me enjoy my meal," I grumbled.

Had I grabbed her arm that hard? I didn't think so. What the fuck was wrong with her wrist? Not that I gave a fuck. I should have broken the damn thing. Then, she'd have to leave.

"You're being an asshole. That girl looks ready to burst into tears."

Good. I hoped I had her sobbing before the day was over.

"You don't know the past," I told Trinity.

"Neither does she." Trinity had her hands on her hips, looking like she might slap me at any moment.

"Don't fucking care. Doesn't change the past, now does it?" I replied, looking at the food she'd brought up.

"Gage, seriously. The girl has amnesia. You can't be angry with her if she can't remember anything."

I sighed, wishing I could reach my food. "Not anger, sweetheart. That was a long time ago. I moved on. I just don't want to be reminded of my past mistake."

Nor did I want to be reminded of how fucking hard it was not to look at her. She had taken all the shit I said to her and not reacted. She hadn't even fucking flinched. The Shiloh I knew would have slapped me and told me to go fuck myself. Then strutted her sexy ass out of here and not looked back. The way she was acting now screwed with my head. Another reason she needed to leave.

EIGHT YEARS AGO

How had I gone from never laying eyes on this girl to her being every-fucking-where I went? It was as if the universe was screwing with me on purpose. Taunting me. I couldn't even go get a damn meal without running into her.

I grabbed the burger on my plate and took a bite, trying not to look back over at Shiloh fucking Ellis.

After Talia had sucked my dick at the party, Shiloh had kept her distance. She'd stayed close to Jackson's side, but whenever she got too far from him, he'd chase her around like a fucking puppy. I'd usually blame that shit on a magic pussy, but I got it. Hell, if I could bang that cunt, I'd chase it around too.

Picking up my drink, I fought the urge to look over at her again. She hadn't noticed me, and I needed to keep it that way. I didn't have a Talia buffer today, and she wasn't with Jackson. She was alone.

"Hello, Gage Presley."

Her fucking addictive voice still reminded me of honey. Maybe honeyed bourbon.

I looked up as Shiloh slid into the seat across from me. Blue eyes danced with delight, as if she were fucking thrilled to find me here. That damn dimple, which I wanted to lick, flashed at me. If I didn't get my food and go, I was fucked. A man was only so strong, and God had decided to create kryptonite in the form of Shiloh Ellis to destroy me.

"Aren't you out past your bedtime?" I asked, trying to sound annoyed.

She raised her eyebrows and pursed her lips. The things I wanted to do to those lips.

"No, Daddy, I'm not," she purred, and my cock was instantly hard as a motherfucking rock.

I chuckled. "I'm a man. That shit might work with the boys, but I've had my share of hot ass." But not her level of hot ass.

I'd stung her again, but she barely let me see it. She held the smug smile in place well. The girl knew she looked like an angel. She owned mirrors.

"I've heard all about the hot ass you've had. Didn't take much asking around to find out about you. Seems you've got a reputation. You and your friends are rather well known," she said, then leaned against the table in my direction.

My eyes immediately dropped to her chest and the cleavage that was now clearly in view. Damn, those tits were incredible. I could see the suntan line from her bikini top.

Lifting my eyes back to hers, I didn't try and hide the lust. "Stop asking about me. You've got a great body and a pretty face, but you're just a little girl."

She leaned even further. "Not all females want to fuck you, Gage Presley. That's presumptuous, don't you think? I have a boyfriend, and he takes care of my needs."

Straight Fire

My grip on the glass in my hand tightened. I did not want a fucking mental picture of Jackson taking care of her needs. I didn't want to think about her needs. "Good. Now, go home. It's getting late," I told her.

She tilted her head to the side and smirked at me. "I heard you were bossy in bed too," she said.

"Then, whoever you're getting your information from doesn't know me because that's not accurate," I drawled, leaning back in the booth and crossing my hands over my chest.

She pulled her bottom lip between her teeth. I knew she was doing that shit on purpose, but my dick did not care. It was throbbing.

"So, you're not bossy and controlling in bed?"

I shook my head. "I'm controlling and demanding when I fuck," I told her. "And I don't fuck in bed."

Her lips made a small O, only making my cock jerk in response.

I had to get away from her.

Sliding out of the booth, I stood up, then glanced down at her. "I'm five years older than you, Shiloh. Keep your distance next time."

I headed for the door when I heard her slide out of the seat. I didn't look back, but shoved the door open and walked out.

When I saw her again two days later, I had Gina, Blaise's stepsister, on her knees with her lips around my dick. Blaise was outside at the pool with a few friends he had over. I hadn't been in the mood for a party tonight, but then I hadn't known Shiloh would be there.

"I thought you didn't fuck on beds," she said, giving me a challenging look.

Gina stopped and turned to look at her. "Is she joining us?"

Fuck. Didn't need that mental image with Shiloh standing right there.

"No. She's a kid," I said, "who needs to go away."

Shiloh gave Gina an annoyed look, and then her eyes lifted to meet mine. "You could do better," she told me.

This baby and her teeth. Fuck if it didn't turn me on when she got nasty.

"You don't have to pay for it," she added.

Damn, she was brutal.

Gina started to get up as she glared at Shiloh. I pushed her back down, pressing my hand to the top of her head.

"She's a baby. You can't go claw her face off," I told her while grinning at Shiloh.

"She called me a prostitute."

"I know," I said, shaking my head. "She's just jealous."

Shiloh's eyes widened, and I knew I'd hit a nerve.

"You gonna watch and get some pointers or leave?" I taunted her, although the idea of her watching was gonna make me come a hell of a lot faster.

She slung her long, dark hair over her shoulder and glared at me. "No thanks. That's something I don't need a lesson in."

She didn't wait on a response before closing the door with more force than necessary.

I was going to come so fucking hard.

Chapter SEVEN

SHILOH
PRESENT DAY

Mentally and emotionally exhausted after dealing with a man who hated the sight of me all day, I did not want to cook anything when I got back to my apartment. I changed into a pair of jeans and a fitted black sweater before turning to leave. I didn't have a car because driving wasn't considered safe for me, due to the seizures. Even though it had been a long time since I'd had one. It still made me nervous to even take driving lessons. So, I'd chosen an apartment within walking distance to restaurants and a grocery store.

When I stepped back into the hallway, the door across from me opened, and I smiled, happy to see a friendly face. Wilder Jones had become my first friend when I moved back here. He'd helped me grocery shop the first time, taught me how to order the perfect burger, and showed me how to get streaming television, all within the first week of my meeting him. Wilder was in his early thirties and divorced. He had a six-year-old daughter, Sarah, who I always baked cookies or cupcakes with at least once every weekend she spent with her dad.

"Where are you headed?" he asked, leaning against his doorframe.

"To eat. Wanna come?"

"Pizza?" he asked.

"Half buffalo chicken and half cheeseburger," I said, as if I even needed to tempt him with his favorite.

He'd go eat pizza any time of the day.

He winked, then reached inside and grabbed a coat before closing his door and coming to walk with me. "You worked later than usual," he said. "Long day at the office?"

Wilder worked from home most of the time. He owned a media marketing company that dealt with the web. He knew my schedule better than me.

"Not exactly. I had to go take care of one of my uncle's private patients. The ones he makes house calls to. Anyway, the patient doesn't like me for reasons I do not know, and he doesn't care that I don't remember my former self. Uncle Neil is going to take over the job until he can get another nurse to go do it."

Wilder opened the door to the outside for me. "Sounds like an ass."

I nodded. "From what I have learned, former me wasn't always a nice person."

Wilder glanced down at me. "Is he a past boyfriend?"

I shrugged. "He's older than me, and the age gap back then makes that unlikely. But to despise someone as much as this man does me, there had to be another emotion involved once, I think. Either that or I robbed his house, ran over his favorite pet, or shot him in the balls," I replied.

Wilder chuckled. "Ouch."

"I was going for reasons to loathe because this man loathes me."

"I find it hard to believe a heterosexual male can loathe you," he said as we crossed the street.

Wilder made no attempt to hide that he thought I was attractive. However, he didn't push me for more than friendship. He seemed to get that I wasn't there yet in my new life.

"Trust me, this one does," I told him.

"Even after you flashed him that dimple?" he asked as he stepped in front of me and opened the door to our favorite Italian restaurant, then moved back for me to enter.

I walked past him and inhaled deeply. I was starving, and it smelled like heaven.

Luca, the owner's oldest son, saw us and nodded his head in greeting. "Pick a seat," he called to us, and we headed toward the tables near the windows.

"Did you ask the guy what you did to make him hate you?" Wilder asked as he pulled out my chair for me.

I sat down. "No. I'm not allowed to ask questions. Uncle Neil's rule."

Wilder was frowning when he took the seat across from me. "Strange rule."

I didn't elaborate. It wasn't like I could explain it anyway. The rules were in place for a reason. *Don't talk about them* was one of the rules.

"Sarah is coming this weekend, right?" I wanted to change the subject.

He nodded. "Yep. We need to go by the store on the way back and get your baking supplies. It's cupcakes this weekend. She wanted me to tell you so you'd be prepared."

I smiled. "Perfect. Icing is my favorite."

Luca arrived with both of our waters and Wilder's favorite beer. "Are we doing pizza?" he asked.

"Yes, please," Wilder replied.

"The usual?"

Wilder nodded.

When Luca left again, he turned back to me. "I have a thing next week. Dinner with a new client and his wife. They told me to bring a date, and, well, you know I'm not currently dating anyone," Wilder began. "Any chance you'd go with me? It's Tuesday night at seven."

This wouldn't be the first time I'd done this for him. He rarely dated. The last woman he had gone out with more than once was Kelly, the redhead. They had lasted almost two months. He didn't have a reason for their breakup other than it just hadn't worked for them.

"Of course," I agreed.

We talked about his work, and he told me a funny story about one of his employees. I was finally able to relax again after today. The pizza arrived, and I took my piece from the buffalo chicken side. Wilder preferred the cheeseburger, but he would eat both. Which was why this had become our go-to order here.

I was on my second bite when I looked out the window and saw Huck standing outside my apartment building, scowling with his arms crossed over his chest. Why was he there? I put the pizza down, feeling my stomach knot up. I couldn't think of one reason he'd have come to find me. I hadn't done anything wrong today. I wasn't even coming back. They had made it clear I wasn't welcome, and I'd accepted it.

I glanced at Wilder. I couldn't tell him or explain this to him, but I also didn't want him in danger, if there was danger. Uncle Neil had said to me more than once that the people living in the house with Gage were not to be crossed. I hadn't crossed them. At least not in the last two years.

I set my slice down and turned to look at Huck again, thinking I should call my uncle. The door to the building opened, and the sight of Trinity gave me a little relief. He wouldn't have brought her if I was in trouble. At least, I didn't think he would.

She was saying something to him, and he placed his hand on her lower back in a possessive way. They began walking toward a black SUV that was on the side of the road. It wasn't until he opened the door for her that he lifted his gaze, and it locked with mine.

I froze, unsure if this was bad or not. He looked directly at me, then swung his eyes to Wilder. I needed to call Uncle Neil. Wilder didn't need to be in the middle of this. I didn't know these people or what they were after.

Huck finally climbed inside the vehicle, and it pulled back onto the road. I let out a sigh of relief and turned my attention back to Wilder. He was texting with a smile I recognized on his face.

"Tell her I'll get the pink sprinkles," I told him.

He glanced up and grinned, then began texting again.

Chapter EIGHT

GAGE

The bedroom door opened, and I dreaded looking over at it. Another day of Shiloh being in this room with me sounded like hell. The heavy footsteps weren't Shiloh's. Thank fuck. I turned to see who was here.

Huck was putting my breakfast down on the rolling table that had come with the hospital bed.

"What time is it?" I groaned.

"Seven thirty," Huck replied.

"What time does she get here?" I asked.

"She quit. Doc will be here by eight."

"What?"

"What are you confused about—the *Shiloh quitting* thing or Doc being here at eight?" Huck asked.

I scowled at him. "You know what the fuck I'm asking."

"You wanted her gone. She told the doc you weren't going to get better if she was here. Her presence was clearly not helping you, and he is closing his office to come stay with you."

This was good. I didn't want to see her again. She had made it so I didn't have to. So, why the fuck was I pissed? I glared at the food Huck had rolled in front of me.

"You gonna eat it or kill it?" Huck drawled.

The urge to throw the fucking plate across the room was strong. She had thought she could just walk back into my life, remind me of shit I had worked a fucking long time to forget, then just walk right back out.

"Fucking bitch might have lost her memory, but she hasn't changed any," I growled.

Huck sat down in the leather chair where Shiloh had sat and read yesterday. "Oh, I don't know. The Shiloh I remember would have thrown something at your head for leaving a bruise on her wrist. No way she would have nursed that fucking wound on your chest. Or quietly accepted the hatred you seethed when you spoke to her. I was fucking rude to her, and she didn't react at all."

I glared at him. "Are you fucking kidding me? That bitch almost destroyed me. I had to join the motherfucking Marines or rot behind bars."

Huck shrugged. "Yeah, I remember. But did you ask her why she came back here? Why she didn't marry her boyfriend? Why she's working for her uncle when we both know her parents are loaded and she was never expected to work a real job in this lifetime? I don't think the Shiloh that woke up from that coma is the same person we knew."

No, I hadn't asked her that shit. I didn't care. Her fucking perfect life she'd planned had fallen apart.

"She didn't get something she wanted. About fucking time."

"I guess that's one way to look at it," Huck replied. "But if she doesn't remember that she wanted those things, then I think that cancels it out. There're probably new things she wants now, and clearly, with the new Shiloh, you didn't make the wanted list. Lucky you."

SEVEN YEARS AGO

One more hour, and I was out of here. Huck needed to hire more employees. The damn *motorcycle repair* shit had been his idea. I wanted something with less manual labor and more women. A strip club had sounded like an excellent idea. But, fuck no, we were running a damn bike shop.

I shoved open the door to the garage, ready to send whoever had just pulled up away. We didn't have enough manpower for any more business this week. The bikes were backed up as it was. Stepping through the door, I swung my gaze to the guy walking inside. The words *we don't have fucking time* were on the tip of my tongue when Shiloh Ellis walked up beside him and I forgot what I was saying.

It had been a year since I'd seen her last. She'd stopped showing up everywhere once her boyfriend was off at college. But this was not Jackson she was with. I watched her wrap one of her arms around his when our eyes met. A corner of her mouth lifted up, and, fuck me, she'd somehow gotten even more stunning. The crop top and tiny shorts she was wearing left little to the imagination, but I wasn't fucking complaining. Had her tits gotten bigger? Shit.

"You work here?" the guy asked. He was tall, lean, and looked like another fucking high school jock.

"Yeah," I replied, annoyed that I wasn't sending him away simply because I wanted to look at her.

"I, uh, wrecked my bike, and I need it looking new before my dad sees it," the guy said. "I'll pay whatever I need to get it done ASAP."

I shifted my eyes back to Shiloh. She was studying her fingernails, as if she were bored. No flirting these days, it seemed. She had given up on me and left it alone. Just like I had wanted, but if she didn't let go of him, I was going to take his fucking arm off.

"We're backed up right now," I told him, shifting my gaze back to his.

"Dude, please. I swear I have the money. Whatever it takes to get this fixed," he pleaded.

Shiloh lifted her eyes again and looked at me. I smirked, thinking about how pissed she was going to be before turning back to the guy.

"Shiloh might be able to convince me," I told him.

He frowned, the confusion on his face clear before he looked at her. She was looking at me, wide-eyed, and, damn, I wanted to laugh. I also wanted to throw her over my shoulder and get her the fuck away from that kid. The fact that this didn't seem to piss her off only made me want to push it more.

"Uh," he said, still looking at her.

She finally turned to him.

"You know him?" the guy asked.

She lifted a shoulder, then nodded. "Kinda."

"Uh, how could she convince you?"

He was nervous now. I could see it in his eyes. He needed the bike fixed, but he also didn't want to piss off the hottest piece of ass he'd ever touched.

"Shiloh." I said her name, and her gaze snapped back to mine.

There was defiance gleaming behind those depths, and I wanted to pull those little shorts down and spank her ass.

"Yes?"

That voice. Jesus Christ, the sound of it went straight to my dick.

"He leaves, you stay," I replied.

"Whoa, dude," he said, but I ignored him, keeping my eyes on her.

She narrowed her eyes, and I couldn't keep from grinning. I'd tossed it out there, and she was wanting to take it.

Not studying your nails like you're bored now, are you, sweet baby?

"Fine," she replied, letting go of the guy's arm.

He looked down at her like she was crazy. "What? No. I'll drive to Orlando or some shit. I don't have to use them. Just go get in the truck."

She glanced up at him, then back at me. "I'm staying," she said, and that dimple flashed.

Damn.

"Shiloh? What the fuck? Are you serious?" His voice took a tone I didn't like.

When he reached out and grabbed her arm, I moved. I took his arm and twisted it, and he let out a shout.

"She's staying, and if you don't want me to snap your arm, you'll walk back to your truck and leave."

I could see the moment he decided his life was more important than a girl. He nodded, and I let him go with a shove that caused him to stumble.

"You got ten seconds," I warned him as he looked at me, then Shiloh.

"I gotta get my bike out first," he said. "It's in the back of my truck."

I laughed and shook my head. "Not fixing your fucking bike. Not after you put your hand on her."

"What? Dude! Are you serious?"

Straight Fire

I took a step toward him, and he took off running to his truck.

When he was inside of it, I turned back to Shiloh. "You can do better," I repeated her words she'd once said to me back to her.

"Is that so?" she asked.

I nodded and walked toward her. She was still too young, but I just wanted a taste. I wouldn't fuck her, but I wanted to see how she tasted and felt. That should get this thing I had for the girl out of my system.

When I reached her, I ran a finger along her jawline, and she shivered. Those blue eyes staring up at me. Fuck, this was probably a mistake. I just didn't seem to care at the moment.

"It's been a while," I whispered.

"Ten months and two days," she replied.

I paused. She knew the exact number of days since I'd seen her last? If any other female had said that to me, I wouldn't be able to get away from her quick enough. But this one? She could admit whatever she wanted with that pretty mouth, and I would stay.

"You miss me, sweet baby?" I asked, liking the idea she'd thought about me enough to know something like that.

"Yes."

How was I not going to fuck her? Who was I kidding?

"What happened with Mr. Football?" I asked.

She shrugged. "He got on my nerves."

He had gotten on my fucking nerves too.

"Come inside with me."

She nodded, and I put my hand on her bare back, then led her back through the door I'd exited earlier. Huck was upstairs in his office, but everyone else was gone. I took her to the meeting room and closed, then locked the door behind me.

She walked farther in, and my eyes went to her ass as I thought of the many different things I wanted to do to it.

I came up behind her and pulled her hair back off her shoulder, then leaned down to her ear. "Why did you come in here with me?" I whispered.

Chill bumps appeared on her arms, and I smiled. Fuck, I'd bet her pussy was wet.

"You brought me here," she said softly.

I ran a finger down her neck. I loved her skin. It looked like porcelain but felt like silk.

"It's not a good idea to follow a man like me to a room alone," I continued to whisper close to her ear.

She inhaled sharply, and I could see her eyes close.

"You're still too young for me to fuck." I slid a hand around to her stomach and moved it inside the front of her shorts.

She tensed, and her eyes opened as she looked down at my hand.

"Unbutton them, Shiloh."

There was no hesitation when she went to the button on her shorts and undid it, then pulled the zipper down.

"Good girl," I whispered, keeping my mouth near her ear as I slid my hand inside the silky panties and over her smooth mound. Then, I ran a finger through her slit.

She jerked and let out a small cry.

"Damn, that's a wet pussy."

She made another little sound. I pressed my erection against her back and shoved the rest of my hand between her legs.

"I'm gonna need to play with it and taste it now that I know it's wet."

The short, quick breaths she was taking made her tits bounce. Hard nipples pressed against the fabric of her top. I was going to have to suck on those too. Get them out of my system.

This wasn't good enough. I had to see this hot little cunt. Fuck knew I'd gotten myself off, thinking about it enough. I pulled my hand out of her shorts and spun her around to face me. She tilted her head up to look at me, and I let her watch as I sucked her juices from my finger. Her eyes were driving me crazy, watching me with fascination.

Damn, she might fucking ruin me, but right now, I didn't give a shit. I bent my head and claimed her mouth, licking at the seam, then thrust my tongue inside once she opened. Her hands went to my chest, and her fist held on to my shirt as she pulled me against her. A groan came from deep in my chest, and I cupped her face with my hands. She tasted like sunshine and peaches. I was fucking jealous of every stupid boy who had gotten to kiss her. Hold her. None of them had been worthy of this. She was fucking delicious.

Pulling back, I looked down at her dazed expression and felt her pulse in her neck against my hand.

"A good guy—the kind of man you deserve—would stop at that, but, sweet baby, I'm not a good man," I told her, then took her shorts and panties and jerked them down.

When I knelt in front of her, the slick pussy was so close to my face.

"Open your legs for me."

She did it without question. Not smart. Someone should have taught her better than this.

I opened her up and leaned in to lick the wetness coating the inside of her upper thigh. Her knees slightly buckled, and I grinned as I began to lick along her sensitive folds. If her mouth tasted like peaches, then this pussy was fucking cream. Her little cries of pleasure had my cock throbbing against the zipper of my jeans.

"I can't," she panted. "Gage, I can't stand up."

Standing, I picked her up and sat her on the conference table. "Lie back and bend your knees." My words came out in a growl. The need to taste her some more was clawing at me.

When I buried my face between her legs again, she instantly cried out my name and pulled at my hair as she lifted her hips off the table. Her body was shuddering as I continued to indulge in the sweetest fucking pussy I'd ever had.

"Please, I can't," she cried, jerking under me.

When she stilled, I lifted my head to look at her. She gave me a content, happy smile. Fucking dimple.

"Did you just orgasm?" I asked. I'd barely even gotten started.

Her blush colored her pretty skin, and she nodded her head.

Fucking hell.

"I need more of this cunt. I'm not done yet."

She bit her bottom lip. "Okay. I didn't—I mean, I've just never ..." She looked embarrassed.

What had she never done?

"No one's ever done that to me before," she finally said.

That was when I found out there was a fucking beast inside of me, roaring to life. The fact that no other mouth had tasted this sweet pussy was messing with my head. I didn't want anyone else to know what she tasted like or looked like when she was like this.

She shifted her hips slightly, and I forgot about all the other shit. I just wanted some more of her. Kissing my way down the inside of her thigh, I inhaled deeply, soaking in her scent.

"So sweet," I whispered against her clit, then licked it and pulled it into my mouth to suck.

"OH," she cried out, and her hands went back to my head. "That feels so good."

My cock swelled in my pants, to the point that it was painful. I reached down and unzipped my jeans and freed myself. I wrapped my fingers around my rigid dick as pre-cum leaked from the top. Using it to lubricate, I slowly began to pump it in my hand as I continued eating her hot little cunt.

"Please," she moaned. "Gage, AH!" I pumped harder, listening to her cries.

"Oh! Oh! That's—oh! Gage."

"Ride my face," I told her as I stuck my tongue inside her.

"Oh God," she moaned and began rocking her hips. "That's so good."

I flattened my tongue and let her rub her clit against it as she grabbed my head, holding me there. My hand jerked my dick in hard, fast pumps. Every moan and cry of pleasure sent me closer and closer to my own release.

"GAGE!" she cried out, lifting her hips off the table and shoving my face against her pussy as she trembled.

I groaned as my cum erupted.

Her hands fell away, but I kept my face pressed against her hot pussy as I continued to spurt out more than I ever had before.

Chapter
NINE

SHILOH
PRESENT DAY

Waking up early was something that only new me did—or at least, that was one of the few things I'd learned from Isaac before I broke things off with him. I liked being up to watch the sunrise and watch the day awaken. People getting out to go to work, walking their dogs, running, just being alive. I took another sip of my coffee while I sat in my window seat that Wilder had made and given to me on my birthday last year.

My gaze went to my wrist and the purple-and-blue bruise that had come from Gage's tight grip yesterday. Luckily, it was winter, and most days, that meant I needed long sleeves in Florida. I didn't want Uncle Neil or Wilder to see the bruise. It would fade away, although I doubted the memory from the day I'd spent being hated would leave me.

I wished there were someone not associated with Gage who knew what I'd done to him. It bothered me. I'd apologized to him for it, but whatever it was went far deeper than an *I'm sorry* could fix. I was truly sorry though. The things I was learning about former me weren't any better here than they had been in Boston.

My cell phone rang, which wasn't normal this time of day. Uncle Neil must have thought of something I needed to do in the office today. He'd left me a list, but that didn't mean he wouldn't add to it. I stood up and walked over to the kitchen counter to get my phone. His name lit up the screen. My life was predictable.

"Good morning, Uncle Neil," I replied, happy to do whatever he needed me to.

"Good morning," he replied, although his tone sounded more like an apology. "I've been to visit the patient today, and we seem to have encountered an issue."

That didn't sound good. My grip on the phone tightened, and I sat down slowly on the barstool. "What is it?"

"Gage is refusing my help. He demanded that you return," Uncle Neil replied. "I'm aware you don't want to be there, but as we spoke about before, these aren't people you refuse."

This didn't make sense.

"He wanted me gone. You were looking for a replacement," I pointed out.

"Yes," Uncle Neil sighed. "I said the same thing. He isn't being cooperative, and frankly, I'm not thrilled about you going back there. However, it is safer for you to obey him and go than to refuse to go."

"But I told you, he didn't even want me touching him. I can't help him or take care of him if he's unwilling to allow me to."

This was crazy. I didn't want to go back there.

"He said he would be easier to deal with," my uncle replied.

I let out a laugh. "What is wrong with this man?"

I heard my uncle sigh again. "The thought that you two have some sort of past is bothersome. Not just because of who he is. You left here when you were barely nineteen years old. Whatever happened, it had to have been when you were a teenager."

And Gage hadn't been. Frowning, I tried to think of what I could have done to make him so angry. I had been nineteen, and he would have been twenty-four. That seemed strange that he was the one who hated me. The only scenarios I could think of would be the other way around. The man was beautiful. I had no doubt that my teenage self could have been attracted to him. Was it a *fatal attraction* thing? Had I stalked him and maybe ruined a relationship for him or something?

"I'm headed to your apartment now. I'll pick you up and take you," Uncle Neil told me before hanging up.

This was not ideal, but I could survive it. Uncle Neil could still find someone to replace me. Gage hadn't said he wanted me the entire time. Right? Or was that what he had decided? Better question was, why had I been involved or even known a guy that age? One who my uncle was scared to tell no? What kind of person had I been?

I pulled out my notebook and pen, then began to write these things down. I'd make a list and see if I could figure out the answers without asking questions. Perhaps I could do some research another way. I chewed on the end of the pen while trying to decide if I should make a list for that too.

Huck opened the door before I reached it. His gaze wasn't as harsh today as he stared at me. I wondered if he was going to mention showing up at my apartment last night. I hadn't told Uncle Neil because I was trying to keep him safe from these people even if I wasn't.

"You came back," Huck said, looking surprised. "Wasn't sure you would."

Straight Fire

I shrugged. "Did I really have a choice?"

If Huck could smile, I'd think he almost did—maybe. I wasn't sure. He was hard to read.

He stepped back so that I could go inside. I walked past him and then turned to see if he wanted to say anything more before I went upstairs to face the patient.

"About yesterday evening," Huck said. "Trinity told me about your wrist. She was worried and wanted to check on you. She was appeased when I told her I saw you on a date across the street." He paused, then added, "Don't tell Gage we were there."

That hadn't been a date, but I didn't correct him.

"I won't," I replied but wondered if he was scared of Gage too. Couldn't Huck just pick him up and toss him across the room?

"Hold out your wrist. I want to see it."

I didn't want to show Huck, but this hadn't been a request. His tone had been a clear demand. I pulled up my sleeve and held it up.

His eyes narrowed, and he muttered a curse. "I'll make sure he doesn't touch you again."

Then, he walked past me and back down the hall that led to the kitchen. Guessed our brief conversation was over. I had no doubt Huck could ensure my safety with Gage. I started for the stairs just as a door to the left—which was always closed—opened, and Levi walked out, followed by a younger guy. He had pale blond hair with more tattoos than Huck.

"You came back," Levi said with a grin that caught me off guard.

Did they think I wouldn't do as told? According to Uncle Neil, it was dangerous to anger them.

"This is Shiloh," Levi told the guy with him. "Shiloh, this is Kye."

"Nice to meet you, Kye," I replied, then turned back to Levi. "Yes, I came back. Although I'll probably regret it," I replied honestly.

Levi looked surprised, and then a bark of laughter followed. Glad this was funny to him. I did smile, however, because his laughter was kind of infectious.

"He'll be better today, I think."

I doubted it, but I was willing to hope. "Good," I replied.

He continued to smile as they walked away.

When I reached Gage's floor, I noticed his door was open. I walked down the hall, then stopped before reaching it. I took a deep breath, then reminded myself this would be fine. I could do this before taking the next few steps that would put me in his doorway.

The light was on, but he was sleeping. Uncle Neil had said he had given him some pain meds when he was here. Maybe they would keep him asleep for a while. I walked into the room and set my bag down by the sofa, took out my e-reader, then went to sit down on the leather chair closer to the bed.

Although I wasn't looking at him, I knew the moment he opened his eyes. The fact that I could feel his gaze on me was disturbing. I shouldn't be that aware of the man. Yesterday, even after he'd looked at me with disgust and bruised my wrist, I had still found him attractive. I was starting to think the *fatal attraction* scenario might have some truth to it. God, I hoped not.

I met his gaze. "Good morning," I said as politely as I could.

He didn't respond, so I turned my attention back to the e-reader.

"You came back," he said.

I looked back up at him. "You demanded I return," I pointed out.

He frowned. "That's a harsh description."

No, it wasn't, but I didn't say anything.

"Do you need something? Ice water? Food?" I asked.

He shook his head. "I'm good."

I went back to my e-reader, although reading was going to be hard.

"You really don't remember anything." He said this as if he didn't believe it.

I shook my head without looking at him. I had already answered that question yesterday. The answer wasn't going to change today.

"Why did you come back to Ocala?" he asked.

He wanted to talk today? Fine, we could talk.

I slipped off my shoes and tucked my feet under me, then looked at him. "Because I didn't like the life I had there."

His frown deepened. "How did you know to come here? Your parents aren't here anymore."

That was a decision that had caused much drama. I wouldn't tell him that though.

"My uncle Neil is here. I needed somewhere that I wasn't expected to be a certain way or to do certain things. Old me liked things that I don't enjoy."

My friends had been shallow and elitist. My fiancé had been worried about appearances, wealth, and connections. I hadn't worked and had never had a job. However, none of that was his business, and I wasn't sharing that much of myself with him.

"I take it, your boyfriend was one of those things."

I shrugged, then nodded. I didn't add that he'd been my fiancé.

"We were too different."

And how had he even known I had a boyfriend? That seemed strange. I started to ask and remembered I wasn't supposed to ask questions. Dang it.

"You work at your uncle's doctor's office."

I wasn't sure if it was a question or a statement, so I just nodded.

He let out a short laugh that didn't meet his eyes. "Yeah, that's nothing like the old you."

How well had he known me? If I had been a batshit-crazy female stalker, would he have known me or what I was like? Other than that I was mentally unstable.

"Would you get me the TV remote?" he asked.

Our talk was over. I wasn't sure if I was happy about that or not. I stood and walked over to get the remote from the dresser, then brought it back to him. He didn't say thanks, or anything for that matter, but I honestly hadn't expected him to.

As the sounds from the television filled the silence, I reached for my notebook and pen. I needed to make a list of the few things I'd learned. Like the fact that Gage had known about Isaac. He had also known I hadn't worked. As I stared at my list, there were so many things I wanted to know. The questions that I had no answers to were all taunting me.

Unable to stop myself, I finally looked up at him. "Can I ask you a question?"

He didn't look at me. His gaze stayed locked on the television. "You can ask, but that doesn't mean I'll answer it," he replied.

I hadn't expected him to agree to even letting me ask, so I was now stuck with deciding which question to throw at him. Asking him what the heck I'd done to make him hate me was a question I knew he'd shut down. If he wanted me to know, he'd have told me already.

"Why did you want me to come back today?" I asked. That question wasn't on my list, but it should have been.

"Not sure," he replied.

"You're not sure why you wanted me to come back when you had made it clear yesterday how you felt about me?"

That was as bad as not answering it. He might as well have said nothing at all.

He turned his head to look at me, and I wanted to shiver from the cold gleam in those amber depths.

"Watch yourself," he warned.

I nodded and looked back down at my list, then closed my notebook, put it away, and picked up my e-reader. My heart was beating so hard that I could hear it in my ears.

Chapter TEN

GAGE

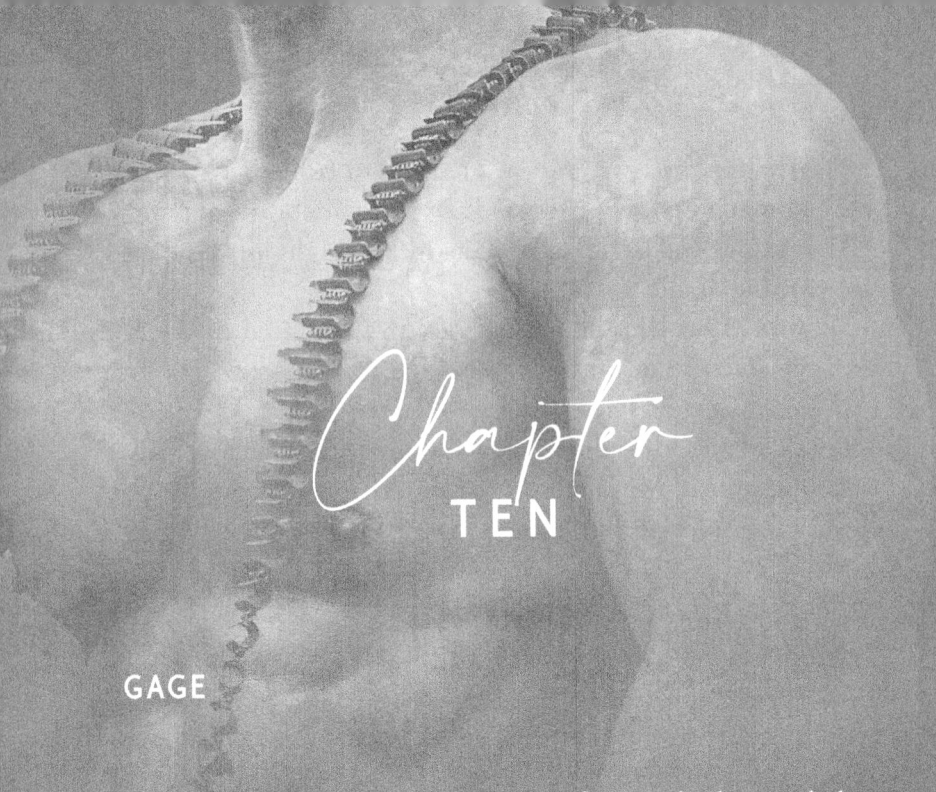

Silky raven hair had fallen over her face as she lay, curled up in the leather chair, asleep. I scowled at her.

After her question this morning, I'd barely spoken to her. She'd been equally quiet. The few times I'd needed to take a piss, she had gone and gotten Huck to help me. I was letting her do the other shit, but she wasn't going near my fucking dick. She'd brought up my needing a sponge bath, and I shut that down quick. I told her I'd make a call and get someone over here to do it. And I'd already texted Huck to get me someone who could bathe me.

Trinity had brought me lunch and pulled her away to go downstairs and eat. Which had pissed me off.

Why was Trinity being so damn nice to her? Because she hadn't known Shiloh before—that was why.

I fisted my hands in the sheets as I watched her slow, even breathing. Admitting that I'd demanded she come back today because the idea of not seeing her again made me fucking livid didn't help matters. Why couldn't I just ignore her? I didn't feel anything for her but hatred.

The fact that she didn't remember me—*us*—was unfair. Memories of her seemed to cling to my damn soul. I fucking despised her, but it didn't mean she hadn't owned a piece of me once that I never got back.

Carmichael appeared at the door. It was time for her to leave.

He glanced at her, then back at me, frowning. "I'm sorry about that. I'll talk to her about remaining alert."

He walked over to her and shook her shoulder gently.

Anger stirred in my chest because he was waking her up. What the fuck was wrong with me? She had fallen asleep on the job. He should wake her ass up. I should have woken her ass up instead of watching her sleep.

I watched as she pushed the hair from her face and looked up at her uncle. Her eyes were still so fucking expressive. I could see the panic when she realized she'd fallen asleep. She sat up quickly, then turned to me.

"I didn't—I mean, I didn't mean to fall asleep. I'm sorry," she said, looking so fucking afraid that I needed to punch something.

Shiloh had never been afraid of anything. Especially me.

She stood up and then swayed slightly. My fucking reflex was to catch her, and when I tried to move, the pain slammed into me. I let out a string of curses. Carmichael caught her and was sitting her back down, whispering something to her. She nodded and gave him a weak smile.

Why was she pale? What the fuck was wrong with her?

"She needs a minute. I'll check that wound and see how things are looking with you," he said as he walked around the bed.

My eyes stayed locked on her.

"Why is she pale?" I didn't like this one fucking bit.

"Uh, well, that happens from time to time. She has some other things that come with the trauma to her brain," he said, then began to work over me, checking my bandage he'd changed out this morning.

"What other things?" I demanded. Why hadn't they mentioned the other things?

Carmichael cleared his throat, and I could see he was uncomfortable. "I'm sorry. I should have been clear about all her health issues. If you prefer I come from now on, I will."

I glared at him. "No, I want her here, but what are her other issues?"

"Gage." Huck's voice filled the room, and I shifted my heated gaze to him.

"What?" I snarled, pissed the fuck off about not being told everything.

He nodded his head toward Shiloh, who had her arms wrapped around her waist, watching me with wide, terrified eyes. Dammit! I was scowling, but I couldn't help it.

"Stop looking at me like I'm about to do something to hurt you! Jesus Christ, you don't have to be scared of me."

That outburst clearly didn't ease her mind. She nodded and started to stand up again. I didn't miss the way she held on to the chair and placed a hand on the wall for stability.

Carmichael stepped away from me and gave me a tight smile. "All looks good. If you don't need anything else, we will leave for the evening," he said and made his way over to Shiloh.

She went to get her bag, and Carmichael stopped her silently, then picked it up. She was too damn pale. And I still didn't have any fucking answers as to what all was wrong with her. The rage slowly churning inside of me had to stop. So what that they hadn't told me? Why the fuck did I care?

This shit ended now. Caring about her led to other things. Shutting down my emotions completely was the only way to handle being around her.

They headed for the door with Carmichael holding on to her arm. There was no real support in that. The old man wasn't going to be able to protect her if she fell. I bit my tongue so hard that I tasted blood to keep from telling Huck to help her.

I refused to let myself give a fuck about Shiloh Ellis's health.

SIX YEARS AGO

A cover band was singing George Strait as I walked inside of Bandits, the local bar in town. They were ruining a great song.

My eyes scanned the crowd for Blaise and Levi. They'd texted me to meet them here an hour ago while I was closing up the shop since Huck had left early to go see his younger brother in Alabama.

There were girls surrounding them when Levi waved his hand to get my attention. I headed over to them, ignoring the women as I slid into the booth side of the round table that had chairs on the other side, then reached for a handful of the pretzels.

"Gage, this is Chelsie, Shanda, Becky, and Tina," Levi introduced the girls, like I gave a fuck.

I didn't acknowledge them but looked over to get the waitress's attention. I needed a beer. I had texted Shiloh and told her where I was headed, but she'd only responded with, *Okay*, and nothing more. I knew she had senior shit at school this week. All fucking spring was full of things that took her away from me. Thinking about the possibility of her going off to college made me fucking ill.

The waitress arrived. "What can I get you, sugar?" she asked.

"Corona," I said. "Salsa and chips too."

"Got it," she replied, then looked at the others to see if they needed anything.

Levi asked the girls if they wanted something, and he ordered them drinks. Blaise ordered a drink, then sat back so that one of the girls could sit on his knee.

When she left, one of the blonde ones reached over and ran her long pink nails down my arm. "You look like you need cheering up," she said, leaning toward me.

I didn't bother looking at the cleavage she was trying to get me to see. Not interested.

"He's grumpy by nature, girls," Levi told them, then winked at the one sitting on his right.

I was sure his hand was giving the one on his left some attention. Rolling my eyes, I leaned back in the booth and looked down at my phone again. Still nothing. What the fuck was she doing?

"I like grumpy," the blonde said and stood up to walk over to me.

I looked up from my phone as she started to take a seat on my knee.

"Didn't invite you to sit," I told her, moving to stand up and make myself unavailable.

I'd go sit in the chair on the other side of Blaise, where no one could get beside me. When I started over to the empty chair, my gaze locked on the raven-colored hair that I knew so well. She was sitting on a stool at the bar, laughing at some fucker who was looking at her like he was gonna get a taste.

Straight Fire

"Call Garrett," I said as I started to the bar. "I'm gonna need bail money."

"What the hell?" I heard Levi say, but I didn't stop.

My eyes were on Shiloh, making sure no one touched her. The fucker who did wouldn't see another sunrise. Just before I got to her, she turned to me. Amusement danced in her eyes as she watched me, knowing I was pissed off.

"Oh, you found time to notice me," she said with a smirk on her face.

"I didn't know you were here," I bit out.

"Clearly. You were busy with admirers." She tucked a strand of hair behind her ear and picked up the drink in front of her to take a sip.

I jerked it out of her hand, then threw the glass down, shattering it against the concrete floor.

"Hey, jackass, I bought that drink," the man blurted out angrily.

Shiloh's hand wrapped around my arm. "Gage, don't."

She had caused this, but then again, she enjoyed doing shit like this.

The man's outraged expression slowly changed to uncertainty as I stared at him. "You can leave and get a head start. Or you can make the mistake of staying here."

His brows drew together.

"Gage, I was just playing. You had a group of women all over you." Shiloh's pleading voice was the only thing keeping me from snapping.

The man pointed at the broken glass on the floor. "This man broke the damn glass on purpose," he told the bartender, who glanced at me, then back at him before turning back to filling drinks. "What? You aren't going to have him clean it or pay for it? Maybe fucking leave?" the man asked, annoyance in his tone.

"No, that won't be happening," Blaise informed him as he came to stand beside me.

The bartender looked at Blaise, then at the man before walking away to get someone else a drink.

"What the fuck?" the man shouted.

Blaise moved in closer to him. "You need to leave," he said in a low voice.

The man's face paled, and it was then that I knew Blaise was pressing a knife against the fucker's ribs.

The man swallowed hard and barely nodded his head. "Okay," he whispered, clearly afraid to move.

The man stepped back, then turned and headed for the door.

"I had it handled," I told Blaise, not liking that he'd dealt with this.

Blaise glanced back at me, then at Shiloh. "None of us needs to end up in jail tonight." He said the words in a low voice while shifting his gaze back to mine.

Shiloh's antics had caused several instances that ended with me needing to be bailed out.

Shiloh moved in front of me then and wrapped her arms around my neck. "Dance with me," she said, smiling up at me like none of this shit had happened.

Blaise turned and headed back to our table.

I stared down at her, wishing like fuck I wasn't so damn obsessed. She made me insane, but the thought of someone else touching her sent me into a blind rage.

I brushed her hair back off her face. "You love pushing me."

She licked her bottom lip. "Maybe I think it's hot. Seeing you be possessive turns me on."

I wrapped a strand of her hair around my finger. "You flirt with anyone else tonight, and I'll kill him," I warned her. I'd probably have to protect her from Blaise if she did anything else to set me off. I didn't say that though.

"Everything good?" the bartender asked, and I turned my head to him and nodded.

Garrett had the owner of this bar under his thumb.

"Let's go dance, and then I'll sit in your lap to keep those mean girls away from you," Shiloh teased, knowing she shouldn't have tested me.

When I scowled, she laughed and took my hand and pulled me toward the dance floor.

Chapter ELEVEN

SHILOH
PRESENT DAY

Uncle Neil walked me to my apartment and made sure I was good before he left me there. Today had been somewhat easier, but only because Gage had seemed to accept my being there. He still loathed me. When he had let me ask a question, I should have asked if I had been a crazed stalker who screwed up his life.

A knock on the door came before Wilder opened it and stuck his head in.

He smiled at me. "Neil asked me to check on you this evening," he explained. "Can I come in?"

"Of course," I replied. It would be good not to be alone.

"I'll go get us some dinner. What are you in the mood for?"

I didn't have to think hard about that. Eating at that house wasn't easy for me. I'd barely touched any food. Tomorrow, I was going to take some protein bars with me. I was pretty sure the lack of calories was why I had gotten dizzy, and I'd told Uncle Neil as much in the car.

"Thai," I told him.

He grinned. "Pad thai with tofu?"

I nodded.

"I'll call it in."

I leaned back on the sofa and reached for the television remote while Wilder called in our order. Replaying every moment I had spent with Gage was clearly not healthy, but that was what I kept doing. He had been confusing today. I still wasn't sure why he'd wanted me to return.

"Done," Wilder said, slipping his phone back into his pocket. "Want to watch another episode of that zombie detective show?" he asked.

I flipped on Netflix and scrolled until I found what he was talking about. "Warning: I might have watched a few episodes without you," I admitted.

"That's not cool," he replied, but I knew he was teasing.

He truly didn't care about the plotline. I was invested.

We were halfway through an episode when he left to go get the food. I paused it and went to get a bottle of water from the fridge. My phone dinged, alerting me of a text message, and I picked it up from where I'd left it on the counter.

I didn't know the number. It was probably some spam, but I opened my phone anyway to read it.

What else is wrong with you?

I read that several times, trying to decide who this was exactly. Could this be Huck? I doubted that Gage would have my number, and if he did, he wouldn't text me.

I typed back:

Who is this?

The response was almost immediate.

Gage. Put my fucking number in your phone. You're my nurse.

Oh. Well, I was wrong then. He would text me. I saved the number under a new contact before replying.

Is this about my dizzy spell? If so, there is no reason to worry or be concerned. I can handle the job. But if you don't feel comfortable with me, I don't have to return.

It annoyed me when people thought I couldn't work. I got migraines or dizzy. The seizures could be an issue, but I hadn't experienced one in months.

That's not a fucking answer, Shiloh.

This man was infuriating.

My brain suffered trauma. I get migraines and dizzy occasionally.

I was not telling him about the seizures. Not his business.

Is that it?

No, that's not it, but that's all I'm telling you.

When I wasn't there, I didn't have to deal with his attitude. Yet he was now texting me when I was at home, relaxing.

Yes. Is there anything you need help with? Should I call my uncle?

There was a pause, and I picked up my bottle of water and took a drink. Still no response, so I laid my phone back down, then picked it back up, just in case. Sinking back onto the sofa, I glanced down at the back-and-forth texts with him. If I was being honest, I was more annoyed with me than with him. Because I wanted those little dots to appear to show that he was texting me back. That in itself was dangerous.

The door opened, and Wilder walked in with a white bag in his hand. I started to ask him if they had the fried sweet potatoes today, but my phone dinged. My stomach did a little flutter thing at the sound, and I winced. What was wrong with me? I should not be reacting like this.

Pulling my phone out, I saw his name on the screen and debated on ignoring it. Just eat my dinner and watch some more television. For a moment, I thought I could do it, but that passed when I opened my phone, unable not to give in.

What are you doing?

I stared at that and reread it three times before replying.

Eating pad thai and watching iZombie.

My thumb hesitated over the phone before I gave in and pressed Send then slipped the phone into my pocket.

"They had the fried sweet potatoes you love," Wilder told me, putting the bag on the coffee table.

"Thank you!"

I reached for the bag and pulled out the boxes of food. When my phone dinged again, I didn't get it out of my pocket. I finished setting up our places, then sat back with the fried sweet potatoes in my lap. My phone felt like it was a magnet, pulling me to it.

Unable to keep this up, I took my phone and opened it up.

That sounds fucking awful.

A laugh escaped me, and I covered my mouth, then put my phone down.

"You never text. Who is that?" Wilder asked, sounding curious.

I glanced over at him as he sat down beside me, opening a bottle of water. We were friends, but I had to be careful what I said about Gage or my job. I'd read the NDA, but it made me nervous that I would mess up.

"The patient I'm taking care of," I said.

He frowned. "The guy you said despises you? He texted you?"

I shrugged. It had surprised me too.

"Guess he doesn't hate you if he's making you laugh. Today must have gone better. Although I wish you had told him no and not returned," Wilder replied.

"It's a job, and he's still not fond of me." I said before putting a fork full of pad thai in my mouth.

"He wanted you to come back, and now, he's texting you," Wilder pointed out. "He doesn't hate you."

I finished chewing my food and started to respond when my phone dinged again. My eyes swung over to Wilder's, and he was giving me an *I told you so* look.

Opening my phone again, I bit my bottom lip to keep from smiling. Why was this making me want to smile?

She eats fucking brains from a morgue?

I had to bite down harder to keep the grin that wanted to break out on my face.

Are you watching it?

I stared down at my phone in disbelief. The thought of Gage Presley lying up in his bed, watching *iZombie*, was funny. If I laughed, Wilder would hear me.

Yes, unfortunately.

I couldn't help it. I laughed. I could feel Wilder's eyes on me, and I knew he was going to ask questions, but I was as confused by this as he was.

Give it a few episodes and see if you don't get hooked.

This was when I needed to put my phone down and eat my food. Instead, I stared at the phone screen while my stomach did strange things. The little dots appeared, showing that he was texting me back.

I can promise you, I won't be getting hooked on this shit.

I should leave it at that. Not say anything more. I placed my phone down on the coffee table and picked up my pad thai. Wilder was still watching me, so I looked over at him.

"Don't look at me like that," I tell him.

He raised his eyebrows. "What do you know about this man?"

Not a lot.

"NDA," I replied.

He frowned. "Just be careful."

"Trust me, I am. What just happened was weird, but he's probably had his pain meds for the night, and they're making him loopy."

Wilder didn't seem convinced. I picked up the remote and turned the show back on. Talking about this with him was not a good idea.

Chapter Twelve

GAGE

Texting her last night had been fucking stupid. I'd ended up dreaming about her, and that shit had to stop. I should have let her go and kept Carmichael here and forgotten she'd ever shown up. My head was fucked.

The more awkward she acted today, the more I got off on it. She hadn't brought up the texting, and I wasn't about to.

I was curious about this version of Shiloh. The more I lay around here, unable to fucking do anything, the more time I had to think about it. She wasn't the same. Sure, she was still the hottest woman I'd ever laid eyes on, but the other things were gone. The way she'd used her beauty to control and manipulate. How she had loved to fucking flirt—and not just with me. The rush she had gotten from getting close to danger. I hadn't seen a glimpse of any of those things in the woman currently getting shit ready to change my bandages.

"I need to piss."

Her cheeks turned pink, and damn if that wasn't funny.

"I'll go get someone," she replied.

"They're gone," I lied. Why the fuck was I lying? I didn't know where the hell they were.

"Oh, well ..." She looked unsure of what to do now.

"You're the nurse, Shiloh," I said harshly. I didn't need her thinking this was something I wanted her to do.

"Right," she replied and went to get the urinal.

I watched as she got the other supplies. When she slipped the rubber gloves on, it made me fucking angry. She was worried about touching my dick? She'd had it shoved down her throat more times than I could count.

She walked over to me and pulled back the covers to find me naked. She gasped and turned her head away. That was funny as fuck, but those damn gloves kept me from laughing.

"You're gonna have to look at my dick in order to help me," I taunted her.

She nodded. "Yes, right. I just, uh ..." Then, she picked up the urinal and started to slip it into place.

My semi was starting to grow with her this close. "Gonna need to help my dick out. Seems to have other ideas."

Her eyes flew up to meet mine, and I smirked. She dropped her gaze back down to the situation at hand and took a deep breath. When she started to reach for my cock, I snapped and grabbed her hand.

"I'll do it," I snarled, grabbing and positioning it.

Her small gasp was distracting. I clenched my teeth and thought of anything but her. She was making this harder than it needed to be, just by standing there. My dick was wanting to do other things. Like sink into her mouth.

STOP! I closed my eyes and managed to shove her out of my head.

When the flow finally started, I was relieved.

I opened my eyes and watched her when I was finished. She took a wet cloth and wiped between my legs, then paused, glancing up at me, as if to question if she was supposed to clean my dick. I snatched the cloth from her and cleaned myself while keeping my gaze locked on her.

"Done," I said, handing her the cloth.

She pulled the covers back up, but she didn't miss the fact that my cock was hardening. I'd done this shit to myself. I was a sick bastard for even wanting her to do it, but she made me unhinged.

"It's a dick, Shiloh. When a female looks at it like that, it's gonna get hard."

She wasn't fucking special.

"You got a pussy and a mouth. That's all a man cares about."

She went to the bathroom to flush my piss. I glared at the ceiling. What next? I'd fucking texted her, had her help me piss. How much more of her being near me could I take before I did something really fucking stupid?

When she walked back into the room, I didn't look at her. I closed my eyes and tried like hell to shove her out of my thoughts. My cock was throbbing, and I was gonna need relief. I'd tried jacking off last night, but that had hurt my chest and ribs too bad.

"Hand me my phone." The tension in my voice made it sound like a growl.

Shiloh jumped up and got my phone, then brought it to me. I snatched it from her hand and didn't look to see her reaction. I wasn't gonna look at her any more today.

I sent a text to Destiny, a stripper at one of the clubs we visited. We'd all used her many times. She came with no strings or drama. We enjoyed fucking her, and in return, when she needed her ass spanked with a belt, we did that for her. It was some fucked up fetish she required every week or so. Seemed weird at first, but I liked spanking the shit out of her, and so did Levi.

Her text came back almost immediately.

Be there soon.

I might have her suck me off a few times before she left. Get this shit with Shiloh under control. I was horny because I hadn't gotten off in three days. That was all this was about. Shiloh had been the only female around. Destiny would get my head cleared.

Closing my eyes again, I managed to drift off.

"You got company." Huck's voice woke me up, and I turned to see Destiny behind him, smiling at me from the doorway. "Did you ask the nurse if this is safe?"

I could see the smirk he was trying to hide from Shiloh.

"Shiloh, the lovely Destiny is going to suck my dick. Is it okay if I come?" I asked her sarcastically.

There was silence for a moment, and I turned my head to look at her.

She was wide-eyed as she nodded. "Uh, yes, um, that's okay. I, uh … you, uh, shouldn't put any pressure on your chest, but, uh, yeah." She finished stammering and looked at Huck. "I'll just go to the kitchen." Her words were rushed before she exited the room, only pausing to say, "Excuse me," softly to Destiny so she could get by.

Huck shook his head. "Fucked up son of a bitch," he said to me, then turned to leave the room.

Destiny was wearing a zebra-print halter top that barely covered her tits and a shiny black skirt as she sauntered into the room. "Heard you got all messed up," she said. "I'm glad you called. I missed you."

Destiny was full of shit. She liked being fucked. The girl had daddy issues, and I took complete advantage of it.

"Of course you have. I won't be able to beat your ass the way you like for a while, but Levi can handle it."

She pushed her lips out in a pout. "I like it better when it's you. I've always told you that you're my favorite."

"You get off on Levi spanking that ass as much as when I do it. Not to mention, you ride on Levi's dick just as much too."

She leaned down and pressed a kiss to my lips. "All you ever have to do is tell me my pussy is yours. Then, it'll just be your dick I'm riding."

Not ever fucking happening. Where the fuck was this coming from anyway? She'd never said shit like that before. I beat her ass with my leather belt, and she spread her legs when I needed a fuck.

"Just suck my dick," I said with a growl.

She winked at me, then pulled back the covers, then licked her lips.

I closed my eyes, and the moment her lips slid down over me, I groaned. Fuuuck, I needed this. I tried not to think about Shiloh, but the struggle to forget what it'd felt like when she was sucking me off was too much. I gave in.

SEVEN YEARS AGO

Bringing her here was a fucking bad idea. Blaise's parties always got out of hand. The last time she'd come to one, she had been on Jackson's arm. After I'd eaten her pussy, I hadn't been able to stay away from her. She was all too willing to do whatever I wanted.

I glanced down at her in the candy-apple-red bikini she was wearing and fought the urge to cover her ass up. There were topless females here, and Levi was currently fucking one in the corner. None of them looked like Shiloh, and the males were gonna look at her. They'd take home the image of what she looked like in this damn bikini and put it in their spank bank.

"You look angry," her sweet voice said as she turned to face me and placed a hand on my bare chest. "What's wrong?"

I looked down at her and then at the bikini. "Nothing," I lied, but this shit was new.

We hadn't even made it a thing yet. I'd eaten her pussy a few times, played with it until she was crying my name. But nothing else.

A blonde I'd fucked before but whose name I couldn't remember walked up beside me and stopped, placing her hand on my arm as her bare boob pressed against my bicep. "It's been a while," she whispered.

"And it's going to be longer," Shiloh said, stepping closer to me.

The blonde glanced back at Shiloh and laughed. "Oh, sweetie. He knows what my mouth can do."

Shiloh tensed up, and I wrapped my arms around her. It was to reassure her, but also, I knew she could get just as mean if she wanted to.

"I'm sure every guy here knows what it can do too." Shiloh's voice sounded like honey, and I grinned.

Knowing I needed to stop this shit before it got out of hand, I looked at the blonde. "I'm clearly taken," I told her.

She lifted one shoulder. "When you get bored," she said with a wink, then walked away.

Shiloh's angry glare followed her, and I reached down to take her chin, then turned her face toward me. Those blue eyes were bright with jealousy, and I liked it. Damn.

"Easy, tiger," I said, then ran a thumb over her bottom lip, thinking I needed to suck it.

"Take me to a room. I don't care which one, just somewhere," she told me.

"Why?"

"Please," she begged.

Whatever the reason, I was doing it. Shiloh saying *please* was all it took for me to bend to her will. I took her hand, then threaded my fingers through hers before heading back to the pool house. She stayed close to my side as we passed more tits and some fucking.

This was typical, and I was used to the scene, but I knew she wasn't. Once I got her inside the pool house, she turned to face me again, then reached for the waist of my swim trunks.

"What are you doing, baby?" I asked as she pulled them down until my dick was free. It grew and hardened as she stood there, looking at it.

This was not what I had expected when we came in here, but, damn, I wasn't about to stop her. If she wanted to look at my cock, she could, but I might start rubbing one off while she did it.

Shiloh sank down to her knees, and I stopped breathing while she looked up at me. Holy fuck, this wasn't going to last long. Her hand wrapped around me, and she gave me a little smile.

"I've never had one this big in my mouth before," she said.

I growled, "Don't want to hear about you sucking other dicks."

She raised her eyebrows at me. "And I don't want to hear about other mouths sucking yours." The defiance in her tone was so damn hot.

"Then, suck it and make me forget them all," I replied.

Her eyes flashed with the challenge.

Those full red lips opened and slid down my cock while her tongue licked along the way. I placed a hand on the side of her head and watched, soaking in every fucking moment because I was going to remember this for the rest of my damn life.

"Sweet baby," I murmured. "Gonna own me with that mouth."

She moaned as the tip hit the back of her throat.

"FUCK," I growled as my hand moved to grab her head.

This was hands down the best experience of my life. Her head bobbed up and down. Little gag noises when she shoved in more than she could fit. I needed a fucking soundtrack of the sounds she was making.

"Goddamn, baby," I groaned as she let it pop free and then started licking the tip.

Her pretty eyes lifted to look at me.

"Don't tease me," I warned.

She gave me a sexy grin, then slid my cock back inside her mouth while watching my face. My mouth slightly opened as I panted. I ran my knuckle down her cheek and pumped my hips against her lips.

"That's so good. Fuck, your hot little mouth. I want to see my cum dripping from your lips."

Her eyes fluttered as she moaned again. As good as this shit was, I wouldn't be able to hold back. My balls were drawn up tight, and I knew I was close.

"I'm about to come," I warned her.

Her nails bit into the front of my thighs as she sank me deeper into her mouth. More little sounds on my cock, and I grabbed her head and shouted as my cock began to jerk with my release.

"Fuck, fuck, fuck," I panted, watching her suck me clean. "My baby can be dirty," I said, grinning as she let me go and licked her lips.

The smile of satisfaction on her face made my chest tighten.

"Now, when you think about getting your dick sucked, I'll be the one in your thoughts," she said, standing up.

I chuckled and pulled her to me. "Since the moment I laid eyes on you, you're all I see when I think about getting my dick sucked," I admitted.

Chapter Thirteen

SHILOH
PRESENT DAY

Stopping at the top of the stairs, I realized that coming back up here was a bad idea. I had been in the kitchen, but then Huck came in, and I didn't want to sit there alone with him, so I'd planned on waiting in the hallway until Gage was done.

"Fuck yes." Then more grunts. "Fuck! Take it! Take it!" Gage shouted.

The area between my legs tingled, and I stood there, unable to move. This wasn't something I wanted to hear. I had known it was happening, but it was private. I shouldn't be listening to it, and I definitely shouldn't be getting turned on by it.

"Swallow it," Gage commanded. "That's it. Get it all."

I closed my eyes tightly. *Move, Shiloh! Go somewhere else. Stop listening to him and imagining what his face looks like when he's doing this.*

I heard female laughter, and that reminded me that he wasn't alone.

"Again?" she asked, sounding amused.

"Yeah, just lick it softly until I'm ready to go again," he replied.

He was getting her to do it twice? Could you do that?

All I knew about sex was what I'd read and watched. I was sure I'd had sex since I had been living with Isaac when I had the accident, but I hadn't been able to do anything with him once I woke up to this new me. He kissed me once, and I pushed him away. It had felt wrong.

"Like a lollipop," I heard Gage say. "Ah, yeah, that's it."

I was not listening to this anymore. This wasn't one of my spicy books or some movie. It was real, and as his nurse, I needed to give him privacy. When I turned around to leave, my eyes clashed with Levi's. He was smirking at me, and I realized he'd caught me. My face felt like it was on fire.

"I, uh, didn't, um …" I stammered, having no words to make this look better than it was.

He cocked one eyebrow. "You like listening to him get sucked off? He'd probably let you watch if you wanted to."

I shook my head, horrified. "No. I didn't—I don't."

"If you asked nicely, he'd even use your mouth and send her home. He won't admit it, but he would."

My chest felt funny, and I started to rush past him and go down the stairs. Levi's hand shot out and grabbed my arm. I looked down at it, then up at him.

"You fucked him up. Even if you don't remember, you did. Be careful," he said.

I wasn't sure what that meant, but I nodded. He let my arm go, and I hurried down the stairs, wishing it were time for Uncle Neil to get here. There were too many new things going on with my emotions. I stood at the bottom of the stairs, thankful I couldn't hear him anymore. I realized I was wringing my hands nervously and forced myself to stop.

"He's all taken care of now. You can go back in," the female said as she started down the stairs.

I waited until she was down first. I wasn't sure I was ready to go face him after hearing him get off. She stopped when she reached the bottom.

"Don't get any ideas," she hissed. "You're not his type. I'm the only woman who knows what he needs. Gage likes it dark and twisted. He knows I can give it to him, just like he is the only one who gives me exactly what I need."

Even if she expected me to respond to that, I wouldn't. She clearly knew what she was talking about. I might as well have been a virgin for all I knew about pleasing a regular man. Much less a man like Gage. I stood there for a moment after she was gone before walking back up the stairs. The strange turmoil twisting in my chest needed to calm itself. Slowly walking back up, I mentally chastised myself for letting any of this bother me. There was no reason for me to care.

The bedroom door was open when I reached the top, and Levi came walking out. Wincing, I glanced at Levi. If he had told Gage, then I would have to admit it and apologize. This was what I got for being a pervert and not going back downstairs the moment I'd heard him.

Levi gave me a nod as he passed, and I forced a smile before walking into Gage's room. He was sitting up with the remote in his hand when I entered. He didn't look at me. Maybe he didn't know I'd listened. I went to the chair and sat down, tucking my feet up and under me. I turned to pick up my e-reader.

"How long did you listen?" he asked.

My head snapped up, but he was still looking at the television. He appeared bored.

"Uh, I'm sorry about that. I didn't know I'd be able to hear," I said, wishing there were a hole that would swallow me up.

"How long?" he repeated.

"Not long," I assured him.

He said nothing more as he found some violent movie and proceeded to watch it. The rest of the day went much like that. Huck helped him with the urinal. Trinity brought up food. Levi stopped by to say Ms. Jimmie was coming at seven for his sponge bath. I had no idea who that was, but the fact that it wasn't Destiny bathing him made me feel better, and that was my issue I had to deal with. By the time I left, I was mentally exhausted from just being ignored.

Wilder had left me a text, telling me his mother had needed him to drive down to Orlando and help her with a broken dishwasher. Relieved that he wouldn't come over and want to visit when I was not in the mood to talk, I made myself a turkey sandwich. I'd forgotten that I needed to buy more fruit, and I had to dig around in the pantry in hopes of finding some chips. I found one package of microwave popcorn and decided that would work.

Once I had my sandwich, popcorn, and water on the coffee table in front of me, I turned on the television. Not wanting to watch *iZombie*, I chose a horror film about a doll. That would get my mind off everything else.

Five minutes into the movie, my phone dinged. Tonight, it was in my pocket, and I paused with my sandwich in my hand. Did I look at it? Could it possibly be Wilder? But what if it was Gage? I took a bite of the sandwich, then set it down. As I kept my eyes on the TV screen while I held an internal battle, the phone dinged again. Crap.

I reached into my pocket and pulled it out. Gage. Double crap. I was weak. I slid my finger across the screen to open my phone and read the two text messages.

Pad thai and zombie shit?

I'm not liking the silence, Shiloh.

I scowled at the last text. *You sure as hell liked it just fine today*, I thought. I should ignore this, but then was that allowed? Was it dangerous to piss him off? Ugh. I wanted to respond, and those were just excuses to make me feel better about it.

Turkey sandwich, popcorn, and a horror movie.

I dropped my phone beside me and grabbed a handful of popcorn.

You like horror movies now?

Interesting. I guessed I hadn't liked them before, and he knew that. It seemed like something only those close to me would know. I needed to write that on the list.

Yes.

I was not giving him any more words than necessary.

Do you still like rocky road ice cream with potato chips?

What? Seriously? I had eaten that? Now, he was teasing me.

Please tell me you're joking.

Although I was going to have to try it now, just to see.

Nope.

He was telling me things about myself that gave away how well he had known me. It was tempting to keep this up and see what else I could find out.

Hershey Kisses dipped in peanut butter?

That sounded good. I looked over at my pantry and thought about the Hershey Kisses in there. I did like those. I needed to buy some peanut butter.

I'll let you know.

He didn't say anything for a while, and I put the phone down, disappointed our conversation had ended. I wasn't sure what was going on with the movie, but I finished the popcorn while trying to catch up. My thoughts kept going off to places they didn't need to be, and I reined them back in. Any day now, Uncle Neil could get a replacement nurse, and I wouldn't see Gage anymore.

That caused a knot in my stomach that needed to go away. That man was not for me.

My phone dinged again, and I picked it up and read the text.

Watch Gossip Girl. Prime has it. I checked.

I picked up the controller and found it under television shows. I clicked on it and sat back to see what it was about.

Chapter Fourteen

SHILOH

Gage was sitting up with his breakfast on the table in front of him when I walked into the room. Today, he would have to start getting up and going to the bathroom, trying to walk around some more. On the drive over here, Uncle Neil had gone through a list of things to have Gage do, and then he had dropped me off, not coming inside. I put my bag down on the chair and met his gaze.

"You watch *Gossip Girl*?" he asked before taking a drink from the coffee cup.

"Three episodes before I made myself quit and go to bed," I admitted.

He looked back at the television. "Guess not everything's changed then."

"So, that wasn't something you enjoyed and suggested to me?" Although after the first five minutes, I had known there was no way he watched that show.

He scowled. "Fuck no."

It had to have been one I liked before. He knew things I'd liked to eat, what I'd liked to watch. That didn't sound like a *fatal attraction* situation. There was the age difference, but I was beginning to think we'd had a relationship.

"I'm going to get Huck or Levi when you're done eating. You've got to get out of the bed and walk around some today. I have the crutches, but with your ribs and chest wound, they aren't ideal. It will be easier if you have someone to lean on who can support your weight. It's best if you can walk on the leg cast. It will take some work, but it'll help with blood flow."

He didn't say anything, so I left it at that and went to prepare the bathroom for him coming in and out. Right now, there was equipment that we no longer needed in the way.

When I walked back out of the bathroom, he cut his eyes to me. "With one of the crutches and you on my other side, I can get to the bathroom."

I wasn't so sure, but if he wanted to try it, I was willing. I got a crutch and put it by his bed. He threw back the covers, and I closed my eyes to keep from seeing his penis again.

"I'm wearing fucking briefs," he told me.

I opened my eyes and saw he had on a pair of white briefs. *Whew. Okay. That's good.*

Still a little more than I needed to see because, good Lord, his body was beautiful. The muscles in the one thigh I could see was as impressive as the rest of him. Lusting over the man wasn't going to get him out of this bed.

I helped him until his legs were turned toward me. I gave him a crutch for the side his cast was on, and I bent down so he could put his arm around my shoulders for the other side.

He pulled up with just a little grunt from the pain. That was easier than I'd expected.

"Take your time," I told him.

It was slow, but he walked to the bathroom with very little help from me. He used me for balance, but didn't put any weight on my shoulders. That concerned me since I was worried about his chest and ribs.

When we got to the toilet and stopped, I wasn't sure what he wanted me to do here. The last time I'd helped him pee didn't go well.

"Move back," he told me as he took his arm off me and then tried to pull his underwear down, but it wasn't working.

He glanced back at me. "You're gonna have to do it," he said, sounding disgusted by the idea. It stung, but at least it helped keep me grounded with him.

I stepped forward and pulled down the briefs, making sure to keep my gaze diverted. He chuckled as I stepped back. At least he was finding humor in this now, as opposed to being upset about my touching him. I kept my head down as I turned my back and walked to the door, giving him some privacy, but not getting too far in case he lost his balance.

Listening to him pee felt intimate, and I didn't know what to do with that. It shouldn't bother me or affect me in any way. It wasn't like he had a great personality. He was mean. I was just attracted to his looks. No worries about getting attached there.

When he finished, he didn't even try to pull his briefs up, so I went to do it for him. Trying to get them up and over the size of his rather large penis was harder than getting them down.

I was going to have to look and move a little closer. He held on to the side of the wall and turned slightly, making it easier for me. I had to pull the front of the briefs out some to get them up. Once that was accomplished, I stood back up, and my eyes clashed with his.

The expression on his face made it difficult for me to breathe. That was not a look of disgust. Not even close. His eyes dropped to my mouth, and my body seemed to feel it everywhere. Especially between my legs.

"You need to move," he said in a husky voice.

I stepped back but kept my eyes on him to make sure he didn't fall. "I, uh, need to get on your other side," I reminded him.

His eyes flared as he looked at me. "I need a fucking minute, Shiloh."

Okay. I nodded and stood there, waiting.

"Fuck," he muttered and clenched his teeth. "Come help me. I can't keep standing much longer."

I hurried to his side and slid under his arm, and then we made our way back to his bed. Turning so he could sit down without falling, I went slowly, and finally, he put some weight on me. When he was back in bed, I stood up, and he let me help him scoot back, which was a first. Then, I moved his cast back onto the bed.

Feeling accomplished and like I was doing my job for once, I leaned over him to adjust his pillow. It had slipped down. He said nothing while I did it, but his deep intake of breath made me pause. I pulled back and looked at him.

"That's enough," he said quietly.

I stepped back and made my way back over to the chair.

"Fucking peaches," he muttered.

Did he want peaches? I waited for him to say more, but he didn't say anything. When the silence continued, I reached for my e-reader. He slept some, and Huck came by to check on him. I used that time to go to the bathroom myself and get a bottle of water. When I returned, they were talking in hushed voices. I paused at the door, and Gage's eyes locked on me.

"I can come back later," I said.

Straight Fire

He shook his head. "No, we're done."

I walked in and went back to my chair. Huck gave me a nod on his way out.

"How's your pain? Need anything for it?" I asked him. It had been well over the time he usually needed pain medicine.

He shook his head.

I felt my phone vibrate in my pocket and pulled it out to check my messages. It was Wilder.

Back home. Dishwasher crisis is over. Want me to bring home barbecue and we can watch some more iZombie?

I smiled at the dishwasher crisis and started to text him back.

"Who is it?" Gage's question startled me.

I looked up at him, and he was glaring at the phone in my hand. I wasn't supposed to use my phone here. Crap, I had forgotten.

"I'm sorry. I forgot," I replied and went to put it in my bag.

"Who is it?" he repeated more forcefully.

"A friend," I replied.

"Male?"

I nodded.

His jaw tensed as he stared at me before turning his attention back to the television so he could glare at it.

"I never get texts during the day. It was an honest mistake."

He continued to look at the television as if it were his next victim. I wasn't going to keep apologizing. I was here because he'd wanted me to come back. I'd forgotten a rule. He could get over it.

"How many *friends* do you have?" he asked.

"Male or female or both?" I straightened in my chair.

"Male."

"One."

He let out a hard laugh. "Yeah. Guys aren't friends with women who look like you."

I narrowed my gaze. "Yes, they are, and that doesn't even make sense. How I look doesn't factor into it."

His head turned back to me. The look in his eyes made me shiver. "Is he heterosexual?"

I nodded.

Gage's jaw worked back and forth, and his nostrils flared. "Then, he's thinking about sinking his dick into your hot little pussy every fucking time he's around you and jerking off with you in his head when he's not."

Several things happened to me. I was taken aback by his choice of words. My nipples got hard, and I had to press my legs together to ease the throb caused by Gage Presley referring to the area between my legs as a *hot little pussy*. Oh my God, what was wrong with me? I didn't respond this way—ever.

He was staring at my legs and breathing heavily. If he didn't stop, I was going to need a time-out—alone.

"You're pressing your thighs together." He sounded angry.

I said nothing. I wasn't about to explain that one.

He lifted his eyes to mine. "Are you wet?"

I swallowed and stared at him. He was asking me about that? Wow, yeah, not answering him.

"Shiloh!" He raised his voice, and I jumped. "Are you fucking wet?" he growled.

I closed my eyes tightly so I didn't have to look at him. "Why are you asking me that?"

"You're pressing your thighs together. You do that when you're wet and horny."

Another thing he knew about me. Which meant … which meant we had done things. If I had left at nineteen, he'd have been twenty-four—my age now—when we might have done things. I opened my eyes to stare at him. Had we done sexual things when I was that young?

"I left here at nineteen," I said, my voice sounding as if I'd just run a mile. "You would have been my age now."

His grin looked evil, and because I was messed up in the head, it was also sexy. "Trust me, I know when you fucking left."

That hadn't answered my question.

"You need to go," he said, looking like he would strangle me if he could.

I stood up to leave the room.

"Take your shit. Go home," he barked.

I picked up my bag, then looked back at him. I wanted to ask him what about my question had made him angry. The fury in his expression stopped me from saying another word. I hurried out of the room. Uncle Neil wouldn't be here for a few more hours. I wasn't going to explain that to Gage though. I went downstairs and walked toward the kitchen with my phone in my hand. I'd text Uncle Neil and see if he could come now.

Levi was standing at the fridge when I walked in the kitchen, and Kye was at the table, looking down at his phone.

"You leaving?" Levi asked, looking at the bag on my arm.

"Yes. He told me to go home."

Levi frowned and looked at the time. "It's only three."

I nodded. I was aware of that.

"He give you a reason?" Levi asked me.

I pressed my lips together and tried to decide how to word this. Levi stood there, waiting on me to say something. I wished he'd just ask Gage himself.

"Uh, well, I think a conversation we were having went in a direction that made him angry."

Levi closed the fridge and cocked an eyebrow. "What was the conversation?"

I tucked some hair behind my ear. "It, uh, well, you see, he said some things about, uh, that guys can't be friends with girls like me and that my friend Wilder is secretly attracted to me. It just got out of hand, is all."

Levi smirked and shook his head. "He's not wrong, but that's not shit he needs to discuss with you."

I didn't respond to that. Instead, I held up my phone. "Is it okay if I text Uncle Neil to see if he can come get me early?"

Levi nodded his head toward the door. "I'll take you home," he said. "Kye, let's go."

Kye stood up and waited on me to follow Levi as he started to walk toward the other kitchen door. I didn't argue because he wasn't waiting on a response from me. I figured it was pointless. We walked through the living room and to another door leading into the garage.

Levi pulled out his phone as he walked toward a black sedan. "Yeah, check in on Gage. He sent Shiloh home, so I'm giving her a ride. Kye is with me." He paused. "You ask him." He ended the call.

I noticed the Mercedes symbol on the front of the car as the lights flashed on it and the doors unlocked.

"Let's go," he said to me as he opened the driver's door.

The thought that this could be the last time I saw Gage occurred to me, and it didn't feel good.

Chapter FIFTEEN

GAGE

The brunette Levi had brought home last night was draped over him on the sofa while they slept. Both of them were naked.

She'd sucked my dick and straddled me on the bed so that she could sink down on me without putting pressure on my ribs or chest. Then, I watched her and Levi fuck for over an hour. It had been a good distraction, but when I was coming, it wasn't the brunette I had thought about.

When Carmichael had called last night to tell me the replacement nurse would arrive today, I'd agreed because I knew, for my sanity, Shiloh had to go. That hadn't kept me from throwing the remote across the room when I hung up or the fact that it fucking physically hurt to think I wouldn't see her again. Sitting in that damn chair. Fixing my pillow and torturing me with her scent.

I ran a hand through my hair and glared at the ceiling. Not even a fucking week, and she had me screwed up. Why?

What was it with this one woman? It didn't help that she was different now. Especially since all the shit that had changed was the stuff that had led to our destruction. Gone was the spoiled princess with a cruel streak. She was now fucking perfect. Fate was a bitch.

"Mmm," the female whose name I could not remember moaned and stretched on top of Levi.

He reached up and grabbed a handful of her ass. Not even the sight of an available pussy put me in a good mood.

"Morning," Levi said sleepily. "Gonna ride my dick before we get up?"

She laughed and reached over to take a condom from the floor. Tearing it open with her teeth, she rolled it down on his morning wood like a pro, then shifted to sit on top of him.

"AH!" she cried out as he filled her.

I watched her bounce on him as he grabbed her waist and began slamming into her hard. She screamed and moaned while her fake tits barely moved. I laid my head back and closed my eyes, letting them finish. It wasn't doing anything for me.

She shouted that she was coming, as if we couldn't tell. Levi groaned as he got his nut, and then I heard him slap her ass.

"All right, sugar, get on up. I got shit to do."

There was a good chance the new nurse would arrive with them both naked in here while used, tied-off condoms littered the floor still. That should make her feel comfortable.

"What about you?" the brunette purred as she ran a hand under the blankets.

I started to tell her *no thanks*, but I reconsidered. Thinking about Shiloh while the brunette had sucked me off made for a fucking good orgasm last night.

The door opened.

"New nurse is here. Get dressed and pick up the fucking condoms," Huck said.

"I was gonna let her suck my dick before she left," I told him.

He shook his head at me. "You'll fucking scare off the new nurse. Carmichael is with her. He's got other people to see."

Then, Shiloh would have to come back. I didn't let that thought take root. I shoved that shit out of the way. Having her here was going to be my downfall. I couldn't do that again.

Levi started picking up the used condoms as the brunette put her clothes on. I glanced at the empty chair, not liking the idea that someone else was going to sit there. I hadn't even been able to let the brunette sit in it last night. Another thing that told me I was doing the right thing by not having Shiloh come back.

Levi left the room, still naked, carrying his clothes, while the brunette followed him. I glanced at my phone and thought about texting Shiloh. I had almost done it last night while I was getting my cock sucked. This morning, it was a little more tempting. Especially since I wouldn't see her today. I wanted to have some contact.

Fucking weak. I glared at my phone and my damn lack of self-control.

"Good morning," Carmichael said as he walked into the room.

I looked from him to the woman beside him. She was fifty and built a lot like Huck. He had been full of shit—I wasn't sure anything would scare off the woman.

"Gage, this is your new nurse, Doreen. She's been in the health care business twenty-five years and specializes in patients that need the kind of care you do," Carmichael began.

I nodded at Doreen, and she nodded back at me. No smile. All business. Fine, she would work. Hell, she could bathe me too. Fuck knew I wouldn't be getting a stiff dick with her. This worked out for the best. Carmichael continued to talk, and I tuned him out, then reached for my phone.

The new nurse is bigger than me.

I sent it. Why the fuck I'd sent it, I didn't know. I'd just needed to connect with her somehow.

No response. I gave it a couple of minutes, and the longer I waited, the more my chest tightened up, and I fucking hated that.

Don't go silent on me.

If she didn't fucking respond, I was calling her as soon as her uncle got out of here.

Shiloh.

Then, finally, the dots appeared. She was texting me back.

You're bossy.

The memory of her asking me if I was bossy and demanding in bed when she had been sixteen came back to me. Fuck, I should have left this alone.

And demanding.

I pressed Send because I wasn't leaving it alone.

I'm well aware.

I smiled down at her words.

You were the one squeezing your legs together yesterday.

Yep, I was going there. She'd been fucking wet, and it had made me feel an insanity I hadn't felt in a fucking long time. I had wanted her sitting on my fucking face so bad that I could hardly breathe.

Why are you doing this, Gage?

I stared at her question.

Can't seem to stop.

I answered her honestly. She didn't reply, and I forced myself to put the phone down.

Carmichael said his goodbyes and left. It was clear that he was in a much better mood now that Shiloh wasn't here. I couldn't blame the man.

"Smells like sex in here," Doreen said bluntly. "You want to go wash the woman off now or wait until later?"

She was right. It didn't smell like peaches and cream. I wanted it gone. It was grating on my nerves.

Chapter Sixteen

SHILOH

The next week and a half went by as if the days with Gage had never happened. Sarah came to stay at Wilder's, and we made cupcakes. I walked with them to the park Saturday afternoon. Tuesday night, I went to dinner with Wilder and his clients. I went back to my office job for Uncle Neil. Things fell back into a pattern I was used to. The one I had made for myself that was comfortable.

Except, now, it seemed empty.

Before meeting Gage, I had been perfectly content with my life. How had only a few days changed it all? They hadn't even been a good few days. They had been painful, confusing, and frustrating. Yet here I was, still missing this guy who had gone out of his way to make sure I knew he hated me.

I grabbed the bag of potato chips from the pantry and poured them over my rocky road ice cream, then went to watch *Gossip Girl*. I was on season three, and I freaking loved ice cream with potato chips. All things I would never have known if Gage hadn't told me.

I glanced at my phone lying on the coffee table. It had taken me four full days of checking my text messages constantly to accept he wasn't sending any more. I'd asked him why he was doing it, and he had said he couldn't seem to stop. That was it. Nothing more. He stopped. Out of sight, out of mind for him. Wished I could do that as easily.

As if I had summoned my phone to do something, it rang. I stared at it, confused, because that was rare, then reached over to pick it up. Gage's name lit up the screen. I glanced at the time. It was after nine. For one brief second, I considered not accepting it.

"Hello?" I said, realizing this was stupid.

"Hey." His deep voice came over the line.

Dang, that was a powerful jolt.

I waited since he was the one who had called me.

"How's your week been?" he asked me.

I frowned, looking down at my ice cream. Had he called to see how I was doing?

"Uh, good. Regular routine," I replied. "How are you and the new and improved nurse?"

He chuckled. "I wouldn't go that far. She's a hard-ass."

I was smiling. Dang it, why was I smiling?

"She can take care of you better."

He sighed. "Yeah, I wouldn't say that either."

His tone made goose bumps break out all over my arms and legs.

"The view isn't appealing anymore," he added.

Yes, I was grinning like a fool. I put my bowl on the coffee table and wrapped an arm around my legs, pulling them up to my chest.

"I seem to recall your former view not appealing to you either. In fact, it made you angry."

He let out a soft laugh. "I tend to get angry when I feel like I can't control something."

I didn't work there now. Questions were allowed.

"Gage, you verbally admitted to hating me," I reminded him.

"Yeah, I did," he replied. "But then you weren't you ... or the you I hated."

This was a setup for questions. "How am I different? For you, that is? I still have no idea what I did or what we were."

He was quiet for a minute. "What do you think we were?"

I chewed on my bottom lip, thinking about it. Then decided to go with the less likely theory. "Well, I wondered if maybe, since I was younger and you are hot, I had some sort of *fatal attraction* thing. Like a crazy stalker who ruined your life."

The laugh that resonated over the line made my chest feel warm. He had a great laugh. I was sure this meant that I hadn't been a crazed stalker.

"No, but damn if I wasn't slightly tempted just now to make you believe that."

I laughed this time. "That would have been cruel."

"I'm surprised that was what you came up with," he said.

I sighed. "Well, you're five years older than me. I couldn't think of a scenario that made sense."

"Yeah." He chuckled. "You were giving me too much damn credit then."

Frowning, I tried to figure out what he'd meant by that. "Care to explain that?"

"I was weak when it came to you. Not sure delving any deeper into the past is good," he replied.

For him. But he had his memories.

"Then, tell me why you called me at least," I said.

"Because I missed your voice."

I closed my eyes tightly. I hadn't expected that response.

"You going silent on me now?" he asked.

"No, I ..." I put my hand on my heart. It felt funny. "You, uh, have an effect on me I'm not used to."

"That right there. That's different. The old Shiloh, she wouldn't say what she was feeling. I was always fucking guessing."

"If she felt like this, then it was because she was scared. She was a teenager, and, well, you were you." I let out a laugh. "That's intimidating."

"Fuck, Shiloh," he groaned. "That's about all I can take for one night."

I instantly regretted saying anything. I had said too much. Maybe I did understand the old Shiloh better than I'd thought I did.

"I'm sorry," I said.

"Oh, no. You're not doing that. Don't apologize for being honest." He sounded tense.

"But it was more than you wanted to hear."

He made a deep sound and muttered something I couldn't make out. "I fucking wanted to hear it. It's my fucking body that can't take any more. Don't get the two confused."

"Okay," I replied, but I wasn't sure I understood that.

"I'm going to hang up now before I do something stupid. Good night, Shiloh," he said.

"Good night," I replied, and then the call ended.

I stared at the phone and sighed. That was a roller coaster I hadn't been prepared to ride. I wasn't sure how I was feeling now.

I set the phone down and stood up to take my melted ice cream to the garbage disposal. I wasn't in the mood for television now. A warm bubble bath and bed. I turned out the lights and locked up, then went to run my bath water. Remembering I'd forgotten my phone, I went back and got it from the living room. There had been a time two weeks ago that I didn't keep up with my phone at all. Barely checked it. Now, I was unable to stay away from it.

Chapter SEVENTEEN

SHILOH

There were only two patients left on today's schedule. It had been busy, but then it was flu season on top of other things. Strep seemed to be making its way around. Ace, Uncle Neil's ten-year-old golden retriever, nudged my leg with his nose as I put the last patient file away.

I smiled down at him. "You've had enough treats today."

His big brown eyes stared up at me, as if to remind me I was a pushover and that was why he loved me most.

"Ten-year-old doggies do not need to eat too many treats. It's bad for you," I explained to him.

It was clear Ace didn't care about canine health. He just liked the taste of bacon.

The front door to the office opened, and I stood back up straight to see a lady walking toward me with a pink box in her hand. She wasn't either of the patients who had appointments coming up.

I stepped up to the desk and greeted her. "Hello."

"I have a delivery for Shiloh Ellis," she informed me.

I looked at the pink box. I hadn't ordered anything.

"Uh, I'm Shiloh Ellis."

She gave me a bright smile that made the corners of her eyes crinkle. "Here you go. Enjoy!"

I reached out and took the box, confused as I read the imprinted silver logo on the top—*Huckleberry Treats*. Where was this place? I lifted my head to ask her who had sent them and realized she had already turned and was headed out the door.

"Excuse me. I've never heard of this place. Did someone send them to me?"

She stopped at the door and looked back at me with a strange frown. "Yes. We haven't made those in a few years, but the gentleman who ordered them said they were your favorite. He even paid extra to have us make those."

My eyes dropped back down to the package. There was a little quiver in my chest, and a grin spread across my face that I couldn't seem to help. Setting the box down, I glanced back up at her. "Oh, well, thank you," I told her.

She nodded, then turned and left.

Ace came over to put his face up on the edge of the table to check out the box too.

I moved the box back enough so that there was no danger of him reaching whatever was inside before I opened it up and looked down at the contents. Although I'd never tried one, I knew they were called whoopie pies. A coffee shop Isaac had gone to daily had them on display. Except these weren't chocolate or red velvet. They were a light violet in color and had pretty pastel sugar crystals on the center of each top. Isaac had said I hated whoopie pies when I tried to order one once. So, I never tried them.

The sweet vanilla-bean smell made my mouth water. Ace whined beside me. I glanced down at him, then back at the box. I knew who had sent them. For a moment, I'd thought perhaps Wilder had sent me something. Until she had said the man who had ordered them said they were my favorite. Wilder wouldn't know something like that.

"What smells so good?" Uncle Neil asked, walking out of his office and standing on the other side of the desk. He leaned over to look down at the gift in front of me. "Lavender whoopie pies from Huckleberry. I'd forgotten about those. Haven't seen them in years." He looked up at me. "Who sent them? A patient?"

I shrugged. "The person who delivered them didn't say."

He frowned, then headed toward exam room one. "You take them. I can't eat sweets at this age."

"Okay, thanks," I replied, then closed the box and put it in a safe place.

Finishing my workday was difficult. I glanced at my phone a hundred times, wondering if I should text Gage. Maybe call him when I got home. In the end, I did neither.

I placed a lavender whoopie pie on the coffee table in front of me and sat down on the sofa with the television remote in my hand. Wilder hadn't stuck his head out when I got home, and I hadn't knocked on his door. I was curious about the lavender treats and wanted to try one. Having Wilder asking questions about them would ruin the moment. I hated I felt that way. I'd never drawn a line in our friendship before. We had always talked about everything. Gage was the first thing I didn't want to share with him.

My phone dinged beside me, and the tiny spark of joy I felt made me pause for a moment. This was not how I should react to this man. I wasn't even sure it was Gage. I picked up my phone, and his name lit up the screen. I'd be lying if I said that didn't make me smile.

So, how are they?

He'd sent them. I had known it was him, but having him confirm it was better.

Be more specific.

I pressed my lips together as I hit Send.

Almost immediately, he began typing.

You know what the fuck I'm talking about.

I giggled, then winced at the sound of it. I was acting like a girl with a crush.

If you mean the lovely lavender whoopie pies, I am about to try one now.

You got them hours ago.

I was working.

There was a pause.

I'm waiting, Shiloh. Try it.

I reached for the plate and picked up what was basically two fat, soft cookies with cream in the middle. Opening my mouth, I took a bite. It was the most unique flavor I'd ever tasted. It was almost as if I could taste the lavender, but I wouldn't have expected it to be this delicious. I'd expected it to taste like the vanilla-bean smell, but it was the cream that was vanilla.

I picked my phone up.

This is incredible.

The dots that he started typing popped up, then just as quickly went away. I took another bite as I waited. This time, I let out a little groan. I couldn't think of one thing I'd ever tasted that compared to this.

Good.

That was all he had sent. Nothing more. Disappointed, I thought about not responding, but felt like he at least deserved a thank-you.
Thank you.
A moment later:
You're welcome.
Then, nothing.

Chapter Eighteen

SHILOH

This was the second night I'd given Wilder an excuse for not going to get dinner with him. Part of me felt guilty. Wilder was my friend, and ignoring him because Gage might or might not text me tonight was crappy of me.

However, the night after the lavender whoopie pies, he'd texted me, asking about my day. Then he had watched the episode of *Gilmore Girls* I was watching while making fun of what was happening. The only time he'd gone quiet was during the sex scene.

Last night, he'd texted, asking me what I was eating for dinner. We had gone back and forth, covering everything from the basketball game that he was watching in the living room with Levi to Doreen wrapping up his cast so he could shower himself. He could go downstairs now and get around on his own more.

My thoughts seemed to get stuck on him throughout the day, and as confusing as this man was, I didn't seem to be able to stop myself from texting with him. When I had been around him, he'd seemed to hate me, but now that we never saw each other, he texted me daily. I wondered if there was a female alive who could ignore this man.

After eating a sandwich, my last whoopie pie, and watching two episodes of *Gossip Girl*, I had to accept the fact that Gage wasn't texting me tonight. The disappointment that came with that sank in my chest like a brick. I hated this feeling, and the more I texted with him, the more power over my emotions he seemed to gain.

Opening a bottle of pinot noir, I poured a glass and went to run myself a bubble bath. Perhaps some hot water, wine, and music could ease this uncomfortable ache. I had only myself to blame for this. The man had kicked me out of his house, and I still continued to respond to him when he texted. Not because I was scared either. I did it because I wanted to. It was almost as if I physically could not ignore him. No matter how badly he humiliated me.

Taking off my clothes, I stepped into the bath and sank down into the bubbles. Just as I was getting comfortable, my phone dinged, and I sat up, dried off my hands, and picked it up while that stupid flutter of giddiness replaced the heaviness that had been there.

It no longer hurts to jerk off.

I read that three times and squirmed in the tub. Okay, he was going to talk about this. I should ignore him. Put the phone down and act like I hadn't read that. If I were smart, I wouldn't let myself interact with him. Especially not about anything sexual. I was an idiot though.

I texted him back:

I hope you got some relief then.

No more, Shiloh. Leave it at that. Be smart.

More than once.

I felt my nipples harden. *Ugh, Gage Presley, why?!* I was weak.
And you are telling me this ... why?
Because I wish you weren't. I didn't need this visual.
When I closed my eyes, it was the image of your mouth on my cock that did it. Felt like you should know.

I sucked in air as I reread that. My body hummed with pleasure just from words on a screen.
Me? I sent back to him.
Yes. You.

I laid my head back, breathing harder as I thought about him moving his hand up and down his cock. The sound of him groaning, thinking of me as he did it. His ripped chest flexing along with his bicep. Good Lord, I was only human, and that was too much. I slipped a finger inside me and let out a moan. My phone dinged again. I wanted to finish this, get my own relief first. I looked over at my phone lying beside the tub and read his text.
You going quiet on me again?

I didn't want him to disappear. Not when I was about to give myself an orgasm with him being the inspiration. Biting my lip, I reached over and typed out.
Just following your lead.

I pressed Send. I thought that was more vulnerable than I needed to be with Gage. He could shut me down and hurt me so easily. He'd proven that over and over.

The loud ring of the phone caused me to jump. Looking down at Gage's name, I felt as if I'd been caught doing something wrong. He was calling me. The thought of answering him after I sent a text like that was equally frightening and exciting. It wasn't like I would be seeing him again. There was comfort in hiding behind a phone.

"Hello?" I sounded breathless.

"Are you fucking yourself?" he asked roughly.

"Well, you said you did, and I'm taking a bath, and it sounded nice," I replied, feeling defensive.

"Fuck," he groaned. "Finish. I want to listen."

I sat up and shook my head as if he could see me. "I can't do that." But I wanted to.

"Yes, the fuck you can. Now, stick those pretty fingers back inside that sweet pussy and fuck yourself. Now, Shiloh." His hard, demanding voice made me tremble and the ache between my legs throb.

"Okay," I breathed as I picked up where I'd left off.

"I want to hear you," he growled.

"Okay," I panted.

My breathing became erratic, and I could hear myself moan as I rubbed my finger over my clit. The fact that he was listening to me seemed dirty, and I liked that. It wasn't something I'd done before.

"Fuck, I wish I could see you. Run my tongue up and taste that sweet cream." His voice was low and husky.

"Oh God."

His nasty talk was hot.

"I've had my tongue all over that pussy. Couldn't fucking get enough of it. I know how addictive it is."

I wished I could remember that.

"I didn't think we'd—" I couldn't make sentences. My hips bucked against my hand.

A low chuckle left his chest. "You have no idea."

I wanted an idea. In my state of arousal, I didn't care that he was cruel and mean. I didn't care that he had women come and suck his dick. Right now, I wanted to be that woman.

"Did we ..." I panted. "Is that all we did?"

"No, that's not all. I was the first dick to sink into that tight pink pussy. It was my dick you came on the first time. So fucking sweet. That night still tortures me."

My orgasm hit me, and I cried out, sloshing water over the side of the tub as I jerked against my hand.

"Still sounds as fucking sweet," he breathed into the phone.

I gasped and lay there, staring at the ceiling, not believing I'd just done that.

"Good night, sweet baby."

Then, the call ended.

I laid the phone down and closed my eyes.

I had given my virginity to a guy five years older than me? One who was dangerous?

I covered my face with my hand. Former me had been crazy. But I couldn't blame her for it. That man could make a nun act stupid.

Chapter Nineteen

GAGE

Getting my cast cut down to below my knee made things a hell of a lot easier. Finally getting to come downstairs again was one step closer to getting my life back. Doreen wasn't needed anymore, and today, I was free of her bossing me around.

Several of the guys had money riding on the basketball game that was on the flat screen, and Destiny had been keeping my whiskey glass full.

Fucking pissed me off that none of this put me in a good mood. Levi had already said something about my foul mood. I'd told him to fuck off, and he'd laughed like it was hilarious. Asshole. He'd left to go get food. Huck and Trinity were out of town, so we had no one cooking for us.

Destiny ran her nails through my hair, and I fought the urge to shove her away from me. She didn't deserve my shitty attitude. Fuck knew she had put up with a lot from me, yet never bitched about it. She never pushed for more or sulked. That was the kind of easy a man needed.

I tipped my glass back and took a long drink. The fact that I'd fucking listened to Shiloh get herself off on the phone three nights ago was still driving me crazy. I had purposely not texted her again. She was dangerous. I'd been a fucking idiot, thinking I could be near her or even have contact with her and not get pulled in. Wondering what the fuck she was doing on a Friday night made me tense. The itch to get my phone, go outside, and call her was clawing at me.

Why couldn't I just be happy with Destiny? There was no threat there. She wouldn't mess up my head. There would be no fucking crazed monster emerging when she flirted with another man. No possessiveness. It would be worry-free. Drama-fucking-free.

Destiny reached down and ran her hand over my shoulder and traced patterns on my arm. I wasn't sure when she'd picked one of us, but it was clear she had. Levi hadn't even been on her radar the past few times she came over. It had been all me. Not that Levi cared. He wasn't territorial either. Never had been.

"You need anything?" Destiny purred in my ear.

Yeah, to forget Shiloh Ellis.

I shook my head.

My phone dinged, and I jerked it out of the pocket of my jeans like the crazy fucker I was, only to see Levi's name. Opening it, I expected him to be asking something about what he was picking up. Although he was the one who had ordered the food. I hadn't given a shit.

Looks like Shiloh found her a man.

And there was a photo of Shiloh sitting at a table, smiling at some fucking guy across from her.

The pounding in my temples as I glared at the image on my screen was going to lead to fucking violence. I hadn't needed

Straight Fire

to see this shit. Why the fuck had Levi sent it to me? And who the motherfucking hell was that guy?

"Isn't that the nurse you fired?" Destiny asked over my shoulder, and I sat up, moving away from her.

"Don't fucking look at my messages," I barked at her.

Who is he? I texted back.

Don't know. Want me to go ask?

I took several deep breaths, mentally battling with myself over the answer to that.

Yes.

Destiny began to massage my shoulders. "You're all tense. Let me make it better," she whispered in my ear.

I needed her to get the fuck away from me. The vibrating in my chest was not a good sign. No one needed to be near me when I fucking snapped.

I shoved myself out of the chair and stood, hating this fucking cast and the limitations with it. Destiny stood up and came to curl up beside me.

I turned to glare down at her. "Get away from me," I warned through clenched teeth.

She pouted and stepped back. "I can make you forget her."

No, the fuck she couldn't. No one could. I'd fucking tried that for years.

Chapter TWENTY

SHILOH

I officially felt like an idiot. Gage hadn't contacted me again, and what I'd let him listen to me do was all the more embarrassing. I tried to block it out and keep busy. That was easier said than done.

Wilder met me at my door and suggested we go get dinner. That was better than sitting at home, watching *Gossip Girl* and trying not to remember the call with Gage. Tonight was one of the warm winter evenings in Florida, and we went to the seafood place in town that had rooftop seating. Wilder had stopped asking about Gage, and he seemed happier that I was working back at the office.

The thought that Wilder wanted in my pants bothered me some, thanks to Gage putting the idea there. But Wilder never stepped over the invisible line I'd drawn. Other than him talking about the fact that he found me attractive at times, he was a friend and only that.

When the server placed our food on the table, I looked up to thank her, but my eyes collided with another pair I hadn't been expecting. Levi was sitting over at the bar with a glass in his hand, looking directly at me. It was weird, seeing him somewhere besides the house he lived in with Gage.

I smiled and gave him a small wave. He returned the smile, then turned his attention back to the women sitting beside him. I doubted he was on a date. That didn't seem like something he would do. He wasn't a relationship guy, much like Gage. They liked girls they could text for blow jobs.

Wilder was looking at me, then turned to see who I had waved at. Levi glanced at Wilder a moment, then turned to say something to the server who had spoken to him.

"You know him?" he asked.

"Yeah, he's a friend of the guy who I had to do the *home nurse* thing for." That was the only way I could think of to explain it.

"He didn't seem to hate you," he said, picking up his fork.

I shrugged. "I don't think he ever did exactly. We didn't talk much, and I rarely saw him."

Wilder seemed appeased by that, and I was thankful he was letting it drop. It was hard to talk around this stuff. I was used to just telling Wilder everything. Other than Wilder, my only real friend in town had been Lynn. She had moved, and I hadn't gotten close to the other ladies in the office.

I listened as Wilder started telling me about his phone call with Sarah today. She had gotten a new puppy and was thrilled. Her grandmother, however, was the one who had bought it and was keeping it at her house. Her mom didn't want to keep it.

"Hello, Shiloh." Levi's voice surprised me, and I looked up to see he'd walked over to us. I hadn't been paying attention.

"Levi, hello," I said, smiling up at him. "Oh, uh, Levi, this is Wilder, my friend and neighbor. Wilder, this is a friend of one of Uncle Neil's patients."

Levi chuckled. "I've been his patient before too," he replied. "Carmichael is the only doctor to ever stitch me up."

I hadn't thought about that.

"It's nice to meet you," Wilder told him.

Levi gave him a once-over, then looked back to me. It was rude, but I wasn't going to correct the man.

"Hope we see you around soon," he said, then winked before walking away.

"That was weird," Wilder said once he was far enough away.

I frowned, then nodded my head in agreement. "Yeah, it was."

My phone dinged in my purse, and I tensed. I saw Wilder's gaze on me, and I continued to eat my meal. I wasn't touching that phone. Not here. What if Wilder looked at it and Gage said something about the other night? No way. That would be humiliating.

The phone dinged again. I put another fry in my mouth and met Wilder's gaze, then smiled. This wasn't his business. Why was he being so nosy?

The phone dinged again.

"You gonna answer that? Sounds like someone needs to talk to you," he replied.

I sighed and stood up. "I'll be right back," I said, then took my purse and headed for the restroom.

Pulling my phone out of my purse, I saw Gage's name with three notifications. I pushed the restroom door open and stepped inside as I opened the text.

On a date with your friend?
Not gonna even look at your phone?
Do I need to send Levi back in there?

I sighed and hoped Levi wasn't back.
I was eating. Yes, it's my friend. Why does it matter?
I chewed on my bottom lip nervously.
Leave.
What?
Leave. Go get your food and go home. Alone.
No. That's rude and crazy.
Shiloh, go the fuck home.

I stuffed the phone back in my purse, silencing it. *He doesn't contact me for three days and then thinks he can tell me what the heck to do. I don't think so, mister.*

Taking a moment to calm myself, I stared in the mirror. I might have just pissed off a man I wasn't sure if I should be scared of or not. But no one was going to talk to me like that. I would deal with the fact that it might have turned me on later. Right now, I was mad about it.

I headed back out into the restaurant and saw Wilder was done eating and drinking his beer. Maybe leaving was best. I pulled out my chair and sat down.

Wilder frowned at me, looking concerned. "Everything okay?"

I nodded. "Yeah. If you're done, I can get the rest of mine to go. Sorry about that."

He leaned forward, resting his elbows on the table. "You look shaken up. Who was texting you?"

I wished he'd stop being nosy. Granted, up until now, I had told him things, but my life had been boring then. It was currently anything but.

I shook my head. "Not something I can talk about, but I am fine."

"You can't talk about it, or you can't talk about it with me?"

I understood his question, and he deserved honesty.

"I don't think it's something we should discuss."

He nodded. "That's what I thought."

I waved at the server and got a to-go box.

Wilder paid even though I'd tried to pay for my half. I felt guilty about him doing it. This night had turned out to be a bit of a mess. We walked back to the apartment in silence. It was awkward, and I didn't like feeling that way with Wilder.

When we reached my door, I looked up at him. "This got weird. I don't want that."

He sighed. "Yeah, me neither. Listen, it's my fault. I handled it wrong. I'm sorry."

I hugged him and stepped back, feeling better. "Thanks for dinner," I told him before unlocking my door and going inside.

I set my food on the counter and pulled out my phone, nervous about what all it was going to say.

Only one text.

Call me when you get home.

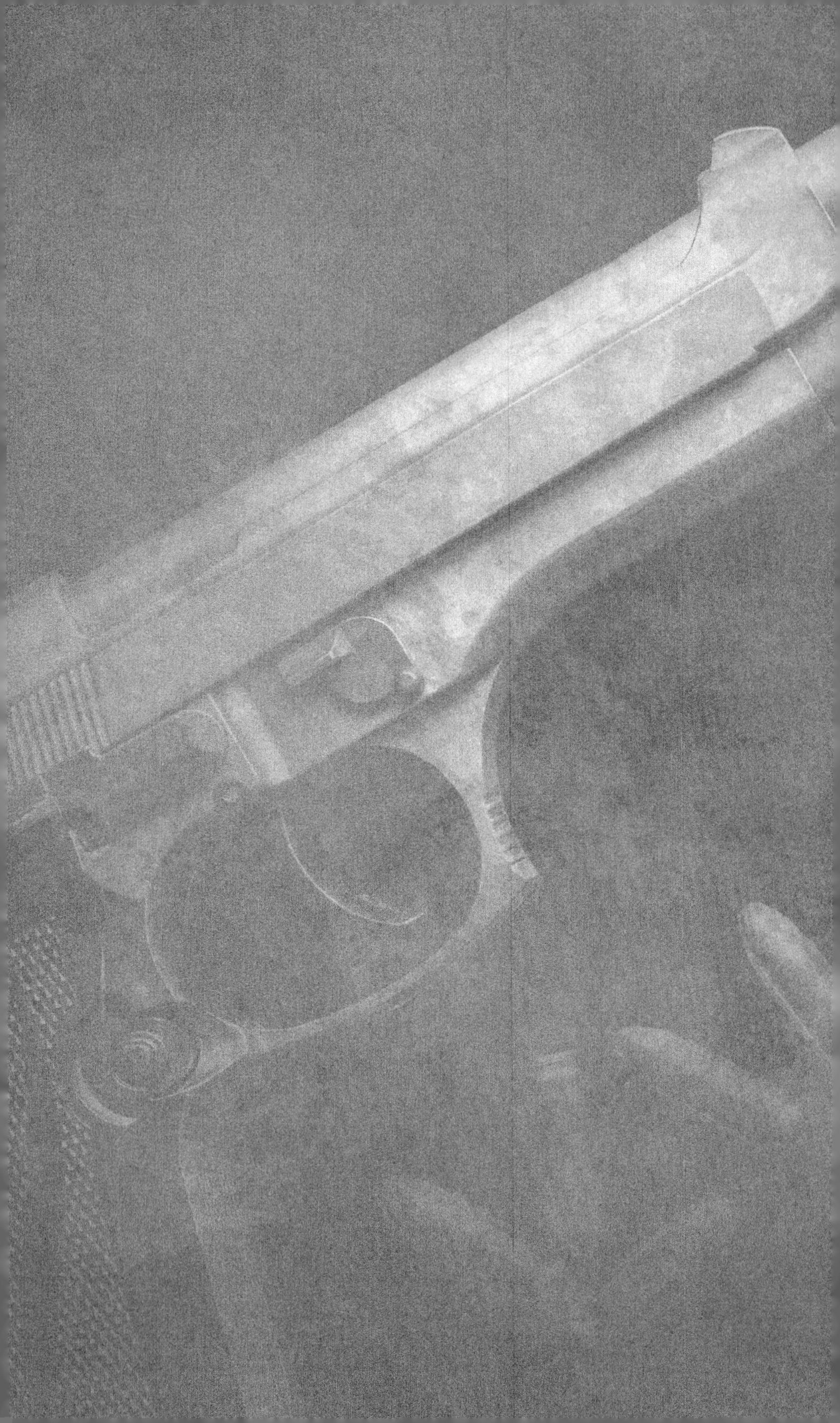

II

It isn't fair to claim that it was toxic when obsession is but a deeper realm of love.
— Abbi Glines

to try:

Rocky Road ice cream with potato chips

~~Whoopie Pies~~ lavender? yum!!

Questions for Gage -

Chapter Twenty-One

SHILOH

Letting my anger get the best of me, I pressed Gage's number.

"That took too long," he said.

"You don't have the right to demand I do something."

He chuckled.

"Why is that funny? I am serious."

"Because you did it, and now, you're yelling at me about it."

I clenched my fists. I hadn't meant to do it, but, yes, it'd happened.

"Why do you care who I go out with?" I asked.

He didn't respond right away. I waited because I needed to hear an answer.

"Who do you think about when you finger-fuck yourself?"

This was not a fair question. "You are answering a question with a question."

"Who, Shiloh?" His voice was softer now, and it caused the fluttering feeling in my stomach.

"You."

"Right, and I don't want you around any more fucking cocks." His tone made me shiver.

"He's a friend."

"Don't care."

I closed my eyes, frustrated by all of this. "Gage, you haven't contacted me in three days. Before that, it was sporadic, at best. You didn't want me as your nurse. I'm getting mixed signals, and it's confusing."

He was quiet for a moment.

"Would you come back here?" he asked me.

"To be your nurse?"

"Yes."

"What about Doreen?"

"I want you."

Whew, this was tempting. "I'm not sure Uncle Neil will allow me to."

He chuckled. "Carmichael will do what I say."

This was a bad idea.

"Please, Shiloh."

Oh good Lord, how was a woman supposed to deal with this? It wasn't fair. I was trying to be smart and make good choices. Gage Presley was not a good choice. But in the two years since my life had basically begun, he was the only person to make me feel all these things.

"Are you going to be nice to me?" I asked.

"Very."

"No more getting angry and sending me away? No more hating me for something I don't even remember?"

"I'll be on my best behavior."

The deep timbre in his voice had some kind of power over me.

"What is it that we are doing?" I asked him.

"You're gonna be my nurse."

Somehow, I didn't feel like that was the case, but I didn't care. My vagina was currently in control right now. "Okay."

"You'll need to bring your overnight bag. Huck and Levi have to go out of town. Trinity is going to stay elsewhere."

Overnight? That sounded like a terrible idea.

"Okay," I whispered.

"Good night, Shiloh," he said into the phone before the line went dead.

This was insanity.

Uncle Neil said very little as he drove me to Gage's the next morning. He had frowned at the overnight bag in my hand, but said nothing.

When we pulled through the security gate, he finally broke the silence. "He's a dangerous man. You understand that, right?"

I nodded. "I do."

"And you want to do this? You're sure?"

As if he could save me if I didn't.

"I want to. He's not forcing me. He asked, and I agreed."

Uncle Neil glanced at me. "I can't protect you from him. Any of them."

"I know," I told him and reached over to squeeze his arm. "You don't have to."

He pulled up to a stop outside the house and let out a weary sigh. "Be careful, Shiloh."

I hugged him. "I will."

Taking my bag, I opened the door and stepped out into the sunshine. It felt more like spring than winter. Heading for the stairs, I wasn't surprised when Huck answered the door before I got to the top.

He looked about as happy as Uncle Neil. "You know what you're doing?" he asked me.

"Yes."

"How much has he told you about your past together?"

I shook my head. "Not a lot."

His scowl wasn't anything new. I thought it was permanent when he looked at me.

"You might want to find out more."

Noted.

He stepped back and let me come inside. "He just went back up the stairs. He's been coming down to eat, and he goes to the living room to watch television. He knew you were coming and went back up."

"Okay," I replied, then headed for the stairs.

The Gage who flirted and didn't seem to hate me I'd only really experienced on the phone. Seeing him in person after things had changed had me feeling nervous. What if Wilder was right? What if this was a mistake?

I reached his bedroom door and went inside. The hospital bed was gone, and in its place was a king-size bed with a black iron frame. When I turned my head to the right, I found him watching me. He was sitting up on the sofa with his broken leg no longer in a full leg cast, and it was propped up on an ottoman that hadn't been here before. It was clear he was doing much better.

"Looks like you've made a lot of progress."

He grinned at me, making me feel light-headed. "Doreen was a drill sergeant."

That was exactly what he needed.

"She was good for you then."

"I like her replacement a hellavua lot better. Come here, Shiloh." His voice dropped slightly.

Walking over to him, I set the overnight bag down and then started to take a seat on the other end of the sofa. He shook his head at me and patted the spot beside him. My nerves were on overdrive now. I sat down.

"Shiloh."

"Hmm?"

"You're fucking tense. Relax," he told me.

I tried, but it was difficult. "Your moods make me nervous. I don't know what I'm getting with you. This is a new mood, so I need adjustment time. Not to mention, I'm not sure you need a nurse anymore." I figured being honest was best.

He reached out and squeezed the top of my thigh. "I gave up on hating you. It wasn't fucking working. I thought that was clear from our phone conversations. And I didn't need Doreen, but I do need you."

I laughed softly and looked down at my hands. Wow, okay. Was he saying he needed me sexually? Good Lord, I wasn't ready for that.

"Yeah, well, the phone and in person are completely different. Like I've said before, you're intimidating."

He lifted his hand and grabbed my chin between his thumb and finger, forcing me to look up at him. "I don't want you nervous around me." His amber eyes held my gaze.

I smiled. "Not sure that can be helped."

His thumb brushed the single dimple in my cheek. "Fucking love this dimple. Always have."

It was a strange dynamic. Having had a sexual relationship with a man who was very intense and not remembering any of it. This had never been an issue with Isaac. He'd not made me feel this way. Looking at him didn't make my stomach flutter or my heart race. Not once had he said or done something to make me need to squeeze my thighs together. A part of me wished I remembered this—*us*—but then I'd remember what I had done. I didn't think I wanted that on my chest.

Hearing what I had done and living through it would be two different things.

"I can't lean forward yet, baby," he said, looking down at my lips. "Hurts too bad. You're gonna have to come to me. I've waited five long fucking years, and I need this mouth."

My entire body felt feverish. With my heart pounding in my chest, I scooted closer and leaned in, careful not to touch his chest or ribs, and pressed a kiss to his mouth. I'd caught myself staring at his mouth while he slept more than once. Wondering what it would feel like to kiss it. Feel his lips move over mine.

He cupped my face as his tongue slid into my mouth. The warmth from our breaths mingled, and I smelled the mint of his toothpaste. He moved his head slightly and plunged deeper. I wanted to press myself against him and get closer. Feel his body heat. I was careful though, not wanting to cause him any pain.

I felt his hand slide up my leg, then inside my shorts. My breath caught, and I started to pull back. His eyes locked on me, and he shook his head. Leaning back in, I felt small little flicks of his tongue along my bottom lip before he pressed his mouth to mine once more. His hand pushed open my legs, and I stopped breathing completely as he moved his fingers inside my shorts until his fingertips brushed my damp panties.

He broke the kiss, his breaths coming in hard, but his forehead rested on mine. "You're already wet," he whispered against my lips.

"You excite me," I replied honestly.

"Fuck, you're gonna kill me," he groaned.

A knock on the door startled me, and I moved back, turning toward the door and pressing my open legs back together just in time for Levi to enter the room.

He glanced at me, then at Gage. "We're heading out."

"Good," Gage replied tightly.

Levi gave him a knowing grin. "You sound anxious to get rid of us."

"Yeah," he agreed.

Levi looked back at me. "Feels almost like old times. Except you're not a bitch."

"Levi." The warning in Gage's voice made me tense.

However, Levi laughed, clearly amused.

"Take care of him, Nurse," he drawled, looking amused as he closed the door.

"I wasn't done." Gage's tone was husky.

I turned back to him, and his gaze dropped back to my mouth.

"Give me that mouth, Shiloh."

Chapter TWENTY-TWO

GAGE

They were fucking gone. Two days of having Shiloh all to myself. I'd listened to Huck and Blaise remind me how badly this girl had messed me up the last time. Levi had been the only one to point out how different she was now. Blaise hadn't been around this version of her, but he'd said that wasn't the point. They all thought I was fucking crazy anyway, and there was a part of me that knew I was wired differently from others. That, compounded with my obsession with this woman, had made me fucking mental. They acted like I'd forgotten, but I remembered.

What would happen when this Shiloh saw how dark and twisted I could be? If she got a glimpse of the me I kept just under the surface? The girl she'd been before freaked the fuck out. Turned on me and never looked back. The spiral that had come from that, I never wanted to repeat it.

Blaise had said I didn't love her, and I knew he didn't think I had it in me to love. He'd said what I'd experienced with

Shiloh was infatuation on a level that was dangerous. If that was what she had on me—this fucking insane pull—I didn't care. I'd tried to hate her, I'd tried to quit her, and then Levi had told me she was on a motherfucking date. I snapped. The outcome hadn't been a pleasant one for anyone in this house.

She was here now. With me. And damn if she was leaving me again. Not until I was done. When I could get my fucking fill and let her go, then she could leave. If that day came.

Watching her prepare the bed for me to stretch out on and get the pillows piled up made the damn beast inside of me roar. He only seemed to wake up in her presence. No one else had ever triggered it. When she had it to her liking, she turned to look at me. I was trying real fucking hard to slow myself down. Demanding she walk around naked the next two days wasn't going to go over well, and I knew that. But damn if I didn't want to demand it.

"Ready?" she asked, walking over to me.

I reached for the one crutch I used and stood up before she could get to me.

She pursed her lips. "I could have helped you."

Damn, she was sexy.

"Then, help me," I replied, waiting on her to come over and put my arm around her shoulders. Which I no longer needed. She didn't know that though.

Once I had her on my side, I let her think she was getting me to the bed. Meanwhile, I enjoyed the way she felt up against me. When we reached the bed—much slower than if I'd have just walked over here—I turned and sat down, then scooted back.

I looked up at her, and she was frowning.

"I'm not sure you need me."

"Trust me, baby, I need you," I assured her. In so many ways.

She didn't seem convinced but went to adjust the pillows behind me. They were fine, but if this was going to get her tits in my face, she could fucking do what she wanted. Reaching up, I cupped one of her full tits in my hand and squeezed. She froze and looked down at me.

"Take your time," I said, rubbing my thumb over her nipple, wishing this shirt were off.

She stood up slowly, as if she hadn't wanted to move but she was finished with the pillows. "Can I get you something to eat? Or drink?"

"You can lie down beside me," I said.

She bit her bottom lip and glanced over at the chair she used to sit in. Like hell was she sitting over there now.

"You sure it'll be comfortable for you?"

"Swear."

She slipped off her shoes and walked around to climb onto the bed.

"All the way over here," I said, knowing she was going to stop too far away.

She moved until the side of her body brushed up against mine.

"What do you want to watch?" I asked, picking up the remote and turning on the television.

"Doesn't matter."

I flicked through the movies until I found one we'd once watched on a date. She wouldn't know that, but I wanted to see her watch it. There were some heavy sex scenes in it, and I'd had a memorable time with her in the back row of the dark theater.

Turning it on, I stretched out my arm and looked at her. "Come here."

She paused. "Will this hurt your ribs?"

"Not if you're gentle."

Straight Fire

She moved closer and laid her head on my shoulder, turning into me. I slid my good leg between her legs. She finally curled into me. Fucking hell, I'd missed this. Turning, I pressed my mouth to the top of her head and kissed it. Soaking in her scent.

The movie was starting, and her attention was focused on it completely. My eyes, however, were on her long, smooth legs that my leg was resting between. My tan skin against her pale skin had always stirred my possessive side. Didn't know fucking why, but with Shiloh, nothing had ever made sense.

Finally tearing my eyes off her body before my dick got any harder, I watched the screen. It was thirty minutes before the first sex scene started. The explicit nature of it caused her cheeks to flush. She wiggled a little, and I bent my knee, moving my leg up until it pressed against her pussy. I felt her body freeze. I rubbed my leg against her, and she gasped, and then her eyes went back to the screen.

Slowly, she began to rock against my leg. The hand I didn't have wrapped around her fisted at my side. She pressed down harder, and I pushed against her.

"Rub it off on me, baby," I whispered close to her ear. I watched the goose bumps cover her arms.

Her little pants were going straight to my dick. I stuck my hand down the front of my shorts and adjusted myself. The scene ended, but I wasn't done with this.

"Take off your shorts for me," I said.

She tilted her head back and looked up at me.

"Get them off and let me play."

Her sharp intake of air caused her bottom lip to fall open slightly. I wanted to suck it into my mouth. I pulled my leg out from between hers, and she lifted her hips and tugged the shorts down until she could kick them off. The pink cotton bikini-cut panties taunted me by covering up what I wanted to see. She wasn't ready yet, and I knew it.

I waited until she lay back down beside me. "Open your legs for me," I told her while my hand moved down her stomach and slipped under the front of her panties.

When I slid my finger inside, she let out a moan.

"You're soaking wet," I told her, and she let out a soft little cry. "Watch the movie and let me play with this hot little pussy."

Another sweet sound. Her eyes were locked on my hand beneath her panties.

"You like seeing my hand spreading you open?"

She nodded, her chest rising and falling fast. I wanted her tits bared so I could watch them. Her eyes closed, and she pressed her head back against the pillow and moaned. Fuck, how had I gone five years without that view?

I pulled my hand out and sucked on my fingers. Her eyes flew open, and she watched me.

"What do I have to do to get you to sit on my face?"

She frowned. "What?"

"Take off those panties and sit on my face, Shiloh. You used to love to do it," I assured her.

She inhaled sharply and bit her bottom lip. I could see her thinking about it. I had wanted to go slow, but, damn, I needed to bury my face in that hot cunt.

"I did?" she asked, sounding unsure.

I grinned. "You were as addicted to my tongue on your pussy as I was to the taste of it."

"Oh," she breathed.

The hesitation was starting to shift toward nervousness. Before I let her think too hard, I turned on my side, hoping she didn't notice how easily I could do that now, and pressed my lips against hers. Softly taking nips of her full bottom lip until her tongue brushed against mine. A whisper of a moan escaped her, and I continued to deepen the kiss. The taste of fucking peaches was still as intoxicating. Her fingers delicately swept across my cheek before they tangled in my hair.

My hand drifted down, past her smooth and flat stomach, and back inside the panties she still hadn't taken off for me. A small whimper came from her throat as she opened her legs. The slick heat that met my fingers caused the fucking beast inside me to stretch and rumble. This belonged to me. I could feel the urgency to possess her grip me.

"Give me your pussy," I whispered against her lips as my fingers pressed and stroked in the places I knew would make her desperate.

Her heavy breathing was warm against my skin as her eyes met mine.

"Please," I added, ready to fucking beg her if that was what it would take.

When she moved to sit up, I pulled my hand back out and licked her from my fingers while she tugged her panties down, then discarded them. I was still enjoying the taste of her when she turned to me. She dropped her gaze to my middle finger as I ran the tip of my tongue up it.

"How do I do this?" she whispered.

I laid my head back on the pillow and held my hand out to her. "Straddle my face like my mouth is my cock."

Her hand slipped into mine, and she pulled herself up onto her knees. After looking down at me one more time, she followed my directions.

I let go of her hand and grabbed her ass, tugging her closer. "Hold on to the headboard, baby."

When she was in place, I trailed my tongue slowly through her slit before circling her swollen clit. Fuck, that was sweet.

I felt her tremble, and my dick throbbed in my sweatpants. Pulling her down closer to my face, I inhaled her, rubbing my nose against her sensitive folds while fucking her with my tongue.

"Oh my God," she panted, slowly moving her hips as I tasted and sucked. "Gage." The desperate plea went straight to my dick.

I took one hand off her soft, round ass and shoved the front of my pants down until my swollen erection was free. I could feel the pre-cum already leaking from the tip. I gripped it in my fist and began to pump as I drowned myself in the sweet taste of the best pussy I'd ever had.

"Ride my face," I told her.

She looked down at me and shuddered.

"Feel good, baby?" I asked her, taking my other hand and running my finger through the wet folds.

"Yes," she moaned. "God, yes."

Her eyes stayed locked with mine as she rocked her hips back and forth over my mouth.

"Fucking love this pussy," I growled, sinking my finger further into her tight hole.

"AH! I can't," she cried out. "Oh, oh, oh! Please don't stop."

This place could burn down around us, and I wouldn't stop until she climaxed on my face. Her little pleas had my hand working harder over my cock.

"That's it, sweet baby. Come all over my tongue. I want to fucking drown in it."

Her body jerked over me then, and I watched her head fall back. Goddamn, she was gorgeous. She screamed my name, pressing down hard on my tongue, and I shouted as my own cum shot onto my stomach. I reached up and grabbed her ass once again and held her there while the last tremors ran through her body.

Straight Fire

When she stilled, I took one more long lick that caused her to shudder before she lifted herself up and off me. I watched her face, waiting to see how she was going to react to what we'd just done. Her eyes slid down me until they froze on my semi-hard cock lying against my semen-covered stomach. I smiled as those eyes widened before she turned to meet my gaze.

"You came on my face, baby. Smelling like fucking heaven and tasting just as sweet. Yeah, I got the fuck off on it," I said, smirking.

Those pretty blue eyes swung back to my stomach. "Can I touch it?" she asked hesitantly.

"My cum or my dick? Not that it matters. You can touch whatever the fuck you want." I was gonna be hard again in record time.

"Cum," she said softly as her cheeks flushed.

Then, she reached out and ran a finger over my stomach, swirling it around as if my fucking load was fascinating. Holy hell, I wasn't sure how long I could just lie here and watch this.

She let out a small gasp when my cock hardened again.

I laughed, and her eyes swung up to meet mine.

"Shiloh, honey, you're fucking playing with my cum. What did you expect?"

"But I read … I mean, I thought it took longer than that to… you know."

I shook my head.

"Oh," she breathed, then moved her attention back to my cock.

"Keep that up, and I'm gonna have you riding my dick next, baby. I'm trying to go slow, but you aren't making that easy."

She sat back and curled her legs up under her. My eyes went to her still-bare pussy.

"You need rest. This is too much strain on you. Let me get dressed, and I'll go get you something to drink and eat." She paused and looked back at my stomach. "I'll, uh, get you something to clean that up."

I smirked as she scrambled off the bed, giving me a perfect view of her naked ass. She bent over and slipped her panties back on, then grabbed her shorts. I wished she'd leave the fucking shorts off, but I didn't say anything. Pushing her too fast could mess this up. I had to gauge where was too far with her. This wasn't forever, and it wasn't love.

Blaise had once said Shiloh and I were toxic together.

He wasn't wrong. We had been. Even if she didn't remember it.

Keeping a line there that we didn't cross emotionally was the only way we could do this. It was the only way I knew we could survive it. Getting my own fucked up need for her and possessiveness under some form of control was the biggest issue.

She walked back into the room with a damp cloth, and I expected her to hand it to me, but she began to wipe me clean herself. Didn't help my current state of arousal. A low groan came from my throat when she wrapped her cloth-covered hand around my dick and moved it up and down. Her eyes darted to mine when she finished and pulled my sweats back up.

"What can I get you from the kitchen?" she asked.

I could get down to the kitchen, but I wasn't sure telling her that was the best idea. The more she realized I no longer needed a nurse, the more I risked the chance of her leaving. She was mine for two days to hopefully fuck out of my system. Get her out of my head and manage to function without violent urges when I thought about another man touching her.

"With your help, I can get down to the kitchen," I told her. "Why don't we order something and find a movie to watch downstairs?"

She held her hand out to me. "Okay."

Apparently, she was going to help me sit up. I gave her my hand and let her think she was pulling me into a sitting position. It took longer with her help to stand, and not smiling at how fucking cute she was while concentrating was hard.

I was playing a dangerous game.

In the back of my mind, there was, *What if you can't fuck her out of your system? What then?*

I didn't have the answer to that.

Chapter Twenty-Three

SHILOH

"I want the cheeseburger, medium well, with provolone cheese and mushrooms," I told Gage after looking at the menu he'd pulled up on his phone.

"That's not how you like your cheeseburgers," he said.

Frowning, I nodded my head. "Yes, it is."

"No, baby, it isn't. I've ordered you a cheeseburger more times than I can count. You were very specific about how you wanted them."

This was about before me. So far, I had liked all the food he'd suggested. Perhaps I would like this too. "Fine. Order it the way I used to eat it, but I doubt I'll like it as good."

He smirked as he dialed the number. I listened to him order his food, waiting to hear how I used to like my cheeseburgers. "Cheeseburger, medium, siracha mayo, cheddar cheese, and skinny fries on the burger, not beside it."

My jaw dropped. Was he serious?

He cut his eyes at me and winked. How was it that when this man winked, it made anything he said okay? My insides felt all gooey and soft.

When he was done, he dropped his phone beside him, then reached over and pulled me closer to him. I wanted to curl up in his lap and purr like a freaking kitten. This Gage was addictive. I wasn't clingy or needy, but I could easily become that with him. Not a pleasant thought. That was not something I wanted to turn into.

Gage put an arm around me so that I could lean in against him.

"I don't want to hurt you," I said, thinking of his ribs.

"You won't," he replied, taking his other hand and dragging me against him.

Fine. I would just be careful. His bare chest and raised scar from the knife, which was still angry-looking but closed up now, held my attention. I'd touched his semen earlier because I really wanted a reason to feel his stomach. Now, I wanted to run my hands over his pecs and see how his hard chest felt under my fingertips.

"In the mood for a horror film tonight?" he asked me as he flipped through the movie options on the television.

Sitting downstairs in the living room was new for me. I'd barely even been in this room when I was here before. Gage had his cast on a large ottoman in front of him with his other foot on the floor. The cutoff sweatpants he wore hung low on his waist, giving me a view of the cut, defined V below his stomach.

"Shiloh?"

"Yeah?" I asked, tearing my eyes off his bare chest and stomach to meet his gaze.

"Horror movie?" he asked, a smile teasing his lips. He'd caught me.

I nodded my head.

"Just so we're clear," he said, reaching over and taking my hand, then placing it on his chest, "you can touch me anywhere at any time."

That was entirely too much temptation. I looked at my hand on his chest, and he flexed beneath me. A small laugh bubbled up, and I glanced back up at his face. Lord, this man was pretty.

"Go ahead. Explore," he goaded me.

I slowly ran my gaze down his neck and broad shoulders. Gently, I ran my fingertips over the pec that was furthest away from his knife wound. He felt like smooth stone under soft, warm skin. I splayed my palm against his skin and ran it down over each hard ripple of his abs.

"Fuuuck," he whispered.

I paused, and my eyes flew back to his face. His jaw was clenched tight, and his eyes were on my hand. I moved my hand lower but continued to watch his face. The moment I slipped fingers beneath the sweats, his jaw went slack.

My fingertips were barely inside the waistline when I felt the swollen head of his erection. He stopped breathing, and that only urged me on. I continued to feel the deep cut in his lower stomach by sliding my hand underneath his rigid length, all the way to the patch of hair. Running my fingers from one side to the other without touching more. His breathing became short and quick. I could see his stomach rise and fall with each one.

Unable to continue torturing him, I wrapped my hand around the base of his cock and slid it up slowly. Gage jerked his hips and muttered a curse, then pushed the sweats down so he could see my hand on him.

"Jesus Christ, baby," he groaned.

Straight Fire

I ran my hand over the pearlescent liquid seeping out of the top and used it as lube. Gage spread his legs wider and bit his bottom lip as he watched me. This was new for me, and I knew how it worked. I just wasn't sure if I was doing it all right.

"Damn." His voice was husky. "Squeeze it harder, baby."

"Like this?" I asked, looking at him for approval.

"Yeah, fuck. Yeah, like that," he said. His hand slid under my shirt. "Take this off. Bra too. I want to see your tits while you do this."

The power I felt, being able to make him feel like this, was a heady rush. I pulled my shirt off, then unhooked my bra, letting it fall down my arms. When his eyes locked on my breasts, I trembled. Leaning over, I took him back in my hand and continued to stroke him, using the liquid leaking from the head to make my hand slide easier and faster.

Gage squeezed one of my breasts in his hand, and I let out a small cry as he pinched a nipple hard.

"God, I love your tits," he growled, lifting his hips and pushing his cock into my hand with a thrust. "Faster, baby," he begged.

I tightened my grip and began to focus on making this feel good for him. He continued playing with my breasts, but I didn't let it distract me.

"Get on your knees between my legs," he growled.

I moved down to the floor, and he opened his legs wider.

"I want to shoot my load all over those pretty pink nipples."

The fierce look on his face as he drew closer to his climax was making me throb harder. I squirmed some, needing the friction there as I felt him swell in my hand.

"FUCK!" he roared, taking his cock from my hand and pumping it hard as he aimed each stream of cum at my breasts. His eyes looked wild while he watched it.

Even without touching myself, I felt close to an orgasm. When he finished, I squirmed a little more, and then he sat up and took my semen-covered boobs in his hands. He started to run his hands over the cum, spreading it all over my breasts. The moment he smeared some over my nipples, the climax I felt building inside of me erupted, and I cried out, rocking my hips back and forth as it washed over me.

"Holy shit." Gage's deep voice made me shiver as the last tremor faded.

Panting, I opened my eyes to look at him.

"Shiloh ..." He said my name like a low rumble. "Did you just fucking get off?"

I nodded, still surprised this was something that could happen.

"How the fuck am I gonna survive you?" he whispered.

I didn't respond. I wasn't sure what to say to that or what he meant.

We sat there, looking at each other in silence until, finally, he let out a deep sigh. "Put your shirt on so I can concentrate, but leave your bra off and my cum all on your tits. Right now, I'm feeling fucking territorial, and that's the only way I think I can stay calm enough to let you eat."

I reached for my shirt and tugged it back over my head, then stood up.

"Are you thirsty?" I asked him, feeling like I needed to get some air away from the sex-charged energy in this room.

"Could I have a beer?" he asked.

I hurried to go get it and splashed my face with cold water. This was not at all what I'd expected when coming here, and it was going too fast that I didn't know if I should hold on and enjoy it or bolt before it was too far gone.

Chapter Twenty-Four

SHILOH

Pulling the food out of the bags, I placed them on plates, then carried them back into the living room. Gage had paused the movie and was texting someone when I stopped in front of him. I set his plate down beside him, then walked around the ottoman to return to my spot on the sofa. The cheeseburger he'd ordered me was too tall to put in my mouth.

How had I eaten this before? With a knife and fork?

I could feel him watching me.

I looked over at him and pointed to the burger. "How do you expect me to fit that in my mouth?"

A grin tugged at his mouth.

"Do not make a dirty joke out of this. I am serious."

He reached over and pressed down on the burger to flatten it, then winked at me. "That's how you do it."

I scrunched my nose and frowned. "I'll be honest, I think Wilder's way of ordering a cheeseburger is better than my old way."

"Wilder?" Gage asked.

I nodded. "Yes, my friend, Wilder. He taught me a lot when I moved back here. Like how to order a cheeseburger."

Gage didn't say anything, so I figured he was texting again. I picked up the burger and glanced at him before taking a bite. He wasn't texting. He was scowling.

I set the burger back down. "What?"

"Wilder's the fucking guy friend of yours that you don't think wants to fuck you?"

I hadn't meant to piss him off. I'd just been talking. Saying my thoughts aloud. "Uh, well, yes. Wilder is my guy friend who has never once tried to fuck me since I moved back here."

"Has he kissed you?" Gage asked, and his tone made me nervous.

"Never," I replied.

I thought that would fix this, but apparently, it didn't.

"I'm not attracted to Wilder. He's just a friend. I've never wanted to kiss him or touch him."

Gage's jaw was clenched tightly. I wanted to reach up and touch his face. Try and soothe him, but he scared me when he was like this. I didn't know where the line was when he'd snap at me or turn into the man I'd first met.

"Just eat," he finally said and picked up the remote to resume the horror movie he had picked.

My stomach was in knots, but I wasn't about to disobey him. I picked the cheeseburger back up and took a bite. Just like the other things Gage had told me to try, I realized this was delicious. Why hadn't I tried fries on my cheeseburger before? It was brilliant. I took another bite, happy about my new discovery.

"You're smiling," Gage said, sounding amused.

Straight Fire

I turned to him, and the furious look in his eyes was gone. He was pleased. His amber eyes glanced at my mouth, then lifted to meet my gaze.

"Because this is delicious."

He smirked, then turned his attention back to the movie. We continued in silence, and by the time I was finished with my meal, I'd figured out what was happening in this film. Gage put his arm on the back of the sofa and motioned for me to come lie against him again. I curled my feet up, and careful not to touch his ribs, I rested my head on his shoulder. His warm body smelled wonderful, and I closed my eyes. Soaking up how good it felt to be near him like this.

The next time I opened my eyes, the room was dark, except for the hallway light, and my head was in Gage's lap. Turning my head, I looked up to see his eyes closed. Crap. He should have woken me up. It wasn't good for him to sleep like this. Easing myself up, I tried to think of what would be best. Maybe I could turn him around and lay him on the sofa, then get him a blanket and pillow. The recliner would be fine for me.

Gage's hand wrapped around my wrist. "Where are you going?" he asked, his voice thick from sleep.

"To get you a pillow and a blanket. I'm sorry I fell asleep. I'll get you comfortable. Just give me a second," I replied.

"No. Let's go upstairs," he said, moving his cast to the floor and then standing up without my help. He'd done it easily. Not even a need for a crutch.

"You're sure you don't want to just sleep down here?" I asked him.

"Want you in my bed," he replied and wrapped his arm around my shoulders, then began walking us toward the stairs.

This man did not need my assistance to walk. Not even a little. He'd left the crutch by the sofa, completely forgotten.

When we reached the stairs, he glanced at me and grinned. "I can do this."

Of course he could. I stood there and watched as he maneuvered himself up without any help or issue. This clearly wasn't the first time he'd done this. I lifted my gaze to his, and he winked at me. Damn that wink. It made my thoughts scramble.

At the top of the stairs, he put his arm around my shoulders again. Not for support, but to keep me beside him.

Was I even needed in this house?

We reached his door, and he dropped his hand to my back and pressed it for me to go in first.

Gage walked to the bathroom, and I could hear the water running, then the sound of him brushing his teeth. I waited until he walked out to take my overnight bag inside and close the door behind me. I didn't try and help him get into bed because he didn't need it. Tomorrow, we'd talk about this.

I washed my breasts off from our earlier sexual activities, then brushed my teeth before changing into a pair of pale blue pajama shorts and the matching sleeveless top. When I opened the door and stepped into the bedroom, I expected to find him asleep. His eyes were open, and they followed me as I walked to the other side of his bed and climbed inside.

"Beside me," he said, still sounding like he'd just woken up.

I moved closer until he wrapped his arm around me and pulled me against him. His lips brushed the side of my head, and his leg wedged between mine. A content warmth washed over me.

For the first time since I'd opened my eyes two years ago, I didn't feel the hollowness deep in my chest. In the beginning, I'd thought it was because I had no memories. That the relationships in my life were now unknown.

Moving and leaving all of that behind to start new hadn't changed it. The emptiness remained while I tried to build a life around it. Struggling to address it when I didn't understand what it was that had caused it. I had been missing an important piece.

My hand moved over to rest on Gage's chest. If he was what filled that for me, former me had been living with the same vacant ache in her soul that I had been.

Chapter Twenty-Five

GAGE
SIX YEARS AGO

This seemed to be all the time now. A constant state of rage churning inside me. I couldn't control it. I couldn't fucking ease it. Unless she was with me, and even then, it all depended on her mood. She'd graduated from high school, and I hadn't been invited to the ceremony. I gripped the wrench in my hand tightly, hating that she had a life I wasn't a part of.

When she was with me, it was so easy to forget that I didn't get all of her. I'd never seen her bedroom or met her parents—they didn't even know I fucking existed. Shiloh was mine. She was it for me. The days of hiding were over. She'd turned eighteen, and yet she still refused to be open to her family about me.

Thinking about her at some fucking graduation party with guys talking to her, looking at her, I slammed the wrench down and stood up. I couldn't focus enough to work on any damn bikes. I cursed, kicking the bike I was supposed to be fixing, then slammed my fist against the wall.

"Don't fuck the bike up more. Go walk it off or some shit. You're gonna have to get control of your temper," Huck called out.

I glared back at him. He had no idea what this felt like.

Huck pointed at the bike. "Don't fuck up shit," he warned again before turning to go back inside the office.

I fisted my hands in my hair, restless, needing to let the pent-up fury inside of me out before I fucking exploded. This was just going to get worse. I'd snap soon. I knew this feeling.

"I like that hair. In fact, it's one of my favorite things. Please don't pull it out," her voice said.

I spun around to see the object of my obsession standing inside the garage, wearing a pair of cutoff jeans, a blue tank top, and a pair of cowboy boots.

I stalked toward her as she smiled at me. Most people couldn't handle me when I was like this. They backed away, got frightened. Not Shiloh. Her eyes taunted me, daring me to do something. Knowing there was no fucking chance I'd ever hurt her.

"You're not wearing that," I growled as I reached her, grabbing her waist to jerk her against me.

She'd come here first. She hadn't just gone to the fucking party yet. My girl had come to see me.

"If I wanted to, I would, but you're right. I'm not wearing it," she replied as her head tilted back, meeting my gaze.

"Not sure I'm gonna be able to let you go," I warned her.

She wrapped her arms around my waist and raised her eyebrows, as if she was going to challenge me. That was nothing new. Barstools had been broken, car windows smashed in, and a few other casualties because Shiloh had pushed me until I cracked. She fucking got off on it.

"If I wanted to, I would," she repeated her earlier words. "But I don't want to. I want you."

Just like magic, her words were the only fucking thing that eased me. She was the reason for my insanity and the only fucking cure. Blaise had sworn we were toxic, but he didn't think I would ever be sane without her. I knew I wouldn't.

I ran a knuckle down her cheek and jaw, then slipped it under her chin as I lowered my mouth to hers. She would own me for as long as I had a fucking heartbeat. Kissing her was as close to anything spiritual that I'd ever get. The soft moans she made, the way she leaned into me, as if she couldn't get close enough, the way her hands grabbed my biceps and her nails bit into my skin.

"I'm gonna follow you," I whispered against her lips.

I'd been fighting my decision. Choosing her over the life I'd thought I wanted with the family, the one Blaise had fought to bring me into. It was no longer the most important thing for me.

Shiloh pulled back from me so she could look up at me. "What do you mean?" she asked, slightly breathless.

"You go, I go," I told her.

She was deciding on college this week. Every time I thought about her leaving me, I got so fucked up that I couldn't think straight. The only way was for me to go where she went.

She frowned. "You can't do that," she replied.

"Yes, I fucking can. I'll find a job. Get an apartment. A nice one you'll like." I had stayed up most of last night planning this. Accepting that, without her, I couldn't function.

She had stormed into my life and claimed my soul. It was done. She owned me.

A soft smile replaced her frown. "You would leave here? Your friends, who are like brothers to you? This life, your job, everything to follow me to wherever?"

"Shiloh, you shouldn't have to ask me that. You should know I'd fucking do anything to be with you."

She reached up and cupped my face in her hands and lifted herself up on her tiptoes. "I love you," she said with a smile so fucking sweet that my chest hurt. Leaning closer to my mouth, she pressed a single kiss. "I guess it's a good thing for everyone that I chose Florida last night."

My entire body stilled. "Florida? As in University of, in Gainesville?"

She was grinning now as she nodded.

Grabbing her by the waist, I picked her up and let out a shout as I spun her around in circles. Her laughter filled the large space, and my heart slammed into my chest. She had chosen to stay for me. I wouldn't have to fucking choose between the family and her.

"What the fuck did you do to him? I came out here earlier, and he looked like he was going to break the damn bike he was working on instead of fix it," Huck's voice called from the door leading into the office.

"I'm going to Florida!" she shouted.

"Thank fuck," he drawled. "Maybe we can keep him out of prison now."

Shiloh laughed harder, and I pulled her back down to me and slammed my mouth against hers.

Mine. She was mine.

PRESENT

Five years. It had been five fucking years since I'd woken up with her tucked against me. Even back then, this had been rare. We hadn't gotten many nights where she could stay with me. I didn't want to move, although I needed to fucking piss. I stared down at her lying on my chest. When she woke up, she was going to freak out about that. Worried she was hurting me.

Damn, I couldn't get used to this again. I was walking a line that could ruin me. Giving her the power she had once held over me wasn't something I could chance. My life was the way I wanted it. Shiloh couldn't be my kryptonite. Not this time around. I was older. Smarter.

I eased out from under her. It was best I didn't linger like this. Enjoying her against me. That was something I could taste, but I wasn't going to indulge. Fucking yeah, I'd get my fill of fucking her. The other stuff I had to be careful with. It would lead to a place neither one of us needed to relive.

Standing up, I glanced back at her, and she'd curled her body into a ball with her hand fisted in my pillow. The shit that did to my chest was a warning. One I had to fucking heed.

Chapter Twenty-Six

SHILOH

When my eyes opened, Gage was gone. Even his side of the bed was cool to the touch. As I had suspected last night, he didn't need me here to take care of him. He had me here for other reasons. The way I felt about him was clear. He made me want things. He stirred emotions in me that were thrilling and, at other times, painful.

After I showered, brushed my teeth, and dressed, I made my way downstairs. When I reached the kitchen, I found him at the table with a cup of coffee and what looked like a fancy cinnamon roll in front of him. He lifted his eyes from the phone in his hand to meet mine.

"Good morning," he said.

"Good morning," I replied. I cut my eyes to his breakfast, then back to him. "You made cinnamon rolls?"

"Fuck no," he said with a crooked grin that made him look harmless. "Trinity made some before she left and put them in the freezer. I just stuck a pan in the oven. Try one. They're amazing."

I made my way over to the coffeepot, trying to decide when to bring up the obvious, which was that he did not need a nurse. Filling up my cup, I added creamer and then picked up a cinnamon roll before heading to the table. His attention was back on his phone.

He didn't look up or speak to me, and I wasn't sure what to say to him. I chose to eat instead and pretend the silence wasn't awkward. In truth, after last night and all we'd done, I hadn't expected the morning to be like this. The fact that I was dealing with disappointment over not waking up with him beside me wasn't helped by his ignoring me.

I took a drink of the coffee and glanced over at him again. He was texting, so I turned my gaze back to the large windows that looked out into the backyard. Maybe he wanted me to talk first, or was this it? Were we back to being silent strangers?

"Did you sleep good?" he asked me.

I turned back to him as he laid his phone down on the table. He picked up his cup before lifting his gaze to meet mine. Something was different. Very different this morning. This was nothing like the guy I'd been with yesterday. What had changed? Had I caused it?

"Uh, yeah, thanks," I replied. I couldn't even ask about his getting around without my help. A lump I hadn't expected was now in my throat. I dropped my eyes back to the cinnamon roll.

"You're not going to bring up my ability to get around?" There was amusement in his voice.

I glanced back up at him. "I noticed that."

He chuckled and took a drink of his coffee.

"I'm trying to understand why I'm here," I added.

Straight Fire

He set the cup down and smirked. "Because I wanted you here."

Why did he do that? Confuse me with his personality changes?

"Do you still want me here?" I asked. I was beginning to think he'd changed his mind on that.

He nodded his head.

Okay. Well, that wasn't very convincing.

"Shiloh." The way he said my name was unfair. It made my body feel as if a hum of energy were buzzing through it.

"Yes?"

"I'm not a morning person," he said.

He had gotten up earlier than me, but then I had slept later than I normally did. I wasn't sure if that was supposed to be his excuse for being silent or not staying in bed with me. I didn't respond. I didn't know what he wanted me to say to that.

"You're here because I want to fuck you. A lot."

That got my attention. My eyes snapped back to his. He had a serious expression on his face.

"Once, we were more. That's not what I want now. But I do want to fuck you. We were always good at that even if we sucked at the other stuff." He smirked. "What we did yesterday was just foreplay. I wanted to ease you into it."

I opened my mouth and closed it again. The right words were all jumbled up in my head. Somehow, he'd now made everything feel cheap and twisted. When we were together, I felt something that I'd thought was mutual. It just showed how naive I was.

"I'm not like Destiny," I blurted out.

"I know. Destiny and I have an understanding. She's been around for a while. That's not what this is. I'm not asking for you to come fuck me when I need it. What I want from you is temporary. Today, I want to fuck you until I've had my fill. Once I've gotten you out of my system, it'll be over."

Ouch. I should have just given him a knife and had him plunge it into my stomach. I had thought I liked honesty. Come to find out, there were some truths that were too painful. The lie I'd let myself get wrapped up in with him yesterday only made the reality more brutal. I wasn't ready for guys like Gage. I still needed to get the hang of dating normal guys. Less intense guys. The ones who didn't wreak havoc on my emotions.

At least his harsh explanation had cleared up my head. I moved my chair back, needing to get some space and to text my uncle to come get me.

"I, uh, thanks for clearing that up," I replied, not looking at him. "But I came here to be your nurse. I can't—I'm not …" I paused, closing my eyes for a minute to try and put my thoughts into words without sounding vulnerable. "I've not had a relationship. Not one I remember. As much as I enjoyed yesterday and the things we did, I just can't. I'm sorry." I barely glanced at him before picking up my plate and cup, then heading to the sink. I'd hardly touched my cinnamon roll. My stomach was too knotted up to think about food.

I heard the cast hit the ground. He was getting up. Hopefully to go in the living room, where I could avoid him until I left. I put the rest of my cinnamon roll down the food disposal, then rinsed off my plate and cup to put them in the dishwasher. He was walking closer to me. Not farther away.

Closing my eyes tightly, I took several deep breaths, preparing myself for whatever it was he would say to me now. With Gage, I never knew if those words were going to slice through me or make me a puddle of goo in his hands. I didn't turn around to face him as I waited for him to stop walking and just say something already. Get this over with.

I felt his hands on either side of mine, caging me in, and my eyes snapped open as the heat from his body moved in behind me. His warm breath caressed the side of my neck, and I shivered. I hated myself in that moment. I hated how weak I was and how he affected me.

"You smell so fucking good," he whispered, pressing a kiss against my skin.

His mouth brushed against my neck as he left a trail of kisses. "I'm sorry my words came out like they did. They were callous, and I'm afraid that was more for my sake than yours."

I swallowed and sucked in a breath. "I think I should just go. I'm not equipped to handle you."

A deep chuckle vibrated from his chest as he pressed in closer to me. I could feel his erection against my lower back.

"Baby, you're the only woman on earth who is equipped to fucking handle me. You just don't remember."

Had I really been able to deal with this man?

I shook my head. "I'm beginning to think you were the one who destroyed me."

One of his hands flattened against my stomach, pressing me hard into him. "The past is over. We won't repeat it. Those feelings are no longer an issue for me." The deep growl in his voice made me whimper. I wasn't sure if it was fear or need.

"Have you fucked since the accident?" he asked in a soft voice against my ear.

I closed my eyes and shook my head.

"Then, it's only right that I'll be the first one to take this pussy," he said, then shoved his hand down the front of my shorts. "Again."

My knees slightly buckled, and his free hand grabbed my hip, squeezing hard.

"I'll show you how good it's supposed to feel. Teach you what you need and what makes you scream out in pleasure."

Gage Presley was very good with words. My mind was screaming at me that this was a terrible idea. This man was going to mess up my head worse than he already had. But my body was so hungry for what he was promising that I wasn't sure I could fight it.

When his fingers began to slide through my slickness, he groaned in my ear. "Fuck, you're soaking wet. Your body knows how good I can make it feel. Just shut off everything else." He pressed a kiss to my temple. "Forget all the other stuff. Let's just be us for today."

But tomorrow will come, my head reminded me.

Unfortunately, the area between my legs was shouting louder. I was going to have sex someday. Why not let my first be with someone who knew my body? He had already managed to hurt me emotionally. I wasn't going to do this and think that love was next. This was just sex. Why not enjoy it and learn what I liked?

"Okay," I finally replied.

There was a rumble of appreciation as he grabbed my shorts and pulled them down. "Get them off." His voice sounded strained. Impatient.

I shimmied them down the rest of the way, then kicked them out of the way. He gripped the hem of my top, and I held my arms up as he pulled it up over my head. When his hands went to the hook on my bra, I realized I was about to be standing in this kitchen, naked, and I was aching so bad for him that I didn't care.

This was not me. Or was it?

"Hands on the sink," he said, pushing me forward.

I grabbed the edge of the sink, and he pressed my back down so that my butt was up. He placed a leg between mine and spread them apart. I heard the rustle of his shorts as he shoved them down. Then, he cursed.

"Are you on birth control?" It came out tense, as if whatever my answer was would make him angry.

"I have an IUD. Former me had it put in," I told him.

"I don't fuck bare, but condoms are upstairs, and we've never used them together. Not sure I can handle the barrier with you."

I should demand he use a condom. "Maybe it's better if we do," I whispered. "You have been with a lot of different women." That was a reminder I needed. It cooled down my arousal.

His hand gripped my hip tightly, digging into my flesh. "Shiloh, I would never fucking do something to hurt you. I've fucked one woman since I was last checked, and I wore a condom."

That was hard to believe. "One?"

His hand tightened on me. "Yes, one."

"When were you checked?" This was good. I was calming down. I could think clearly.

"When I was injured."

I let that sink in. I knew he'd had Destiny over to suck him off. But that meant he'd also had sex with her or someone. I started to stand up straight. My head was in control again, and I couldn't do this.

"This is a bad idea," I started to tell him.

He grabbed my arm and spun me around, then backed me up against the edge of the counter. His pupils were big as he looked at me. "No," he snarled as his hand slipped between my legs, and he shoved his middle finger inside me.

I grabbed his arms and cried out.

"Stop thinking about it," he said as he continued to pump his finger into me. "Get whatever shit is in your head out. Yeah, I fucked someone upstairs in my hospital bed," he said, leaning down until his mouth was hovering over mine. "And

I closed my goddamn eyes, let her ride me, and pretended it was you."

Shut up. Shut up. Don't say that. I wanted to scream at him to stop, but I couldn't speak. Not with what he was doing between my legs.

"Fucking pissed me off when she didn't feel like you. Her pussy didn't squeeze my dick like yours. She didn't smell like you." He leaned down and kissed my jaw, then my collarbone. "No one ever feels like you."

He won. I had no resistance to this man when he talked like that. I grabbed his face and kissed him. My tongue slid across his lips, and he opened for me. The warmth of our breaths mingled as we fought to taste the other as if we were starving.

He grabbed my waist and sat me up on the counter without breaking the kiss. When he pulled me to him and entered me, I broke the kiss as I cried out his name. It was better than I'd imagined. The full feeling. As if I were being stretched until just before the point where it might be painful.

"FUCK! It shouldn't be this tight," he growled as he pulled back and then slammed back into me. His eyes locked with mine. "I'm beginning to think this pussy's only had my dick." The way his eyes flared as he said it was the sexiest thing I'd ever seen.

One of his hands grabbed the back of my head, and his eyes dropped down to watch where we joined. I held on to his arms as he sank deeper into me with each thrust. A frenzy was slowly sweeping through me. Gage's name, along with pleas, fell from my lips.

"Fuck, I missed this. You're so goddamn beautiful." His words came out in a deep, raspy sound.

The crest was coming. I could feel it as my body drew closer. I held on to Gage's arms, afraid of the power behind it.

This wasn't like the orgasms I'd given myself. It was different. There was an unknown to it.

"That's it, sweet baby. I know that look. Come on my cock." Gage's dirty words triggered me.

"OH GOD! GAGE!" I heard the panic in my voice before the burst of euphoria took over, tossing me into a space I never wanted to come back from.

"That's it." I could hear Gage in the distance. "Fucking hell, baby."

My body shook with his savage pounding, and my pleasure only increased.

"GAH!" Gage shouted, and the warmth of his release rushed inside of me. "Take it," he groaned. "Take all of me." His hips jerked, and he stilled.

My eyes opened as I gasped for air, and his amber gaze was fixed on me. We sat there like that for several moments, silent. I knew even without remembering sex that this was normal. This was special. It had to be. What I had just felt wasn't some cheap way to get off. There had been more to it. I didn't care what he said—this was not just sex.

Gage pulled out of me, and the moment was over. He wasn't going to let it be more. I started to get down, and he stopped me, then wrapped his hands around my waist to set me down. I looked up at him, wanting to see something in his gaze that gave me any clue that he felt this too. That I wasn't alone in this.

He smirked as if he'd done what he had set out to do. Fuck me out of his system. Had he also meant to break me? It felt like my heart was breaking as we stood there. He didn't hold me or say anything sweet. This was what he'd meant by fucking. No emotions.

Well, joke's on you, Gage Presley, I thought.

My eyes stung, and I looked away then. I would not let this man see me cry. This was done, and I would leave here with some sort of pride. When I was alone, I could fall apart.

"Shiloh."

I didn't look at him. I was afraid I'd start crying if I did. How was it possible to hate someone and want them at the same time?

"Shiloh," he said again as he grabbed my chin and forced my head in his direction.

I knew my eyelashes were wet, and I tried to jerk my face free from his grip, but he firmly held on. I was angry that he was making me do this. Taking the tiny little shred of pride I had left, I lifted my tear-filled eyes and glared at him.

"What?" I had meant for it to sound angry, but it had come out as a sob instead.

His nostrils flared. "Why are you crying?"

I laughed then and shook my head hard, finally freeing myself from his grip. "Just let me go."

Gage pushed me back again with his body blocking me in. What now? He'd fucked me. Used me. Proven his point.

"Tell me why you're crying."

"Does it matter?" I asked, looking up at him.

For a moment, it was there. The brief glimpse of something more. A feeling that went deeper.

"Yes, it matters. We just had fucking incredible sex," he said as he brushed a tear away with his thumb.

"I ..." Pausing, I tried to think of how to explain this without opening myself up bare.

But then did it really matter now? Why couldn't I just tell him the truth? He'd been brutal with me. This ended after today. I'd never get a chance to tell him again. I hadn't been one to hold back before. Why let him turn me into that?

"Because I didn't expect to feel something that strong. To you, it was great sex. To me, it was more. You don't feel anything deeper. What we had was over years ago." I wiped at my face as tears continued to escape. "But to me, this is new, and it's not just sex. It's a connection, and I have all these emotions where you're concerned that I've never had."

His mouth covered mine, silencing my words. I tasted the salt from my tears as he made me forget for a moment why my chest hurt. The gentle way his lips moved over mine made the rest of my world fade away. He controlled me in these moments. He owned me, and I thought he knew it.

When he ended the kiss, pulling back, he stared down at me. "I'm sorry. I let my need to be inside of you again, to feel that, control my actions. I didn't consider you. I should have. You're not the same girl who left me. You don't deserve the way I've treated you."

Each word out of his mouth was like a splinter in my soul. I could see the goodbye in his eyes. I had chosen honesty, and this was the price I would pay.

"I can't do this." His voice was tight as he said it. "As much as I fucking want to. As badly as my body is already craving you again. I can't. Go upstairs, pack your things. I'll have a car take you home."

With that, he finished twisting the knife in my gut and then shoved it into my chest.

Chapter
TWENTY-SEVEN

SHILOH

There was no goodbye. He simply texted me that there was a car out front, waiting on me. He didn't watch me leave or say anything more. Every step I took from that house caused the emotional pain to morph into a physical one. One I recognized.

A man appeared at the car door and took my bag, then opened the door for me to get in. I didn't even say *thank you*. The slow pounding in my head was coming on faster than usual. The morning sunlight didn't help. Closing my eyes, I curled my legs up on the seat and tried to breathe slowly. There was pain medicine at home I could take. I would get there. It would be fine.

"Do you feel okay, ma'am?" the driver asked.

I tried to open my eyes, but that was too much at the moment. Instead, I nodded my head. "Yes, fine, just a little tired."

When the car started moving, I was thankful he wasn't going to continue to speak. He remained silent on the drive.

I prayed the nausea that came with this waited. The radio wasn't loud, but it wasn't helping. Speaking to ask him to turn it off seemed too difficult of a task.

The first nauseous wave hit me, and I wanted to cry.

The car came to a stop, and I heard the driver get out. I would have to open my eyes to get inside. Forcing them to endure the sunlight, I squinted as the driver opened my door. Talking myself through the steps, I managed to get out and take the bag he was holding for me.

A muttered, "Thank you," was the best I could do as I walked to the door of my apartment building.

The lights inside weren't as awful as the sun had been, but it still hurt. Everything hurt at this point. Getting inside my apartment was slightly difficult. Getting the key in the lock was a struggle. Wilder wasn't home, or he'd have been out here already.

When my door finally opened, I dropped my bag and headed for the bathroom. Just as my knees hit the floor in front of the toilet, I threw up. Several heaves until there was nothing left. I wanted to curl up on the bathroom floor, but I needed the darkness only my bedroom could provide. The blackout curtains were in there for a reason. Grabbing a washcloth, I ran it under the cool water and did the best I could to clean my face.

The curtains were already closed in my room, and I walked to the bed, falling into it and curling up before I realized I hadn't gotten the pain medicine. I knew I couldn't physically get up and eat something in order to take the pills. Not in the state I was in. Sometimes, it eased on its own. I could wait and see. Give it time.

Tears slipped from the corners of my eyes, and I couldn't stop them. I had to face the emotional pain if I had any chance of getting over the physical. Time seemed to fade in and out.

I wasn't sure if I was sleeping any or not. The migraine wasn't easing up. Twice, I tried to stand up to go get some medicine, but I was too dizzy.

I wasn't sure which direction the door was in, and I lay there to think about it a moment. Before I knew it, the time faded some more. I shivered, wishing it would ease. My mouth was dry. In the distance, I thought I heard my phone ring, but I wasn't sure.

I'd dropped my things when I got here, hadn't I?

How long had I been here? A few hours maybe?

It felt longer when I thought about Gage and the way he had made me feel. Even if it had just been for a moment. Did former me still love him? Was that what this was? My mind had forgotten, but my body remembered? I should have stayed away from him.

But if I had, then I'd never have known him. That thought seemed intolerable. I'd rather know him and live through the pain.

Chapter Twenty-Eight

GAGE

The house was full. It was loud. Some hot blonde, who Levi's hookup had brought, was in my lap. This was my life. The one I enjoyed. The one I wanted. My chest felt fucking hollow, but that was familiar too.

"GAGE!" Huck called out from the kitchen.

"What?"

"Where's your fucking phone?"

"Don't know," I replied. Didn't fucking care.

The blonde was playing with my hair, and it was annoying me. I needed another drink.

Huck stood in front of me. "Who took Shiloh home yesterday morning?" he asked, frowning.

The sound of her name made me tense up.

"Bart." I snarled his name as if it were his fucking fault I'd sent her home.

"Did he say if she went inside?"

The concerned look on Huck's face was sending off alarm bells I didn't fucking like.

"I didn't ask."

Huck scowled at me like I'd done something wrong. I had sent her home. He'd been wanting me to send her home since day one. He started to walk off.

I shoved the girl off my lap. "MOVE!"

She scrambled to stand, and I pushed myself up.

"HUCK!" I shouted his name.

He glared back at me. "What?"

"Why are you asking about her?" I couldn't even say her name. I was afraid I'd snap. It was right there on the edge. Sending her away had been the only way to stop myself. To keep me from going fucking psycho over her. One more minute with her, and it would have been done.

"She hasn't answered any texts or calls from her uncle. He went by to check on her, and she's not answering. Her neighbor has also tried. They assumed she was here still, so he called YOU. When he didn't get you, he called me."

My heart slammed against my chest. Terror squeezed my throat so tightly that I could barely breathe. I had enemies. We all did. If any of them had known …

I shoved past everyone, walking toward the door.

"Where the fuck are you going?" Huck shouted.

"To her apartment!"

"You can't fucking drive yet!"

"I'll go," Levi called out, but I didn't stop.

I continued on, pausing in the gun room on my way out to make sure I was prepared.

"Gage." Levi said my name as if he was trying to talk me down.

There was nothing to talk me down from. Shiloh wasn't answering her phone or door. Something was wrong.

Straight Fire

"DRIVE!" I shouted as I climbed inside the car, slamming the door behind me.

Levi glanced at me once as he pulled out of the garage, and we headed down the long drive toward the security gate. I'd fucking let her drive right off yesterday. Didn't even check to see if she was safe. Make sure she got home okay. I had been too busy trying not to let myself claim her.

If someone had her or something had happened to her ...

The madness was stewing right below the surface.

"Bart drove her?" Levi asked.

I nodded, unable to speak.

He pressed Bart's number on the car's display screen.

"Yes, sir?" His voice came over the speaker.

"Did Shiloh Ellis get home safely yesterday? Anything off with her?" Levi asked.

"Like I told Huck when he called a few minutes ago, she didn't seem well. I asked her if she was okay, but she barely spoke. She was curled up in the backseat the entire ride and kept her eyes closed. But, yeah, she got inside. I made sure before I drove off."

My hand slammed down on the console in front of me. "AND YOU DIDN'T FUCKING THINK I NEEDED TO KNOW SHE WAS ILL?" I roared as I felt myself start to unravel.

"No, sir. I'm sorry, sir. I thought she had a headache or felt sick. Maybe that was why she was leaving. You didn't ask me about her, so I figured you knew ..." He trailed off.

I hadn't asked. Just like Huck had pointed out. I hadn't fucking checked on her.

"Thanks, Bart," Levi said, then ended the call.

My heart was pounding in my ears.

"You're gonna lose it, and that won't help anyone. Remember last time. Rein it in," Levi told me.

"Drive faster," I replied through clenched teeth.

The phone rang, and Huck's name appeared on the screen.

"Yeah?" Levi said.

"It's okay. Her uncle called. The neighbor went to the landlord and got the backup key. He got inside, and she's suffering from a migraine. He said, since the accident, she sometimes gets them, and they can be debilitating. But the neighbor is with her, and she'll be fine."

The neighbor. Wilder. Fuck no.

"DRIVE!" I shouted when Levi slowed down like he was going to go back.

"What are you doing, Gage? She's fine. You don't have to get involved," Huck said.

My body was strung so fucking tight that I wasn't sure which side of sanity I was currently on. He was with her. In her apartment. Taking care of her. Touching her. My vision blurred.

"We don't need to go, man. Let's go back." Levi's voice was concerned.

"Drive," was all I said. It was all I could say.

"Fuck," I heard Huck mutter. "Try to keep everyone alive," he said.

"I'll do my best," Levi replied.

He pulled up to the outside of her apartment, and before the car came to a complete stop, I swung open the car door. Getting out, I cursed the fucking cast for slowing me down.

"Let's talk about this first," Levi called out, then followed me into the building. "Fucking hell."

Her door was locked, and I pounded on it.

"Don't break it down," Levi warned me.

The door opened, and it wasn't Shiloh. It was a guy.

"Oh fuck," Levi muttered behind me.

Straight Fire

The guy looked down at my cast then back at me. "You must be Gage. You're not coming in here." The guy scowled at me.

I ignored him and started to walk inside, but the man stepped in front of me. He narrowed his gaze, and for a second, he looked ready to fight me if he needed to. The moment my Glock was pressed against his forehead, that stance evaporated, and he quickly turned pale.

"You just flipped the damn crazy switch. Congratulations," Levi said to the man as he walked past us. He stepped inside, then looked back at me. "Put the gun away. Blowing his fucking brains out all over her apartment isn't going to help shit."

Hatred seethed through me as I glared at the man who thought he had a right to be in Shiloh's apartment. "Get the fuck out of here," I warned him.

He swallowed hard, and his Adam's apple bobbed, but he didn't move.

"Listen—Wilder, is it? We met at the restaurant. Anyway, my friend is fucking insane, and there is little I can do to stop him. Normally, I can rein him in, but we've added Shiloh to this equation, and where she's concerned, he is batshit crazy. I can assure you, she is the safest female in a ten-mile radius because of him. You, however, might not see another sunrise. Now, please, go back to your apartment. Don't call the cops because they won't come. You're welcome to try, but it'll be a waste of time. But leave, please. I am not in the mood to clean up the mess if you don't."

The man's gaze shifted from me to Levi.

"Put the gun down, Gage," Levi told me.

He was right. Shiloh would be upset if I shot him. I had to think clearly. Losing her again wasn't going to happen. I slowly lowered the gun.

"This is the part where you get the fuck out of here," Levi informed him.

He backed away, his eyes wide, and Levi closed the door, blocking him from my view.

"He's going to call the cops. I'll make the call and handle that," he told me. "Go on and see her for yourself. It's done now. No more stopping this shit. I can see the psycho gleam in your eyes."

I laid my gun on the counter as I headed to the closed door at the end of the short hallway. The room was completely dark. I eased myself inside and let my eyes focus until I could make out her sleeping form on the bed. My chest felt like it was going to explode. I'd done this. She was like this because of how I'd treated her. Someone should have pointed the fucking gun at my head.

Walking over to the bed, I climbed on it and moved in close to her back. Her breathing was slow and steady. I wrapped an arm around her, pulling her to my chest. She stirred, and a soft sigh escaped her before she stilled.

"It's me," I whispered, pressing a kiss to her head.

"Gage?" Her voice rolled over me like a fucking balm.

"Yeah, baby. Go back to sleep."

She turned her head and blinked as she stared at me. "Am I dreaming?" she asked.

I shook my head. "No."

"Why are you here?"

I pressed a kiss to her lips. "It's where I belong."

She sighed. "I'm still asleep."

The disappointment on her face made me smile.

"We will talk in the morning," I told her.

"Okay," she muttered, turning away from me again.

I buried my face in her hair and inhaled.

How the fuck had I thought I could keep this from happening? It'd been fucking inevitable.

Chapter Twenty-Nine

SHILOH

Before I opened my eyes, I felt the warm body pressed against my back. My eyes snapped open, and I looked down at the hand on my stomach. Gage. That hadn't been a dream. I tried to replay what he'd said in my head, but I'd taken the pain medicine. Things were hazy. Who had called him? His being here wasn't going to help. I was afraid I'd end up like this again after he left.

A heaviness settled on my chest. This entire thing was too much. His hand slid up, and he cupped one of my breasts. I looked down at his hand, and I felt his breath against my neck before he pressed a kiss just below my ear.

"Gage?"

"Hmm?"

"Why are you in my bed?"

"Because you're mine."

He ran his hand down the side of my body, then slipped it between my legs. "How's your migraine?" he asked in a husky voice that made me shiver.

"Uh, gone," I replied.

"Do you get them a lot?"

"Not anymore," I whispered.

"Good," he said, rolling me onto my back, then moving down my body until his head was over my stomach. He pulled up my shirt and feathered kisses against my skin.

"You, uh—Gage?" My thoughts were getting all rattled.

"Yes, baby?" he asked, his breath hot against my skin.

"When exactly did you decide"—I gasped as he tugged at the front of my sleep shorts—"uh, that, I was, um, yours?"

Focus, Shiloh. Stay focused.

He pressed a kiss just below the waistline of my shorts. "You've been mine. I just needed to accept it. Take all that came with it." He continued kissing lower.

I squirmed. "I think ... we should ... talk about it." My words sounded like a sigh. "Before you, uh, do that."

He lifted his head, and his amber eyes locked with mine. "Do you want to leave me?"

I shook my head.

"Do you want me?"

I paused, afraid that he'd react the way he had last time I was honest with him.

"Shiloh?" he urged.

"I, uh, we had this conversation. I told you how I felt, and you sent me home." I gasped out the last word as he kissed the spot just above my clit.

"I made a mistake. I'll never make it again. I should have fucked you until you couldn't walk. It's what I wanted to do."

I let my head fall back on the pillow. Good Lord, how was I supposed to keep it together with this man? He was driving me crazy. His hands gripped the sides of my panties and jerked them down with the pajama shorts.

"I can't handle this," I told him. "It hurts too much when you decide you're done and send me away."

Gage pushed open my legs. "I swear to you that I'll never hurt you like that again. The thought of you in pain makes me fucking livid. I'm done trying to save us both from this. I can't. It was done the moment you walked into my fucking bedroom."

His tongue began to tease and lick my clit.

"Oh God," I moaned.

"Let me make you feel good," he murmured, running his tongue against the sensitive folds. "I'm sorry I did this to you," he added.

I whimpered. He was taking his time.

"Will you forgive me?" he asked before he slid his tongue inside of me.

"Yes," I panted.

He groaned, and the vibration made me tremble.

"Things you should know," he said, not looking up at me. "I'm possessive as fuck. Only with you. Dangerously so. Can't help it." He licked again, then pressed a kiss inside my upper thigh. "Some say I'm obsessed." His eyes lifted to look at me as his tongue stroked between my legs. "You're all I fucking want. And that can get demanding."

I watched him struggle to breathe.

"I no longer want to stop it. I need it." He pressed a kiss where his tongue had been. "This belongs to me."

His finger joined his tongue, and he began to slide it in and out of me while his tongue ran back and forth over my clit. My head was pressed back now as my hips lifted to get closer to him.

"Yes, please," I panted. "That's so good. Don't stop."

Gage growled against me as he began to get more aggressive with his mouth. I grabbed the back of his head and continued to cry out his name and plead with him. The crest shattered into bliss.

Gage's hard body moved up over me, and his mouth left a trail of kisses along my skin until he was lying beside me, pulling me into his arms. I snuggled against his chest as I floated back to earth, sighing.

"That was amazing," I said, pressing my lips to his chest.

He ran his hand down my back. "This thing with us, even though you're different and I'm older, it's still intense. I don't always do the right thing. I fuck up," he said.

I lifted my eyes to his. "Is this your way of telling me you sleep with other women?"

He scowled. "Fuck no. Shiloh, this is my way of telling you that I can't stay away from you. Jealousy is a monster that consumes me, and I don't handle it the way you want me to. I'm going to try. Losing you a second time …" He paused. "I won't be able to do that."

This was all hard to take in.

"Okay, but I'm still stuck on you sending me away. And now, you're in my bed, giving me a mind-blowing orgasm. I need time to catch up, I think."

His hand squeezed my butt cheek. "Take all the time you need, but you'll be doing it by my side. With me. All the time."

All the time? I frowned. How would I do that?

"And that means exactly what?" I asked.

A knock at the front door interrupted us, and I started to sit up, but he held me to him.

"Levi will get it," he said, his arms tightening around me.

"Levi is here?" I asked, my cheeks turning bright red. I'd been screaming Gage's name just a few minutes ago.

"He brought me last night," Gage explained.

I heard male voices.

"That's probably Wilder. I should go explain why Levi is answering my door."

His hold on me was like a vise grip.

"Gage?"

"Levi can handle it."

I reached up and cupped the side of his face. His jaw was clenched tight.

"He helped me when I needed it yesterday. He's my friend, and I owe it to him to let him see that I'm okay."

His nostrils flared as he held me.

"Let me do this, and then we can talk some more—in bed." I was bribing him.

Slowly, his hold on me eased, and I smiled, pressing one more kiss to his lips before getting up and grabbing my robe and heading toward the bedroom door.

My apartment door was open, and Levi was standing at it, just like Gage had said. He turned his head in my direction and looked relieved.

"Ah, there she is. You can see she's alive for yourself," Levi said, stepping back as I walked over to the door.

Wilder's eyes scanned me before he locked on my face. "Are you okay?"

I nodded. "Yes. I'm all better. Thank you for your help."

He glanced behind me.

"There were two of them last night," he said to me, then scanned the area behind me like he was looking for Gage.

"The other one is in her bed. You just missed her screaming his name over and over," Levi drawled.

"Levi!" My face was bright red.

He shrugged. "Dude thought we were gonna hurt you last night. Pushed Gage too far. I'm just reassuring your friend that you are being taken care of properly."

I winced at his choice of words, then turned back to Wilder. He looked angry. I'd never seen Wilder angry. It was shocking.

"I'm sorry about him."

Wilder narrowed his eyes. "You're sleeping with that psychopath? Did he tell you that he put a gun to my head?"

Levi made a tsking sound from behind me, but I didn't look back at him this time. I was trying to figure out what I had just heard.

"A gun?" I asked, not sure I had heard him right.

Wilder nodded.

A hand was on my waist then, and I tensed. I hadn't heard Gage walking due to the carpet cushioning his steps. He pressed a kiss to the side of my face.

Wilder's eyes widened, as if he was scared. Had Gage seriously held a gun at him?

"You saw her. You can leave now." Gage's tone wasn't normal. It had a darkness to it.

Wilder looked from him to me.

"You got two seconds," Gage said coldly.

"I'm fine. Thanks for checking on me," I told him, then went to close the door quickly before this escalated.

Levi started to clap. "That was handled like a fucking pro. Damn, if you'd handled shit like that five years ago, things might have gone down differently."

"Gage, did you point a gun at Wilder?" I asked in disbelief.

Gage shook his head. "No, baby, I pressed it against his forehead. I didn't point it," he replied as if this were a normal conversation.

"You did what?" I asked.

He smirked. "After I licked your pussy and had you come all over my face, I warned you about this. Me."

I shook my head. "No, you did *not* mention anything about guns."

He ran his knuckle down my face as he tilted his head slightly. "The monster that consumes me. Takes over. The insane jealousy. I explained this to you. That wasn't a fairy tale, baby."

I ran my hand through my hair. "Being jealous is one thing. But that ... what if you'd accidentally killed him?"

He chuckled. "I've never accidentally killed anyone. Everyone I've killed, I meant to pull the trigger."

I needed to sit down. I felt light-headed.

"She's gone pale," Levi said.

Gage wrapped his arms around me and brushed his lips against my ear. "I warned you many times that I was dangerous. Your uncle warned you." He licked along the outside of my ear. "I'm cruel, unstable, deadly." He ran the tip of his nose along my neck and brushed my hair back. "And I'm fucking obsessed with you." He pressed a kiss on my neck. His warm breath caressing my skin. "For you, I'm willing to try and be better. I didn't kill him last night. The son of a bitch wants what's mine, and I let him live. You'd be sad if he was dead. And I don't want you sad." His hands grabbed my butt, and he jerked me against him. "I want you happy, satisfied, and taken care of, but only by me."

My heart was racing as I placed my palms flat against his chest and tried to push him back. I needed air.

What he'd just said ...

I shook my head, and he didn't budge as I pushed against him. The knife wound, the broken leg and ribs. Someone could have shot him. A completely new panic started clawing at me. This life, what he did, he could die. I could lose him. He'd been beaten and stabbed.

"I can't breathe," I said, looking into his eyes as they watched me.

"You don't get to back out now," he said gently. "We'll go back to that bedroom, and I will give you mind-blowing orgasms until you're clinging to me, begging me to never leave. I'm not letting you go. You're mine." He reached up and tucked my hair behind my ear.

"He's not lying about being better. Five years ago, Wilder would have been dead," Levi said from where he now sat on the sofa.

"Stop saying that," I said, not wanting to think about death.

"Let's go," Gage said, placing his hand on my back and nudging me toward the bedroom.

"Why do you kill people?" I asked, fighting against him.

My uncle couldn't have known this.

Gage held my face with both his hands. His thumb brushed against my skin. "It's what we do if needed. Not for fun."

"When ... why is it needed?"

He pressed a kiss to my lips. "Many reasons. The family has to protect what's ours."

I closed my eyes. He made it hard to concentrate. "Gage, this doesn't make sense."

"We're the Southern Mafia," he whispered against my lips as if he were telling me something sweet. Then, he pressed another kiss against them before using his tongue to lick the swell of my top lip.

Mafia. There was a Southern Mafia? The Hugheses? That was why they were powerful? I let it slowly sink in and realized that it made sense. He was serious. And Uncle Neil had known about this.

"Let's go back to your room."

Panic and fear were starting to take over, and my eyes flew up to meet his. "Why? What are you going to do?"

"I'll start with eating your sweet pussy again," he said, placing a hand on my back and pressing me to move.

I stumbled forward.

"Then, I'll fuck you until you know exactly who owns that pussy."

"Gage, stop."

"No," he replied.

"I need a minute. To think about all this. Adjust to it."

He stopped and pushed me against the wall. "You can't do that with my head between your legs?"

I inhaled sharply, angry at myself for being turned on by that. "No," I said, but it didn't sound convincing.

He started pressing kisses all over my face. "I love how you taste," he murmured. "I'm craving more."

"Gage," I said, placing both hands on his chest to push him back. "Look at me."

His eyes were hooded as he stared down into mine.

"I just need to let it all sink in and find some sense in all this."

"I won't let you go," he repeated.

I closed my eyes, wishing this weren't a completely twisted mess. "I don't want you to."

His eyes looked as if he was searching for a lie on my face. "You swear?"

I nodded, realizing that I was in love with him. That was the only reason I could honestly say that I didn't want out. How could I want him and all the insanity that came with him if I didn't love him? The man had crushed me yesterday, but he'd apologized, and I had been putty in his hands. It scared me that I thought I might be able to forgive him anything if he asked.

His mouth covered mine, and he kissed me like I was his source of oxygen and he couldn't get enough.

Chapter Thirty

SHILOH

"I'm not rushing things, but I got some shit to do. Kye is waiting on me," Levi said, standing up.

"She needs time. You can go. I'll call when we are ready," Gage replied.

Levi shook his head. "I'm not fucking leaving you here. She doesn't know this side of you yet. Someone has to watch your crazy ass until she understands what sets you off."

If it was jealousy, then we would be fine.

"I don't think there's any cause for concern if we're in this apartment," I told him.

Levi smirked. "You have no idea. One text from your neighbor, and this crazy son of a bitch doesn't need a damn gun to do damage. He's trying, but that don't mean he's got it handled."

Gage scowled at Levi. "You can shut up now. You're freaking her the hell out."

I was already freaked the hell out.

Levi shrugged as if it was something that had to be said. "Maybe she needs to make a list," he said.

Gage glared at him. "What the fuck are you talking about?"

Levi held up my notebook and a napkin that had been on the table. "She makes lists. This napkin is a list of Netflix shows she wants to try in order. The notebook has lists—from what she needs to get accomplished that day to a list with questions about her past. You should answer them."

"Levi!" I yelled. "Stop looking at my stuff."

Gage grabbed my chin and pulled my gaze to his. "You make lists?"

I sighed, then nodded. "It helps me get organized."

"You never made lists before. I like that."

I shook my head. How did he get in my head so easily? I couldn't stay focused.

Maybe it was best if they left. Both of them. Some space and time for me to figure out how all this fit now. "I'm fine here. I'll call you later," I started, and Gage turned on me, his eyes narrowed.

"You trying to get me to leave?" he asked.

I shook my head. "I just … I'm fine here. Levi needs to go and—"

"Levi can fucking go," he said as his hand wrapped around my arm. "I'm not leaving without you."

"Gage, I live here." I stated the obvious.

He shook his head. "Not anymore."

This we hadn't talked about.

"Excuse me?"

"You said you didn't want to leave me."

I threw my hands up. "Meaning I want to be with you. In a relationship. I didn't know that meant move in with you."

"Yep, I need to stay. I'll make a list of the reasons why for you," Levi said from across the room.

"Baby, you're mine. With me all the time. In my bed. In my fucking shower. In my lap. Mine."

I stared up at him. "That's not healthy."

"No shit," Levi called out. "I'll add that to the list. It's number fucking one."

Gage grabbed my chin. "I need you." The desperate look in his eyes made me feel helpless. "Please don't do this to me."

I wrapped my fingers around his wrist. "You want me with you all the time? You'll get tired of me. I'll be in your way."

A soft, almost-pained smile crossed his lips, which made my heart ache. "That's not possible. Just you. It's always just you."

I sighed, wanting to rub my chest to give it some relief. This man was a lot. "What about my apartment, my job?"

He shook his head. "You can't keep that job. It's not safe anymore. I've got enemies. The family has enemies. You have to stay with me."

Just when I thought I could accept something, he threw a new obstacle in the way.

"I want to work, Gage."

He nodded, looking slightly panicked. It wasn't something I was accustomed to seeing.

"I'll get you a job within the family. Trinity cooks and cleans the house. Madeline works at the stables. There will be something you can do."

Who was Madeline, and what stables? The Hugheses'?

I felt light-headed again. Pinching my temples, I tried to figure this out. How to make this work.

"Can I have time to ease into this?" I asked. "This is picking up where we left off for you, but it's upending my life and changing it overnight."

He looked so hurt that I wanted to fling myself into his arms and agree to anything. But I couldn't do that. I had to keep my sanity. One of us needed it.

"Don't make me sleep without you." His voice was pleading.

"Okay," I said, trying to find a happy medium here. "How about I keep my apartment and we try me working and then staying the night with you every other night?"

He scowled. "Every night."

"Gage," I sighed. "I can't just move in with you. I don't know you that well. We've not spent a lot of time together. This has been the most unstable back-and-forth ... whatever it's been. We aren't ready for that."

"If you only knew," Levi said from the sofa.

"I'll stay here," Gage said.

"Oh, for fuck's sake," Levi groaned.

"Gage," I started, but he shook his head.

"NO. That's me compromising. I'll let you work at the office for now. We will stay weeknights here and weekends at the house."

"But that's not how you date someone, Gage," I argued.

"That's the next step. The one between dating and marriage."

He grabbed my waist and closed the distance between us. "We aren't fucking dating, baby. We skipped that step."

I laughed. No kidding.

"Shiloh, this is all I can do," he said, lowering his forehead to rest on mine. "Please."

All my good sense. All my list-making. All my planning and being sensible. It all evaporated.

"Okay," I agreed.

He closed his eyes.

"Leave, Levi," he said roughly.

"This is a fucking bad idea," he said.

"It'll be fine," Gage told him.

"You sure you can do this?"

He opened his eyes and looked down at me. "It's what she's willing to do for now, and I'm not sleeping without her."

My stomach fluttered.

"Call before he fucking snaps, not after," Levi told me.

I turned to look at him. "What do you mean?"

"He burned down a fucking house over you once," Levi said. "That's gonna be number two on the list."

Gage tensed and turned to Levi. "GO!"

"You did what?" I asked, wondering if I should pack my things and just go with them.

He turned back to me. "Long time ago. Things are different now."

"I fucking hope so," Levi said as he reached the door.

I waited until the door closed behind Levi before asking him, "Why did you burn down a house?"

Gage lowered his head and pressed a kiss to the corner of my mouth. "Someone touched what was mine," he said softly. "I need to fuck you now, baby."

Chapter Thirty-One

SHILOH

"Seems you forgot to mention something to me," Uncle Neil said, walking out of his office to address me.

I stopped pulling files and looked at him. "What?"

Lately, a concerned frown seemed to be permanently etched on his forehead when he looked at me. "I was going to go to Gage's house to cut the leg cast off and put on a brace today. However, it seems he is coming here because he's not at home." Uncle Neil paused and studied me.

"Gage is getting his leg cast off?" I asked.

Uncle Neil nodded. "Yes. As you know, I have most equipment at their house since it's not uncommon for them to need my services."

Because they're the Mafia and you didn't tell me. I could throw that in his face. He hadn't mentioned that.

"Shiloh, why is Gage Presley staying at your apartment?"

I was going to have to deal with this eventually. Might as well start the first week of the relationship.

"Because I won't stay at his house," I replied with a tight smile, then went back to looking for the patient files we needed. "I assume I should also pull Gage's file?"

"No, it's not in there. I keep their files ... elsewhere."

I looked back at my uncle. He was waiting on me to say more.

"Why do you do that, Uncle Neil? Why can't their files go in here?" I asked, knowing exactly why he didn't keep their files where anyone could access them.

He narrowed his eyes at me. "Shiloh, if you know why, then I need you to admit that. Because I am struggling right now with the fact that you are my niece and your safety trumps all else."

My aggravation with him eased. He wasn't supposed to tell me—or anyone for that matter. Telling me would put him and me in danger—or in other circumstances where I wasn't with Gage, it would.

He blamed himself for putting me in a very bad position. There was no way for him to know younger me had been the one to start this. Not him.

"Yes, I know who and what he is. What they all are. And I am safe. Trust me," I assured him.

"You're seeing him then?"

I nodded.

He sighed and rubbed at his white beard. "He knew you ... before?"

I nodded again.

"There is an age difference. Doesn't matter now, but back then ..." He trailed off.

I smiled. "Apparently, teenage me was adventurous."

"What about him being angry at you?" he asked, but before I could answer, the front door opened, and Gage walked in, followed by Huck.

Gage's eyes locked on mine, and then he winked. Just five short hours ago, I'd been straddling him in bed while he gave me another epic orgasm. I bit my bottom lip, feeling my cheeks get warm.

"I guess that answers my last question," Uncle Neil said under his breath.

Gage walked to me, and I put down the files I had been working on to step over to the counter. He stopped when he reached the other side.

"You look hot in scrubs," he said, then flashed me a grin that made my knees weak.

"You saw me in them this morning," I reminded him.

"Yeah, and thought about it several times."

Uncle Neil cleared his throat. "Ah, um, okay, let's get that cast off, why don't we?" he said.

Gage winked at me before turning to walk over to the door Uncle Neil was standing at. Huck didn't go with them. He glanced over at me, and I could see the concerned look in his eyes.

"Do you need my assistance?" I asked Uncle Neil.

"I'll have Reba help me," he replied.

I turned my attention back to Huck and smiled. "Hello."

He rubbed the back of his neck and studied me. "You know this is bad, right?"

Needing clarity, I asked, "What?"

"This shit with the two of you. Gage is not"—he glanced around to make sure no one else was in the room—"sane when it comes to you. The two of you together is flawed as fuck. He's always been crazy, but with you, he is psychotic."

I glanced back at the closed door. The way he would go from being so sweet to the look he'd get in his eyes that excited and terrified me at the same time had been bothering me. Making me question a lot. I didn't know all of our history, and when I had asked him last night, he'd skirted around it until I was distracted with his body again.

"I love him," I admitted. It was the only excuse I had for this.

Huck sighed. "Did you tell him? If not, you might want to wait. He will get worse if he knows."

I hadn't yet. Things were all very new and had changed overnight. I shook my head.

"Good. You need to be one hundred fucking percent sure before you do. Because you told him you loved him once. And it was a fucking disaster."

We were going to have to discuss the past. It was clear I needed to hear the story before it went any further. I nodded.

"Another thing. When we have to handle things"—he didn't elaborate on what those things were—"we all need you to just go with Trinity to Madeline's. Don't fight him on staying at your apartment. It's already unsafe that he's doing what he is now. But he's made his claim on you clear. You can't stay there alone, and if we need his focus on another issue, he needs to know you're safe."

When it was just us, I forgot about all this. The Mafia, the safety, the other stuff. Hearing someone else say it out loud made it real. Made me wonder how I had ended up in all this.

"Who is Madeline?" I asked.

"Blaise Hughes's wife. You'll meet her soon enough."

I just nodded. I needed a moment alone. Glancing back at the door, I wasn't sure how much longer this would be.

"I'll be back. I need to go to the restroom," I lied.

He crossed his arms over his chest and leaned against the wall. I turned and headed for the break room. I needed a drink of water, a slap across the face, because I had started a relationship with a man I couldn't seem to say no to, who was also a dangerous, crazy person in the freaking Mafia.

Chapter THIRTY-TWO

GAGE

The brace on my leg was annoying, but better than the cast. Just a few more weeks, and I'd have my body back. My gaze went to the front counter the moment I stepped out of the room, but Shiloh wasn't there. I turned to Huck.

He shrugged. "She went to the restroom."

I hated her being here during the day, but pushing her to quit was asking for too much right now. The uneasiness in her eyes hadn't gone unnoticed by me. I was doing my best to reassure her this was okay. I'd swear to her whatever she wanted if she would stay with me. Losing her a second time wasn't happening.

Restless, I shifted my gaze back to see Carmichael walking out of the exam room. "What restroom would she have gone to?"

He motioned for me to follow him, but I could see he wasn't thrilled about this. I didn't give a fuck. He'd get over it. Shiloh was mine. He paused at the open door leading into the restroom. It was empty.

I scanned the area and saw another door open and lights on. Not asking what room it was, I headed toward it. The fucking urgency in my chest to find her began to make my head pound. Reaching the door, I pushed it all the way open, and my eyes locked on her sitting at a table with a bottle of water in her hands.

She smiled at me and stood up, but the troubled look in her eyes wasn't hidden that easily. Had Huck said something to her? She'd been fine when I walked in. I went to her, able to walk faster with the boot on instead of the cast.

"What's wrong?" I asked as I reached her, slipping my hand around her waist.

She smiled. "Nothing. I was just taking a break."

That was a lie. Something was bothering her.

"Go home with me."

A soft laugh escaped her lips, and she shook her head. "I can't. I have to work."

"Please," I begged.

If I had her with me, I could remind her how this was good. More than good. It was fucking perfect. If she wasn't with me, then she had time to get shit in her head.

"Gage, you know I can't." Her voice was gentle as she said it.

I gripped the back of her shirt in my fist. "I need you with me."

She stood on her tiptoes to press a kiss to my mouth. "I'll be home later."

"Now," I bit out, hating being told no.

"I'll see if I can get off early."

Compromise. I had to learn to fucking compromise. I nodded, still not letting go of her. Part of me wished like fuck she could remember. So we could skip all this other shit. The other part, I knew, if she could remember, I wouldn't be holding her right now.

"Let me know, and I'll pick you up," I told her.

"You can't drive."

"I can now."

I wanted to tell her I loved her, but was that what I felt? Love seemed so damn weak. You loved pizza or horse racing or porn. This was consuming. More powerful than a word used flippantly.

Before I left, I made sure to remind her just how good this was with a kiss that got those sexy little sounds out of her.

After leaving Carmichael's office and Shiloh, we headed back to the house to get my car. I was going to need it, having to go back and forth. Shiloh didn't own a car, and we hadn't discussed it. Her uncle drove her around, it seemed. My thoughts were on that while Huck talked to Blaise about an issue we were having that I couldn't participate in since I was still fucking broken.

Tonight, I was going to find out more about Shiloh's past two years. All she'd been through and why she didn't have a car. Not that it mattered now. I'd take care of her. There was shit I didn't know, and it had to be cleared up. When it came to her, I wanted to know everything. If I could just keep my hands off her long enough to ask the right things.

We pulled into the garage, and I got out of the SUV while Huck finished his conversation. Glancing over at my bike, I knew I wasn't taking that. Shiloh had had a head injury already. I wasn't putting her on the back of my bike and taking any chances.

We'd just use my Jeep. Damn, it felt good to have the freedom to drive again. Heading in the back door, I heard the noises, but wasn't completely sure until I stepped into the living room. Destiny was naked and bent over the sofa while Levi stood over her with the leather belt she preferred in his hand. Kye sat in the leather chair, watching them.

"Where the fuck is Trinity?" I asked, thinking Levi was an idiot. If Trinity saw this, Huck would lose his shit.

"Gone to Maddy's," he replied, then grinned. "Want a swing?" he asked, holding the belt out to me. "Kye is next, but we know she prefers you."

"Please, Gage," Destiny begged with her already-red ass in the air.

I shook my head. "You look like you have it under control," I told him, then headed for the kitchen.

"GAGE!" Destiny called my name, and I glanced back. "You know I'd rather it be you."

Levi nailed her ass with a hard lick. "Watch it, bitch. I'll make you regret that." He winked at me. He didn't give a fuck who spanked her, just like I didn't.

"Not interested," I replied and left the room.

The loud sounds continued as he called her names, which she got off on, and beat the hell out of her ass. She moaned and wailed and begged for it. We'd done this so many times that it felt choreographed. I opened the fridge and pulled out a beer.

"What the fuck?!" Huck shouted. "Warn a man first."

"Sorry," Levi replied. "Didn't know y'all were gonna be back here so soon. I was just showing Kye here how to spank a bitch's ass the right way."

I was leaning back on the counter when Huck walked into the kitchen.

He looked at my beer. "You not spanking her ass anymore?" he asked.

I shook my head. "No. Shiloh wouldn't like that."

"No, she wouldn't. But you liked it. Thought you might want to keep that up. Get some of your rage out."

I shrugged. "Not feeling real full of rage at the moment."

"What happens when you do? Shiloh isn't gonna bend over and let you beat the hell out of her ass."

The idea of her perfect, round white ass turning red made my cock stiffen. "Not like that. No. But that shit's a little fucked up anyway. I'd prefer to put Shiloh over my knee and use my hand."

Huck nodded, as if he understood. I had no doubt Trinity had been in that position with him more than once.

"That's for sexual pleasure though. What you do to Destiny doesn't get you off. It releases steam."

"I'll get a fucking punching bag."

The noise finally stopped in the other room.

"She leaving?" Huck called out.

"Not yet. I need to fuck her first before my damn dick explodes," Levi replied.

"Take it upstairs then."

I smirked as I took another drink. Huck didn't want to listen to it. He knew Trinity would be furious if Huck could see or hear Levi fucking Destiny.

"Gage, I need you," Destiny called out. "I want both of my holes pounded."

"No thanks," I replied.

"Let that go. It ain't happening anymore, but Kye here can help out," Levi informed her.

"Shit, you serious?" Kye asked.

"I don't lie about a hot fuck. You want her ass or pussy?"

I chuckled. Levi would have him broken in real soon.

Chapter Thirty-Three

SHILOH

There had been no sign of Wilder all week. Part of me was relieved because I wasn't sure how to handle Gage around him. The other part felt like the world's worst friend. Having to choose between Gage and Wilder wasn't fair. Gage didn't have to choose between me and Levi or Huck. I just had to because Wilder was a man.

When we stepped into the building after Gage picked me up from work, Wilder was walking out of his apartment door. His gaze met mine, then shifted to Gage before returning to me. I could see so many emotions flicker in his brown eyes, and that just made me feel worse. For eighteen months, he had been my best friend.

"Hey, you. How's your week been?" I refused to ignore him.

Gage would have to accept that I wasn't going to cut Wilder out.

He cleared his throat. "Uh, same. Good. And you?" It was such a formal answer. Not one with a funny Sarah story or one about his work. No talk about getting pizza or watching *iZombie*. Nothing.

"Different," I replied honestly.

Gage's hand on my back fisted my top. If that was a warning, he was going to have to back down.

"Yeah, I imagine so." He forced a smile, then looked inside his open apartment door. "I'll, uh, see you around. Have a good weekend." Then, he was gone, inside, closing his door before I could say anything else. He'd been leaving but changed his mind.

I walked faster than Gage could, angry about the entire situation with Wilder. Unlocking the apartment door with more force than necessary, I pushed my door open and went inside. Gage walked in behind me, studying me closely. I didn't meet his gaze, but I felt it on my skin. Grabbing an apple, I bit into it rather aggressively and stood there, staring out the window above the sink. Wilder would have Sarah this weekend. She'd expect me to be here and make cookies or cupcakes with her. How did you explain to a little girl that everything had changed in two weeks?

"You're pissed." Gage stated the obvious.

I nodded and kept chewing.

"Because of him?" The way his tone changed made me stiffen. There was a smooth yet lethal quality to it.

This was what I'd been warned about. What I had overlooked and said I could handle simply because I was unable to stay away from Gage. I would have agreed to anything if I could have him. Now, I had to pay that price.

"He's been my best friend for eighteen months. For me, that is most of my life. I feel awful that I just shut him out. Didn't go explain or talk to him. He's always been here for me, and I just … just tossed him away because of you."

The muscles in his neck flexed as he clenched his jaw. Why was this so hard for him to understand?

"You know it's you I want. Since I met you, you've done nothing but jack around with my emotions, and yet I still want you. How can you think that I would want another man after all this crazy shit you've put me through?"

Gage walked toward me, closing the distance he'd left between us. "He doesn't see you the same way. You think he does, but I assure you, he doesn't." He stopped in front of me and ran his knuckle along my jawline. "Seeing you so familiar with another man makes me feel destructive, murderous." His eyes dropped to my lips. "You've always made me this way," he whispered, yet there was a savage edge to his voice.

"I want you. But I want to keep my friend. Why do I have to give up the only friend I have?"

His right hand grabbed my waist tightly, bordering on painful. "I don't share. Not you. Never you." The dangerous glint in his eyes caused me to shiver.

This was a conversation we needed to have at his house, with his friends there, I realized. Levi was right. I didn't know when he would react or how. Once, I had been the cause of his violence, and I didn't want that.

"Okay," I replied, hoping that would ease him.

He lowered his mouth to mine, but his lips hovered without touching. "Take off your fucking pants and get on the counter."

I realized I was trembling as I slipped off my shoes, then pushed down my pants, along with my panties. Once they were discarded, he grabbed my waist and put me up on the counter. The sound of his zipper made me tense up. I closed my eyes and took a deep breath, trying to calm my racing heart. He was different. I could feel the rage simmering under the surface, like a buzz radiating from his body.

Straight Fire

When his hands grabbed my hips, his fingers dug into my bottom, and he jerked me forward in one quick movement, thrusting inside of me. Startled, I cried out as he stretched and filled me. Because my body reacted to this man, no matter what personality he had, I was more than ready for him.

"Your body still likes it when I'm on the edge of fucking sanity," he growled. "This soaking wet pussy wants it."

He was right. Who had I become? Or had I been this way all along? I just didn't know myself.

My body hummed with pleasure as he pounded into me. There were no gentle words, no love involved. I was being fucked and getting off on it.

Lifting my knees, I leaned back on my hands, opening myself up more for him.

"That's my girl," he praised me.

Our eyes locked, and the untamed beast inside of him glared back at me. The need to possess was so clear in those amber depths. As unhealthy and fucked up as that was, I wanted it. For him to possess me. Own me. The thought caused a shudder to run through my body.

"Gage." I moaned his name, unable to put into words what all I was feeling.

"Fucking hell, this hasn't changed. Needy little cunt likes to be taken." The snarl in his voice excited me. "Pushing me to a place where I can't control myself, then obediently opening these sweet thighs."

Had that been me? Was this what I needed? Oh God, why was it so good?

The electric rush began to unravel inside of me. I could hear myself panting in anticipation of what was coming.

"That's it, baby. Come all over my cock —this tight pussy coating my dick." The dangerous bite to his voice was like a match igniting me.

I screamed his name as my body convulsed with the euphoria that sucked me in. His arms wrapped around me, pulling me against his chest as he slammed into me several more times.

"FUCK, that's what I need. What I always need," he groaned, and then his body jerked as he unloaded inside me. "HOLY FUCK!" he roared, throwing his head back and closing his eyes.

I was sure I'd never seen anything as beautiful in my life. From the veins popping out on his wide neck, to his broad shoulders, to the ripped muscles on his chest. His biceps flexed as he held on to me, as if he planned on keeping me right here forever.

When he began to come down from his own climax, his head dropped to the crook of my neck, and he inhaled deeply. His arms tightened their hold on me. "I fucking worship you." His breath was hot against my skin. "*Love* isn't a strong enough word. It never has been with you. I'm not a religious man, but being inside of you is a spiritual experience." He lifted his head, and his eyes met mine. "Don't fucking destroy me again. Please." The urgency in his words broke me.

Gage was a lot to take in. He was terrifying and thrilling, all at once.

I placed a hand against his cheek, and he rubbed his face against my palm.

"You scare me, terrify me even, excite me, and humble me, all within a few minutes. I imagine teenage me didn't know how to deal with you. She wasn't ready for all this ... but I am."

His hand covered mine, and he closed his eyes as he inhaled sharply. "I need inside you again," he said as he opened his eyes up.

I smiled and slid my legs around his waist.

Chapter Thirty-Four

SHILOH

Trinity handed me a sheet pan that she had pulled out of the oven. "Put those on that red tray over there. I've got to get the hot wings finished. Can you get the dips set out with the chips, veggies, and crackers from over there?" She pointed to the counter behind us.

"On it," I replied.

We had been in the kitchen since before noon. Gage had tried three times to get me alone, but I wasn't leaving Trinity in here to make all this food. It was my first ever Super Bowl party, and although I knew nothing about the NFL—or football for that matter—everyone seemed excited because Florida had a team in the big game. New voices kept arriving, but they were gathering in the living room. Very few had come into the kitchen.

I was arranging the veggies when I felt Gage move in behind me. Smiling, I glanced back over my shoulder to look at him. This weekend had been nice. I liked it here. While

Huck was large and intimidating, his fiancée was warm and friendly. Not that this meant I wanted to move in and become a Mafia girlfriend or whatever, but in the future, maybe this wouldn't be so bad.

"These leggings are fucking with me," he whispered in my ear. "I want to bend you over and fuck you while I grab this ass."

"With a house full of people, that's not the best idea," I replied.

He kissed the side of my neck. "We can go to my room. Take off these damn leggings, and I'll lick that sweet pussy until you pass out."

I sucked in a breath, trying not to get turned on, although that was difficult when Gage was pressed against my back. His smell, the heat from his body, and the thick erection all made it hard to concentrate.

"Get off her so she can help Trinity with the food," Levi complained as he walked into the kitchen. "You can't hump her in the kitchen." He paused, then shrugged. "I take that back. If you want to, I could get on board with that."

Gage growled, "Fuck off."

Levi laughed and took a chip, then winked at me.

"Okay, boys," Trinity said, placing the hot wings on the counter. "Play nice."

I laughed, then bit my lip to stop myself.

Gage's arm, which was wrapped around me, flexed. "You think that's funny?" he asked. I could hear the teasing in his tone.

"A little," I replied.

"Bad girls get spanked," he warned me, his gaze turning dark as he dropped his eyes to my mouth.

"Please don't spank her in the kitchen," Trinity quipped, and I laughed again.

Straight Fire

"Who's getting spanked?" a guy covered in tattoos with piercings in his face asked, walking into the kitchen from the living room. His eyes went to Gage, then me, and I saw them widen in recognition. "Fuck."

"Six, you remember Shiloh," Levi said. "Shiloh doesn't remember you though. Car accident, amnesia. Tread carefully because, well, you know."

Gage's body was tense as he held me.

"Nice to meet you, Six," I said, trying to ease Gage and the situation.

Six nodded slowly. "So, if she doesn't remember … why are they …" He wagged his finger at the two of us.

"Long story," Levi replied.

"No one's business," Gage said at the same time.

Six pressed his lips together, then let out a loud sigh. "All right then. Fun fucking times ahead."

I heard the rumble in Gage's chest and realized it was time to defuse the situation. I turned in his arms and wrapped my hands around his neck. "It's a party," I reminded him. "People are going to be curious."

He slammed his mouth against mine, taking me by surprise. His tongue slid between my lips, and I opened for him. The taste of mint and whiskey teased me. We had an audience, but at the moment, he was making me not care. His hands were full of my ass while he held me against his body.

When he broke the kiss, we were both breathing hard. He slid me back down his body before slowly letting me go, and then he winked at me. The crooked smile made my chest feel warm.

"So, you see," Levi said, breaking the silence in the kitchen, "he's still fucking obsessed with her."

Six chuckled, and thankfully, Gage's body relaxed.

"I need to finish getting the food ready," I told him.

He nodded, then tucked a strand of hair behind my ear. "I'm going in the living room. If I stay in here, I won't be able to keep my hands off you."

I liked that. Knowing he wanted to touch me. I nodded.

"We are almost done," Trinity said. "I'm ready to go curl up in Huck's lap myself."

Gage turned and walked out of the kitchen, leaving me with a lovestruck smile on my face that I couldn't wipe off. I managed to finish my job, then helped Trinity get the drinks set out.

After that, she pulled the mini cheesecakes she'd made from the fridge and placed them on a cupcake stand. "We are done!" She beamed at me. "Thank you so much for all your help. I would have had to start before daylight if you hadn't been here."

It made me feel like I had a place. I fit in with this very strange family.

"I was happy to help," I assured her.

She nodded her head toward the living room. "Let's go watch the pregame with our men."

I followed her into the living room. An attractive man with blond hair pulled back in a bun walked in, and cheers went up around the room.

A few people shouted, "Boss," which caught my attention.

Then, a beautiful woman with pale blonde hair walked up beside him, and he put his arm around her shoulders. I watched as he pulled her close and pressed a kiss to her head. It was then I saw his wedding ring. My gaze dropped to her hand, and the diamond rock on hers was easy to locate. This was Blaise Hughes and his wife, Maddy.

Her gaze found mine, and a soft smile touched her lips. She was the kind of beautiful that could be intimidating, but the expression on her face was friendly. That was a relief. I

Straight Fire

wasn't sure what to expect from the woman who was brave enough to marry the next crime lord or whatever. She glanced up at her husband and said something. His head turned, and his eyes locked on me. The way his jaw flexed made me nervous. He nodded his head, and Maddy left him to make her way in our direction.

"Maddy," Trinity said, stepping forward and hugging her. "Where is Cree?" she asked, then glanced around.

Maddy laughed softly. "Uh, well, the way these parties can go, I thought it best that he stay with Ms. Jimmie at the big house."

Trinity nodded. "Yeah, smart." Then, she stepped back and turned to me. "Shiloh, this is Maddy Hughes, Blaise's wife. Maddy, this is Shiloh Ellis, Gage's girlfriend."

Maddy held out her hand. "I've heard about you. I will admit, hearing that there was a female alive who was Gage's kryptonite—I'm quoting Blaise on that one—was hard to believe. I'm honored to meet you." The sincerity in her words made me relax.

I slipped my hand into hers. "It's nice to meet you too. As for being his kryptonite, well, I was surprised too."

Maddy laughed, and her eyes twinkled with amusement.

"Speaking of Gage," Trinity said, "he's getting unsettled. You might want to go ease that."

I turned to find him watching me. The intensity in his gaze made my body flush and the area between my legs tingle. "I'll chat with you ladies later," I told them and headed through the crowd, stepping over legs as I went to the corner of the sectional sofa he was sitting on.

He patted his leg, and I moved my body between his knees before sinking down onto his lap.

His arms circled me, and I felt his warm breath on my ear. "You smell like fucking cookies."

I grinned. "Because I made three dozen," I replied.

"At halftime, I'm fucking you. We can go to my room."

I shivered, then nodded.

"How's life been, Shiloh?"

I turned to see a man looking at me who had to be of Italian descent.

"That's Mattia," Gage said against my ear.

"Oh, um, it's been interesting," I replied, which made him laugh.

"Glad you're back."

"And she's not a bitch this time," Levi added, walking over to sink down onto a chair to the right of us.

"Levi." Gage's threat was clear in his voice.

I leaned forward and sighed, looking at him. "Levi, don't poke at him."

He smirked and took a drink from the beer in his hand.

A man stood up, taking the blonde who had been with him at the other end of the sofa, and bowed his head at Blaise before going to find another seat. I realized he was giving up the seat to Blaise. He sat down, then took Maddy's hand and pulled her down onto his lap.

Gage slipped his hand under my shirt and began to make little circles on my stomach with his finger. I glanced at him, but his attention was on the television. They were talking about the Buccaneers. I knew enough from listening to them yesterday that this was Florida's team and who they all wanted to win.

I leaned back and relaxed against him. He talked about the players with Levi and Mattia. Huck came in and sat in a large leather chair on the other side of the room. Trinity curled up with him, and he held her like she was something precious and fragile. It had been odd, seeing him with her this weekend. I'd not been around the two of them much before, and

Straight Fire

seeing that massive man turn into someone else with Trinity was interesting.

My attention was back on the television as the game started when a beer appeared beside me and Gage reached up to take it. I glanced up, and my body tensed. Destiny glared at me before walking over to hand Levi a beer, then wrapping her body around him. She was wearing an extremely short red dress that barely covered her boobs. It was so low-cut that I wasn't sure how she kept them from escaping. I jerked my gaze off her as she began whispering in Levi's ear, and Gage pulled me closer to him and pressed a kiss to the side of my face.

Forcing myself to relax was difficult, but I tried. The fact that she'd brought Gage a beer pissed me off. I needed to work on my jealousy with her though because it seemed Levi liked her. Gage moved his hand further up my shirt and tugged the side of my bra down, then began cupping my bare breast. That was distracting. If he was attempting to get my mind off Destiny—or anything else really—it was working.

"She's not you," he said against my ear.

I wanted to tell him I was fine. It was fine. But then I'd be lying. Instead, I just nodded. He pinched my nipple and rolled it between his thumb and finger. My breathing started getting erratic. Gage slowly reached down and pulled my bra back up, then moved his hand back to my stomach, where he kept it.

A large redheaded man shouted at the television, and others cursed at the refs. I had no idea what was happening. Gage didn't shout or yell, which was a relief since my ear was so close to his mouth. I took in the room and watched as people got into what was happening on the television.

Glancing down at Gage's beer, I realized it was empty. I sure as heck didn't want Destiny getting him a new one. Trinity stood up across the room and headed for the kitchen.

I pressed a kiss to Gage's cheek, then whispered, "I'm going to see if Trinity needs help. Want another beer?"

He glanced at me and smirked. "Yeah, baby."

He was aware I didn't like Destiny giving him the beer. I scowled at him, and he chuckled before I headed for the kitchen.

A round of cheers went up in the living room, and someone shouted, "Touchdown."

Trinity was making a plate when I walked into the large, bright room, where it was quieter.

She looked up at me and smiled. "Needed to get away for a moment?"

"Yeah. I'm going to get Gage another beer. I wonder if he wants food."

Trinity laughed. "The answer to that is always yes. He loves to eat."

I hadn't realized that. It bothered me that there was so much I didn't know about him. He didn't seem concerned with meals at my apartment. Was I not feeding him enough? Living here, Trinity knew more about him than I did. I chewed on my bottom lip, trying not to get too worked up about this. We'd just started this relationship thing. She'd been here awhile. Of course she'd know more.

I took a plate and paused, trying to think about what he'd like. There were too many options, and I wanted to get it right.

Trinity stepped up beside me. "The cheesesteak sliders, buffalo chicken meatballs, Big Mac crunch wrap, and the cookies you made," she said.

I glanced at her, and she gave me a reassuring smile. "You'll know these things soon enough. I've been cooking for them since May."

I nodded. She was right. Next time, I'd know his favorites. I fixed his plate, got him a beer, then headed back into the room. His eyes locked on me and followed me until I reached him.

The corner of his mouth curved up, and he patted his knee. I sat down, careful not to spill his food. He took the beer with one hand, then pulled me back further onto his lap with the other.

"Looks like my hands are full." He ran the tip of his nose against my ear as he said it. "You'll have to feed me."

I liked that idea, especially since Destiny was beside us. I picked up the slider and held it to his mouth. He took a bite and licked his lips as he chewed. My gaze was on his mouth.

When he swallowed, he leaned forward and pressed a kiss to my lips, then whispered, "You keep watching my mouth like that, and we're gonna leave this game so I can fuck your mouth."

A rush of anticipation coursed through me. That wasn't a real threat, but I stopped watching his mouth and tried not to watch him as he chewed. I was getting turned on by feeding him though. Especially when he'd take the last bite of what I was holding and lick my fingers.

When he was done, I set the plate down on the floor beside us.

"Thank fuck," Levi said. "I was getting a hard-on, watching y'all."

Gage glared at him, and I grabbed his face and turned his attention back to me. "He's teasing."

"No, he's fucking serious," Gage said through clenched teeth.

I laughed then and kissed him gently before turning and settling back in his arms. It was strange how, when I was here, everything was fine with us. There was no inner battle that I had to deal with. No wondering if this was healthy or if I was making a mistake. No guilt over Wilder. It was a little world where I could have Gage and nothing else mattered.

While we watched the game, I noticed a few things. The blonde by the man with red hair had taken off her top, and he was playing with her bare breasts in front of everyone. Then, the tattooed guy had a brunette sitting on the floor between his legs with her hand inside his pants, clearly stroking him while he petted her head like she was his pet. As I squirmed, my gaze unfortunately turned to Destiny and Levi. Her dress was pulled up to her waist, and her legs were spread open while she rubbed the outside of his pants, where his erection was obvious.

Jerking my eyes off them and hoping Gage didn't look over and see Destiny's vagina on display, I saw Maddy stand up and Blaise follow behind her as they left the room. Was it because of the soft porn that was suddenly starting to break out around us?

Gage rocked his hips under me, and I felt his hard length on my bottom. His hand slid back under my shirt, and I turned to look at him. Did he expect me to act like this in front of all these people? I felt slightly panicked.

His hands grabbed my waist and stood me up so quickly that I gasped. Gage stood up behind me and guided me back through the room toward a hallway. We passed a woman who was straddling a guy, and I was almost positive they were having sex.

"Where are we going?" I asked when we left the room.

"My room," he replied.

He was walking a lot faster these days, but this was quicker than I had seen him do with the brace on. We made it up the stairs in record time, and he pushed me back toward his bedroom. Once we were inside, he shoved me back against the wall and covered my mouth with his. He groaned into my mouth and jerked my leggings and panties down to my knees, then slipped two fingers into my wet folds.

"Couldn't wait until halftime," he said as he nibbled and licked his way from my mouth down to my cleavage. "I wanted to take my time. Taste you. But, fuck, I need inside you now."

I wiggled and maneuvered my leggings down the rest of the way and kicked them aside. Gage pulled my shirt off, then discarded my bra before filling his hands with my breasts and squeezing.

"Fuck, I love your tits." He bent his head and flicked his tongue over each of my nipples, then ran his nose up the valley between them.

"Go to the bed, put your hands on it, and stick this ass out for me," he ordered as he yanked his shirt off, dropping it, then unzipping his jeans.

I did as I had been told, and he came up behind me, then slapped my butt hard, causing me to jump and cry out. I looked back at him, and his eyes were glowing with a darkness I hadn't seen before. He slapped his hand across the other butt cheek, and his eyes flared brighter. I watched in fascination as he continued to spank me, then run a hand over the red mark he had left. Each time seemed harder than the last, and the inside of my thighs were coated with my arousal. I wasn't sure if it was the spanking or the way he looked at me as he did it.

He dropped to his knees and began to kiss the now-tender skin. His tongue came out and licked at it over and over. I knew there would be handprint bruises on my butt tomorrow, and I hoped he'd be okay with that. I would be. The thought of it only made the pulse between my legs stronger.

He pushed my legs open further, and then he stilled. I knew he was seeing how this had affected me. I could feel how wet I'd gotten. He sucked in a breath, then hissed.

"Damn, sweet baby needed spanking," he murmured, then licked at my inner thigh. "You've made a mess, like a good girl."

I whimpered as he licked everywhere but where I needed his tongue.

"So fucking naughty," he whispered just before his tongue circled my clit, then began to suck it.

My knees buckled, and I cried out his name.

"So sweet," he said, then licked again. "Mine."

He stood up then and grabbed my hips before sinking into me fully.

"God, yes," I moaned, my hands fisting at the cover underneath me.

"Trying to watch a fucking football game, and all I can think about is this pussy," he growled, pumping harder.

The sound of our bodies slapping against each other filled the room. Gage's grunts made me more desperate. I wanted to feel him come inside me, hear the way he sounded when he reached his release. I loved to see his face.

"Hot little ass with my handprints all over it," he groaned. "Makes me feel like a fucking animal. I want to sink my teeth into that soft, juicy ass and bite it. Leave my damn teeth marks in your skin."

That was all it took to send me flying over the edge. His name ripped from my chest as my body bucked wildly with my orgasm. Another hard slap of his hand on my bottom, and he shouted my name as his warm release pumped into me.

I felt marked. Owned. Claimed. And I loved it.

Chapter Thirty-Five

GAGE

I took a beer from the fridge, then turned to see Destiny walk into the kitchen. Where the fuck was Levi? If he was going to bring her to shit, then he needed to keep his leash on her. I opened the beer and took a drink, ignoring her while I went to get a chip.

"You missed the last part of the first half," she said, walking toward me.

"Yep," I agreed and stuck a chip in my mouth, then moved farther away from her.

She didn't take the hint.

"It was a good one. I wish you'd been there," she said, closing the distance I'd put between us.

"Don't," I warned her.

She was going to ruin my good mood. I'd just found out that Shiloh still liked her ass spanked. Destiny needed to back off and let me revel in it.

"I need you," she whined, pressing her tits against my back.

"I said, don't."

She ran her hands over my sides and down the front of my shirt until she reached my pants. "Please, spank me, Daddy. I've been a bad girl," she purred.

I shoved her back and got the hell away from her. This shit wouldn't work now. I had what I wanted. I had what I'd been fucked up over. No one else was going to fill that hole. Not when I had the real thing.

"Gage, she's going to bore you soon. I know you. We've been doing this dance for a while. You'll need to feel that leather belt in your hands and hear the hard slap of it against an ass. She's not going to let you beat her. Not like I do. I want it. I crave it. That twisted-up sickness you have? I love it." She pulled her dress up to her waist and stuck her finger inside her pussy. "See how wet just talking about it makes me? You remember. I know your dick was throbbing hard the other day while you watched Levi beat my ass. You wanted to do it to me so bad." She grinned and flashed a triumphant smile over my shoulder. "Oops."

My stomach dropped, and I turned, hoping like fuck that wasn't who I thought it was.

Shiloh stood there. Her eyes wide and full of pain. I moved to her, and she backed away, shaking her head.

"Shiloh!" I had to get her to listen to me.

"He didn't do it. Don't be so dramatic. He just watched Levi beat my ass while I was bent over the sofa, naked, what was it, two days ago?" Destiny kept talking.

"SHUT UP!" I roared, glaring back at her.

When I turned back to Shiloh, her eyes glistened with unshed tears. Fuck no. I shook my head.

"No, baby. That's not what happened," I assured her. "Come here."

Straight Fire

She shook her head and kept backing up until she hit the wall. "Don't," she said, holding up her hands to stop me.

"She's never gonna let you share her with Levi. If this freaks her out, you won't get to fuck a woman sandwiched between you two anymore." Destiny's cold, calculated words made Shiloh flinch and close her eyes.

Seeing the way she was falling apart was killing me. The moment her tears began streaming down her face, I could feel the detonation inside me as the beast consumed me. I turned, stalking to Destiny, no longer seeing her as a female. My hand wrapped around her throat as I slammed her against the wall, holding her so that she couldn't touch the floor.

"You're a fucking whore. One I wish I'd never used. You think that I'll stand here and allow you to hurt what is mine? I warned you only because she wouldn't want me to kill you. But you're as fucking dumb as you look."

"GAGE!" Levi's voice called out.

"Oh damn," I heard Kye say, coming up to my left.

If the kid fucking touched me, I'd lay him out.

I tilted my head and glared up at her with loathing. "You don't matter to me."

Her face was turning blue.

"He's gonna fucking kill her," I heard Levi say behind me, and I laughed. It sounded as twisted as my chest felt. "Back up, Kye. You're not ready for this or his crazy ass."

A large hand grabbed my wrist and forced my hand to lower.

"Let her go," Huck demanded.

"NO!"

Levi was on my other side, pulling my arm back as Huck forced my fingers to release Destiny's throat. I heard her gagging and gasping for air, but I didn't care. I tried to break free and attack her, but they both held on to me, keeping me from getting to her.

"You're scaring the shit out of Shiloh," Huck warned me.

I swung my gaze to her, and her arms were wrapped around her stomach, her red-rimmed eyes wide with horror. She was trembling. I pulled free of them, needing to get to her, and this time, they let me go.

"Baby," I said as I reached her, and she stiffened. "She lied. I never watched. Levi and Huck can back me up on that. I got the hell out of that room. I walked in on it happening, not knowing. She wanted to hurt you."

I put my hand on her hip and pulled her to me. She didn't relax against me, but she didn't fight me off.

"You—you we-were choking her," she stammered.

"She hurt you. I can't—" I swallowed hard. "I can't handle seeing you hurt. It flips a trigger in me. I lose control."

Shiloh tilted her head back and looked up at me. "But you were gonna kill her."

"I didn't."

She blinked. "Because they stopped you."

"And I didn't kill her." That wasn't the best defense, but I didn't have another.

She was right. I was gonna fucking kill Destiny.

She glanced over my shoulder. I had heard the others leave. Levi would get Destiny out of this house and away from here.

"Is this what Levi meant?"

I brushed the tears from her face with my thumbs, hating to see her cry. Fuck, I hated it. "About what, baby?"

She blinked several times. "About you … being crazy."

I nodded. Fear had my throat in a choke hold now. We'd been down this road. It hadn't ended happily for me. It'd crushed me in ways I never recovered from. Not without her.

"You can't ..." she said, dropping her eyes to my chest. "You can't just kill someone because they hurt me. That's not ... normal."

I tightened my hold on her. "I'm not normal. You've been told this."

She sighed. "I didn't realize this is what that meant."

My heart was slamming against my chest so hard that it hurt. Fuck, she couldn't do this to me. I couldn't lose her.

"You're all I care about. Just you. I have to protect you, and in doing that, I might not always stay sane. She pushed me. She said shit to hurt you after I warned her to stop."

Shiloh shook her head. "She said things though. She's right. I-I ... don't want to be shared. I don't want that."

I grabbed her face and forced her to look at me. "Shiloh, if another man were to see you naked, see you come, touch you, I'd be put in prison. There would be no way to save my ass from the destruction I'd leave in my path. I don't want to share you."

She still looked so fucking lost. Her eyes were full of pain. It was ripping at my soul.

"Do you want to ... do ... the beating thing? Is that something you need?"

I ran my thumb over her bottom lip. "What we did upstairs earlier, that wasn't new. You used to love it when I spanked your ass. You begged for it. Not with a fucking belt, but my hand. You wanted it hard, and you got off on it. When Levi brought Destiny here the first time, she wanted to be beat with the damn belt. I—" I clenched my teeth, hating I had to tell her this shit. "I did it because, inside me, this fucking monster that couldn't have you needed to hurt someone. She willingly offered for me to hurt her. It helped with my rage. You're the only person who, just holding you, can take that rage from me. Without you, I have no other fucking outlet."

I watched as she let my words sink in. She was quiet, and I wanted to beg her to talk to me, but I was afraid of what she would say. I couldn't push her.

"I'm scared," she whispered.

"Of me?"

"I'm scared that I'll be the cause of you killing someone. I don't think I could live with that."

I brushed hair back from her face. "I shouldn't have lost it tonight. Not in front of you. That's on me. Not you."

She shook her head. "That's not the point. If that was enough to send you into a murderous rage, what if—what if someone hit me?"

My eyes narrowed. "Then, they'd die."

She shoved at my chest. "No! That is not the answer, Gage. That's not something you kill over."

"We disagree on that."

She let out a long sigh and covered her face with both hands. "I want to go home."

"You're not leaving me." I would tie her to my fucking bed if I had to.

She dropped her hands and looked at me. "No, I'm not. I just mean, I want to go back to the apartment. With you."

Relief felt like a fucking wave crashing over me.

I nodded my head and pulled her to my chest. "I'll get your things, and we can go."

She nodded her head against my chest, and the invisible grip on my throat eased away.

Chapter THIRTY-SIX

SHILOH

When I opened my eyes, I was surprised that I'd been able to sleep. I hadn't expected to after last night's events. Gage's warm chest was pressed against my back. In the light of day, was I that surprised by his reaction to Destiny last night? No.

That didn't make it okay. He crossed lines and didn't care. He didn't have boundaries or morals. I wasn't sure if he had a conscience. But knowing all of that, I couldn't imagine going back to a life without him in it. Which made me question everything I knew about myself.

I turned on my back to look at him. Through hooded eyes and those thick lashes, he stared back at me. My heart fluttered, and I felt that thrill I got when I was with him. All the things I'd read about and thought didn't exist, I'd found it. In a psychotic killer.

"We need to talk," I told him with my voice still husky from sleep.

He narrowed his eyes. "If you think you're gonna try to end this, I'm flipping you on your back and fucking you until you can't walk."

A smile curled my lips, and I felt him let out a relieved sigh. "No. It seems I can't quit you. Even though you need some serious mental help. I want to talk about former me. Us. I need to know all what happened."

He groaned and buried his head in the pillow beside my head.

"I already know it's bad. But I need to know how bad this can get."

He lifted his head. "We were different. You were different. We were like a fucking volcano that kept erupting."

"I want to start from the beginning and hear it all to the end. I'm calling Uncle Neil and staying home today. It's time I heard this. Please."

Gage stared down at me. I could see the reluctance in his eyes. "I'd rather you stay home and let me give you more orgasms than you can count."

I shook my head. "Not until I've heard it all."

"But you know how talented I am with my tongue."

"Gage"—I reached up and cupped his face—"I want to hear about us."

He finally nodded. "Fuck."

"I'll go make breakfast first," I told him, then tossed back the covers and climbed out of bed.

Standing up, I looked around for my robe since I was naked. He'd refused to let me sleep in anything.

"Fuck," he whispered as his hand gently brushed over my bare butt. "Damn, baby. I hit you too hard."

I couldn't tell if that was his aroused voice or pained one. Maybe both. I reached for my robe.

"I bruise easy. I'm fine. It's my pale skin. You should have seen my wrist after you almost broke it. I had your handprint around it for almost two weeks."

My feet were off the ground, and I was on my back, staring up at him. Gage hovered over me, his hands on either side of my head, holding himself up.

"I bruised your wrist?"

I nodded, trying not to look at his beautiful body.

"You never showed me."

I shrugged. "You hated me."

He winced and then picked up the wrist that he'd once hurt. I watched as he brought it to his lips and kissed it. My breath caught as his tongue darted out against my pulse.

"I'm sorry," he said, pressing his lips to it again.

I squirmed underneath him. "You're forgiven."

He frowned, then put my arm down. "Your ass has my handprints all over it."

I smiled. "I'm sure it does. Didn't you leave marks on my ass back when you used to spank me?"

He shook his head. "We didn't get to see each other like this. You lived with your parents. Who didn't find out about me until close to the end, but they hated me. I didn't get to see you naked in the mornings. The spanking thing was also later in our relationship. I got mad at you because you fucking flirted with guys to piss me off. I lost it one night at a bar we all used to go to and took you out to my truck, then spanked your ass. I was so fucking angry. Then, you started moaning and asking me to do it harder. I swear to God, I almost shot my load in my jeans. You were so wet that you had to take off your panties." He put his knee between my legs and pushed them open. "Now, I need to fuck you. Talking about that has my cock throbbing."

It had made me wet too. I bent my knees and lifted my hips to take him in fully when he thrust inside of me.

"Did I flirt with guys because the sex after was hot?" I asked.

He paused and looked down at me. "Fuck," he whispered. "Holy fuck." He shook his head. He started moving in and out of me slowly. "You might be onto something. Every time you did it, we fucked like maniacs after. How had I never realized it?"

"Maybe we fucked a lot, so you didn't see the trend."

He began to move faster inside me. "Once I got inside you the first time, I became a fucking addict. All I could think about was burying myself inside you again. And you were too damn young. So fucking sweet. Then, you started playing with my cum when it leaked out of you," he groaned. "It made me unhinged."

Teenage me was an adventurous sex partner. I started thinking about his cum on my fingers as I touched myself, and my clit pulsed. My nails clawed at his back as he became more intense.

"Think of it this way. Today, when you tell me about the past, you can give me explicit details about our sex."

He made another low sound in his chest. "You'll be fucking sore tomorrow. This is hot as hell." He paused and leaned down to brush his lips against mine. "I ate your pussy for the first time when you were only seventeen. I was a fucking starving man. I hadn't been able to fight it off any longer. And it was the sweetest damn thing I'd ever tasted in my life."

Fuck! Why is that hot?

I cried out his name. "Harder," I pleaded.

He pulled out and flipped me over, then jerked my hips up. "Let me look at this pretty, bruised ass while I shoot my load in you."

"Oh God," I moaned into the bed, clutching the sheets tightly in my hands.

He took me so hard that he shook the bed, slamming it into the wall.

"I own this ass!" he roared as his release spilled inside me, taking me with him as I shattered into a million pieces.

After a shower and breakfast, we sat on the sofa for my history lesson in us.

"You sure we have to do this? Can't I just tell you about all the sex, you sucking my dick, me eating your pussy? Those are the highlights anyway."

I laughed and shook my head. "We will end up having sex again."

"You say that like it's a bad thing," he drawled.

"First time we met," I asked.

He sighed, leaning back on the sofa. "Pool party at Blaise's house. You were with the senior quarterback from your high school, who had only been invited because he was … well, last night's game, the other team's quarterback?" He paused, and I nodded. "That's him. You were sixteen. He was eighteen, and although he had women of all ages throwing themselves at him, he wanted you, and I didn't fucking blame him."

My jaw dropped. "I dated an NFL quarterback?"

He tensed. "He wasn't NFL back then. Just headed to play first-string quarterback at an SEC school."

I pressed my lips to keep from smiling. Apparently, this guy was a sore point for him. "So, you took me from him?"

He shook his head. "You were sixteen. Sexy as fuck and a mouth on you. I had some chick straddling me, and you managed to slash her with words said so damn sweetly that it was impressive. Anyway, you showed up some other places and drove me fucking nuts. I couldn't seem to go anywhere without seeing you."

"You said I wasn't a *fatal attraction* thing!" I accused, not liking the fact that I had chased him around.

He chuckled. "I don't think it was on purpose. It was fate taunting me with what I couldn't have. Anyway, eventually, that ended. Mr. Football went off to college, and you were no longer in my circle of people. Then, some time went by, and you showed up with some douchebag at Huck's shop to get his motorcycle fixed. You acted like you didn't know me and were bored. Pissed me the fuck off since you were a year older and fucking better-looking than you had been the last time I saw you. I basically asked you to stay. You did. He left. I kissed you and put myself out of my misery. Then, we ended up in the meeting room inside the shop, and I ate your pussy."

I put my hand up. "Okay, wait. I hadn't seen you in a year, and I let you just go down on me?"

He grinned. "Have you looked at this pretty face?"

"Yes, but I would hope I wasn't that easy."

He leaned forward and ran a hand up my calf. "You weren't easy. You just had a crush on me. You knew that it had been ten months and two days since we'd last seen each other. I used that crush to my advantage."

I shoved his hand off my calf. "No distractions. Keep going. Skip the details on the oral sex this time," I told him.

He smirked. "After that, I couldn't get enough of you. I was too damn old for you, and I knew it. So, I managed to convince you to meet me places alone. We'd go to the springs, drive over to the beach, go anywhere to get away. And I got my mouth between your legs every time. You got as addicted to my tongue as I was to your pussy. When I wasn't licking you like a starved man, we had fun. You made me relax and smile more. Being with you kept back the dark shit in my head. That summer, I started taking you to Blaise's parties, around my friends. The first one I took you to, another girl offered me a blow job, and you got territorial. Sharp tongue and quick to bite. I fucking loved it when you got jealous. Then, you demanded I take you to a room. I did. You then hit your knees and gave me the best damn blow job I'd ever had. Swallowed like a pro and left me shook."

I was unable to hold back my smile.

"Why are you smiling?"

I shrugged. "I'm proud of seventeen-year-old me."

He raised his eyebrows. "Of your oral abilities?"

"Yep."

This time, he laughed.

"Continue," I pushed.

"Okay, fine. Then, after that, I took you everywhere I went. The guys got to know you. I took your virginity in the same pool house you had sucked me off the first time. I can give you details, but I'll need to fuck you. Because it was a lot of buildup, wanting you, and after you recovered from the painful part, we … yeah, I need to hold off unless you're ready to stop this story and let me between those pretty thighs."

I was already getting damp, watching the look on his face as he thought about it. "You can tell me later."

He nodded and took a deep breath. "We fucked a lot after that. Everywhere I could get you alone. Then, the summer ended, and you turned eighteen, and you were a senior in high school. You always flirted with guys and drove me crazy. That wasn't a new thing. But that year, it got worse. You were gorgeous, and guys were always hitting on you. I'd go through it all, but I will just hit some of the worst ones because listing them all could take a while.

"I took a steel bat to a guy's car for following you to the parking lot at school and touching your back. I broke a barstool over a man's head, who was almost thirty, for leaning in and whispering in your ear. He got a skull fracture. I got arrested for that one. Garrett, Blaise's dad and the boss, got me out of it. I threw a guy across a room and into a brick wall for grabbing your arm and pulling you to him when you were walking away from him. Broke his nose and arm. Again, arrested, and Garrett got me out. There were a lot of these instances. You would scream at me to stop. I would do it anyway. You'd storm off. I'd chase you down and kiss you until we were fucking.

"You were all I cared about. Nothing else mattered. Not the family. Not my friends. I just wanted you. I made plans, and when you decided where you wanted to go to college, I was moving there. Leaving this all behind to follow you."

I held up my hand. I was dealing with the fact that former teenage me had in fact been a selfish bitch. Why would I have flirted and let him keep getting in trouble like that? But now, this?

"Did I know you were going to do this?" I asked, horrified that he'd give up what he wanted for me after all the shit I did.

He shook his head. "No, you chose the University of Florida before I told you my plans. You didn't tell me you'd chosen Florida until I told you I was following you. But then you were just forty miles away, and there was no need for me to leave. You stayed home instead of living the dorm life. That summer was one of the best ones of my life.

"Then, the fall came. You had new friends, a life that I wasn't a part of. We were together as much as we could be, but you had study groups, and that was where you met Leo. You wanted me. You made that clear. Our sex life was off the charts. There was no problem for us there. It was the jealousy that made it all turn. Leo was after you. He wanted what was

Straight Fire

mine, and I knew it. I saw it, and I warned you I'd kill him. I meant it too."

I covered my mouth. "Please do not tell me you killed this guy."

He shook his head. "No, I didn't. But I did burn down his frat house. No one was in it. The only casualties were some fish. But ... I hadn't known no one was in it. I'd thought he was."

Oh my God. I took a deep breath. "Back up. Why did you do this? Because he had flirted with me?"

"Fuck no. I'd have only broken his arm or some shit for that. You came to surprise me at the shop. The secretary Huck had hired was hot for me. I'd put her off and told her I wasn't interested a million times. We had a party that night. I drank too damn much because we were supposed to see each other that night and you'd called to tell me you had a study group you couldn't miss. Anyway, Misty, the secretary, got topless and wrapped her arms around my neck. Unfortunately, that was when you walked in the door. I hadn't reacted quickly enough because I had enough liquor in me to kill a man. I was slow to shoving her off my lap, and you were already in your car, speeding away. I tried to run after you. Fell face-first and passed out.

"Woke up the next morning to a raging headache. Couldn't remember shit. Checked my phone, and you'd broken up with me by text. It felt like you'd reached into my chest and grabbed my heart and ripped it out of me. Levi told me what had happened. I got in my truck and went straight to your house. You refused to answer your phone. Your car wasn't at your house. Your mother, who hated me, informed me you'd stayed at the dorms with a friend.

"I went to find you, but the friend you were supposed to be with told me you'd gone to breakfast with Leo. This was when

I snapped. It gets a little foggy for me. But I waited for you to return to the dorms. He drove up, opened your car door, then pressed you up against the car and kissed you. I went to buy the supplies I needed and then headed to his frat house."

"You lit it on fire because I had kissed this Leo guy?" I asked.

He nodded. "I convinced myself you'd been wanting to date him. That you'd been seeing him behind my back. That you'd used the Misty thing as an excuse. No one was killed, but I ended up with a trial date, although there was no firm proof that it was me who had done it.

"While I sat behind bars, you packed your bags and moved to Boston. Wrote me a letter, telling me you couldn't do this anymore. That we were bad for each other. That you didn't love me and you wanted a new life. Your parents were buying a home there, and you'd decided to go ahead and move there now. Get enrolled in college. A lot of other shit that destroyed me. Garrett was able to get me out of a trial and prison time if I went into the Marines for four years. I took the deal.

"Came back a year and a half ago once I finished serving my time. I'd only checked on you once. About six months after I joined the military, I had Blaise run a check on you. He sent it to me. You were in college, dating a premed student, in a sorority, spending time at a country club, attending fancy events for the Boston elite. There were pictures of you with Isaac Jeffrey, son of some political shit, in the paper more than once. I threw the papers away and never checked again." He stopped.

"And then I walked into your house five years later, like I hadn't done anything wrong," I whispered. "I'm surprised you didn't choke *me* to death. I left when you were in jail, and I left you a letter? That's cruel. It ... it's horrible. Why would I—"

Gage's mouth was on mine, silencing me as he pressed me back until I was under him. His hand moved under my T-shirt dress and pulled at my panties. "It was cruel. It fucked me up. But you came back," he said, pressing another kiss to my mouth. "You fucking came back."

His hand slipped down between my legs, and he shoved two fingers inside me. "I knew when I lit the house on fire that I'd pay for it," he said against my lips. "I just hadn't known that payment would be losing you."

I let out a cry as he began to fuck me with his fingers. "Gage."

"Yeah, baby?" he asked, pressing kisses down my neck.

"If I had loved you, I'd have never left."

He stilled and looked down at me.

"Because I love you now and I would never—"

His mouth covered mine again as he ripped my panties off and spread my legs.

Chapter THIRTY-SEVEN

SHILOH

The next few days would have been perfect if I hadn't had another awkward run-in with Wilder and had to rush Ace to the vet because he had gotten into Uncle Neil's chocolate stash. Also, Gage was going to be out of town the next two nights. He and Huck had to accompany Blaise to a ranch in Tennessee to see a horse. Uncle Neil was taking me home after work, and Levi was picking me up at seven from my apartment to take me to stay with Trinity at the house.

Knowing our past and understanding why Gage had treated me the way he had made it easier for me to accept. This life. The family. The secrets, crime, and whatever else they were involved in. It was like I'd told Gage—I loved him, and because I loved him, I wasn't leaving.

Uncle Neil had a late patient come in with a broken arm. I finished closing up things, then got the trash together to take outside to the dumpster. The office would be closed for the next three days, so we always made sure it was clean and food was all disposed of properly. I had to text Levi and tell him I needed a little extra time to pack since I would be getting home later now.

The sunset was getting later the closer we got to spring. It was nice to go outside at five and it not be dark anymore. Smiling at the last bit of sunshine, I walked the bags out to the trash. My thoughts went to Gage and how he'd woken me up with sex this morning. He'd been demanding, and I loved it when he was like that. But then I loved it when he was sweet and when he was dirty.

A noise that sounded like a van door caught my attention. There were no cars back here but Uncle Neil's when I walked outside. I started to turn around when a sharp pain hit my head, and then everything went black.

The throbbing pain in my head made it hard to open my eyes. I tried twice and had to close them. The light in the room was too much. When had another migraine hit me? I didn't remember it. Where was I? I tried opening my eyes again, and I winced. I couldn't do it.

Focus. Where had I lain down? The smell of stale beer and cigarettes made me cringe. Why would I be asleep in a bar? A dirty one at that? Something was wrong. I tried to move, and the coarse rope around my wrists made that impossible. I froze as fear slowly trickled in. Okay, this wasn't good. My ankles were tied together too.

I went still and tried to make my breathing slow and even as I waited to hear something. Male laughter from a distance. I wasn't sure how far away, but it wasn't in this room. Then footsteps coming closer. My heart started to hammer in my chest. Why would someone have me tied up like this? Where had I been last?

The garbage! I had been taking the garbage to the dumpster. How had I gotten tied up and in a strange, foul-smelling room?

"You awake yet?" a male voice asked as the footsteps behind me came to a stop.

"You hit her too fucking hard," another one said, farther away.

They had hit me in the head. I'd been taken. Oh God, oh God. What did I do now? Did I let them know I was awake? Why did they have me?

"She's awake," the first one said, sounding amused. "She's breathing too fast." He moved, and I could tell from the shadow over my eyes that he was in front of me. "You can open those eyes. You're not fooling us."

I winced. "I tried. It hurts too bad. The light hurts my head."

"Told you that you hit her too hard," the other one said.

"Fuck off." He moved closer, and I jerked when he ran a finger down my arm. "You're sure nice to look at."

Tears stung my eyes. *Please, please don't let them rape me.* I'd rather they killed me.

"You can't fuck her. Not yet at least. He might let us fuck her later."

I was going to start crying, and that was only going to make my head hurt worse. "What do you want with me?" My voice cracked.

One of them laughed. "Can't answer that."

A phone rang behind me.

"We got her. She's awake. Uh, she's not talking much. Won't open her eyes. Says it hurts. No, he fucking hit her head too hard. Yes, boss. I will."

"What did he say?" the other guy asked.

"He said to get her some water. See if she's hungry."

"He's gonna get in trouble for that. He must have seen what she looks like." The other one sounded amused.

"Yeah, he did his research."

A hand touched my arm. "I'm gonna sit you up. How about opening those eyes?" he asked.

I squinted, and it was bearable. I gave them time to adjust, then managed to open them up all the way. A man with long, greasy black hair, a matching beard, and a big gut was looking at me. He had a snake tattoo around his left arm, a scar across his nose, like it had been sliced once, and a large mole on his neck. I tried to take in the details in case I made it out of this alive.

"Damn, would you get a look at those eyes?" he said, staring at me.

The other man walked around and stood beside him. He was tall and skinny. Spiky brown hair and a weird goatee. Same snake tattoo on his arm though. "Who does she belong to again?" the skinny one asked.

The fat one shrugged. "We don't know. Boss just said to get her. Not sure he knows why this was what *she* wanted."

The *she* was not me. I didn't want this. I thought about telling them who I belonged to, but then I worried it would put Gage in trouble. I didn't want any of them in danger. I kept my mouth shut. Gage was still recovering.

The skinny guy looked at me with an apologetic frown, as if he was sorry about this. "Which is why you hit her too damn hard. This ain't even Viper-related."

"It is when the pussy that the boss wants demands we get her."

"Boss might change his mind about what pussy it is he wants when he gets a look at this one," the skinny guy muttered. "I've seen them both. This one wins."

The fat guy shook his head. "Nope. Pussy he wants is Acid's sister. He'll pick her."

"Acid might want her." The skinny guy tilted his head toward me.

I wanted to scream that no one was getting me. My skin felt like it was crawling, and I was nauseous. I wasn't sure if it was from the head pain or the fear.

"You want some water? We got some food in the kitchen. Best fucking barbecue you've ever had," the skinny guy told me.

"Just water," I replied.

"If you change your mind, let me know. Juice is a genius on the grill."

I ignored that but put yet another name away, just in case I needed it later. It sounded like I had a small chance I might get out of here alive.

My thoughts went to Gage. Would he know I had been taken? Would he think I had run away from him? No. I'd left my purse, phone, everything in the office. The back door had been left open. He'd know I hadn't just run off on foot. At least if I didn't survive this, then he wouldn't think I had left him.

Chapter THIRTY-EIGHT

GAGE

The plane landed in Nashville just as Blaise's phone rang. I pulled out my own phone to send Shiloh another text. She hadn't responded to the last three. I knew she had been at work earlier, but she'd be home by now.

"When?" The tone in Blaise's voice caught my attention. His body tensed up, and Huck also noticed. "You're sure? What time did he say? We'll head back now. Just landed. They'll need to refuel. I'll handle him."

Blaise ended the call, and his gaze leveled on me. Then, he stood to walk to the front of the plane and talk to the pilot.

"What the fuck is going on?" I asked, feeling a slight uneasiness.

"Not sure," Huck replied, his jaw clenched as he waited for Blaise to return.

We didn't try and get off the plane.

"He looked at me," I pointed out. "Not you. Why me?"

Huck shifted and shook his head.

When Blaise reentered, he looked at Huck for a brief moment, then turned back to me. "That was Levi."

I stood up. My chest tightened. Levi was supposed to pick up Shiloh.

"Shiloh has been taken."

The words were a blow directly to my chest, as if a bomb had exploded.

"She didn't run?" Huck asked.

Blaise didn't turn from me. "No. She was taken from the back lot of Carmichael's office. Her purse, phone, everything was left inside. The back door was left open. The trash she had been taking out was left beside the dumpster. She was taken by surprise while her back was turned."

A wave of nausea hit me, and I dropped my head into my hands.

"Levi is getting footage from security cameras in the entire area, and he has Six checking the tread of the tire. Do you know anyone who would use her against you? Who would know to? I know you piss off people regularly, but who have you pissed off lately?" Blaise asked me.

I needed air. The plane was too fucking small. Why wasn't it moving? I had to get back there. Fucking hell! Why had I let her keep the damn job? This was my fault. I couldn't tell her no, and now, this. I ran my hands through my hair, pulling at it as if ripping it from my scalp would help.

"Gage?"

"I DON'T KNOW!" I roared. "If they've hurt her …" I couldn't go there.

The tightening in my throat got worse.

Touching my neck, I paused and looked back at Blaise. "Destiny."

Blaise frowned. "Destiny couldn't have done this."

"But who does she know?" I asked.

"What did you do to her that would make you think she'd go to these measures? I'm doubting your dick is just that good."

Huck cleared his throat, and I realized he'd not told Blaise about the other night.

"Destiny said some shit to Shiloh. About Levi whipping her ass and lies about Gage watching and getting off. I was there. Didn't happen. Anyway, she then shared some other shit. Shiloh was falling apart and started crying. He snapped," Huck said, nodding his head at me. "Held Destiny by her neck against the wall until she was turning blue. Took me and Levi to get him off her."

Blaise looked murderous. "And you didn't think I should fucking know this?"

Huck bowed his head. "I knew you should know. I just didn't want you to be hard on Gage. He's working this shit out with Shiloh. You know it's different this time. He's had a lot to fucking accept this week, and Shiloh does keep his insanity in check and calm him."

Blaise swung his glare to me. "Were you going to kill Destiny?"

"Yes," I replied honestly.

"And that's him being in check and calmer?" Blaise asked.

Huck cleared his throat. "It's Gage, boss. He's never going to be completely sane. It's why he's a weapon. He's a lunatic."

Blaise put his phone back to his ear. "Find out who Destiny Ward is related to and everyone she's been in contact with. Pull all her phone records. Work hours. Everything from this past week."

He dropped his phone and looked at me. "Don't kill because your woman cries next time. Unless her life is in danger."

I clenched my teeth, and my hands balled into fists. I managed a nod.

Blaise stood up and got in my face. "You fucking lose your shit, and this is what happens!" he roared. "Your woman is in danger, and we've got to find her because you can't control your goddamn temper when it comes to her. Don't make me regret my decisions, Gage. DO YOU UNDERSTAND ME?"

I took a deep breath. He was right. I fucking hated that he was right.

"Yes, boss," I replied.

He nodded and sat back down. "We'll find her. When we do, then you get to fucking kill someone. Happy?"

No. I wouldn't be happy until I had Shiloh in my arms, safe. Even then, I wasn't sure there would be enough people to kill to calm the fury inside me.

"I'm putting fucking trackers under their goddamn skin. All three of them," Blaise muttered as he glared out the window.

The plane was in the air, headed home, when Blaise's phone rang.

"Yes."

There was a pause.

"Motherfucker."

Another pause.

"Let Levi know. We are about an hour out."

He ended the call and dropped the phone, then looked at me.

"Where the fuck did you three find Destiny?" he asked, then glanced to Huck.

Once, we'd all fucked her. She'd been coming around for a while.

Huck pointed at me. "It's fucking pretty boy over there. She is a dancer at a club in Orlando. She latched on to him,

Straight Fire

and we ended up tag-teaming her in a private room. Then, she was coming back to the house with either him or Levi. They shared her, fucked her, but it's his fucking face she loved."

I scowled at Huck. I didn't need fucking reminding that I'd been an idiot. She was a hot piece of ass who spread her legs and got on her knees for me whenever I needed it.

"Her brother is a Viper. Goes by the name Acid," Blaise informed me. "You've been bringing a bitch into the house who is connected to a fucking gang. Who did her background check?"

"Not sure we did," Huck admitted.

Blaise looked livid. "Let's fucking hope Acid doesn't like to hurt pretty faces."

My blood felt like it was boiling under my skin. My fists clenched and unclenched as I sat there, planning the payback. Fucking Destiny was gonna wish she'd never opened her mouth.

Blaise stood up. "Need to go tell the pilot we need to go to fucking Orlando now."

I didn't speak. I let all the fucking rage inside of me simmer and build. When it released, they'd all fucking die.

Chapter Thirty-Nine

SHILOH

As time wore on, my headache started to slowly ease. The two guys had left me in the room alone what felt like hours ago. I was thankful for the silence. To keep from falling apart, I had thought about the past few mornings and nights with Gage. The things he'd said to me. The way he'd looked at me. My throat felt tight at the thought of never seeing him again.

What if this morning had been the last time we would be together in this life?

Footsteps. More than one set. I braced myself for what was to come. I recognized the fat man's voice as he explained they'd tried to feed me and I'd refused food. There was no response from whoever he was talking to.

When they were almost to the room, there was a pause.

"I'll take it from here," a deep voice with an accent I couldn't quite place said.

I closed my eyes tightly. I could do this. I could face whatever happened. Opening my eyes, I waited, and one set of footsteps entered the room. I turned my head to the right to look at him. I wasn't going to show weakness. Gage wouldn't want me to. He'd want me to be brave.

The man was average height with long, dark dreadlocks pulled back in a ponytail. His eyes were a light brown while he had a mocha complexion. A gold lip ring and another piercing in his eyebrow. He wasn't as dirty-looking as the men from earlier. However, the snake tattoo was on not one, but both of his arms and around his neck with the snake's head coming up over his jawline and the pointed tongue reaching halfway up his cheek.

"Unexpected," he said as he walked closer to me. "Shiloh Ellis?" he asked.

I nodded my head.

He bit his lip, and then his tongue darted out to flick the gold ring. "Do you know who I am?" he asked with a smirk.

I shook my head.

"You're not a stripper, are you?"

I shook my head again.

"You're wearing scrubs. A nurse?"

"Yes," I replied.

"That explains the location I was told to have you picked up at." He squinted his eyes and pursed his lips. "I believe I've not been given the entire story." He looked at me and grinned, as if I understood what he was talking about. "You see, I was led to believe you were … different. I'm trying to decide if I care."

If he had abducted me to dance for him, he was going to be sorely disappointed. I waited for his weird conversation he was having with himself to continue.

"Answer me this, Shiloh," he began. "How do you know Destiny Ward?"

I tensed. This was about Destiny?

"Ah, you do know her. It's all over your face. Interesting. Do you consider her a friend?"

I shook my head.

He chuckled. "Well, that seems to be on the correct course. She, in turn, hates you. Which is why you're here. You see, I've wanted Destiny in my bed exclusively for a while now, but she is difficult. She thinks because I still fuck other cunts that she should be given the same opportunity to have other dicks. I don't share, so you can understand why we've been at a standstill."

"Why did you abduct me?" I asked.

He pointed a finger at me and smiled. "No need to rush me. I'm getting there. It's not as if you have anywhere to go." He held out his arms and waved them back and forth to show me the small concrete room with some storage cabinets, a chain that hung from the ceiling, some cuffs and chains on the wall, and a drainage hole in the center of the room.

"Two nights ago, Destiny agreed to finally give in to my desire for her to be in my bed exclusively. However, in return, she wanted one thing." He pointed at me. "You." He shrugged. "Dead."

The tightness in my lungs made it hard to breathe. He was going to kill me.

"I assumed you must have done something terrible to her for her to request death. I expected someone from the strip club she works at or perhaps a former employer. What I did not expect when I handed your name over to my men to collect you was … well, you. That face—you remind me of a porcelain doll. Perfect, angelic, unattainable. What could you have possibly done to make Destiny want you dead?"

She was doing this because of Gage. He'd almost killed her. This was her payback. She didn't want him dead, but me, she did. I couldn't tell this man that. What if he decided not to kill me and went after Gage instead? I couldn't allow that.

"No explanation. Does she have a reason? Perhaps I should get her down here and ask her."

She hadn't told him about Gage. She wasn't going to. Even though he had almost killed her, she still cared about him enough to keep his name out of this. I had to trust she would continue to protect him.

"I'm leaning on the side of this being a crime of jealousy. Did you take a man that Destiny wanted for her own?"

I said nothing, and he let out a laugh that verged on evil.

"That's it. She wanted a man who wanted you." His eyes slowly scanned my body. "Even with those unattractive scrubs on, it's obvious you're a complete package. I like the classy feel to those elegant features."

He played with his lip ring as he studied me. "I bet your pussy is as fine as you are. Sweet, slick, pink." He reached down and grabbed his crotch. "Sorry, I needed to adjust myself. You're making me hard, thinking about what's under those boring clothes."

He closed the space between us and put his hands on either side of my chair as he came level with my eyes. "You won't tell me his name even if it means your life?"

"No," I replied.

He smiled as he dropped his gaze to my lips. "What a lucky man. An elegant beauty who is also loyal. Even when it's her life on the line. That's uncommon with a face like yours. I've found beautiful women to be evil once you get to their core."

He pushed back, standing back up, and I felt like sighing in relief that he hadn't touched me. If he was going to kill me, I wanted it to be Gage's hands that had touched me last when I took my final breath.

He began to pace as he looked at me. I remained silent. Waiting on him to say something. After several minutes, he stopped and pulled out a slim phone from his pocket.

"Bring Destiny to me. Acid too," he said, then ended the call.

Acid was who they had spoken of earlier. There was a man with that name. He wasn't going to actually use acid on me—I hoped. That would be brutal. Not the way I imagined dying. But then I hadn't imagined this either.

"Since you are so tight-lipped and impressively loyal, I will need to hear Destiny's side of the story. Perhaps we can decipher the truth among the lies she tells." He paused and winked at me. "As for Acid, I just like to add to the drama. Family drama is always entertaining. And Acid likes beautiful women. He adores them. When he gets a look at you, well"— he shrugged—"family drama."

The fear of rape hung over me again. I would much prefer the acid death to Acid raping me. I clenched my hands behind my back. The rope had already rubbed my wrists raw. It hurt to move them.

"Are you hungry yet?" he asked, tilting his head with a concerned frown. As if he gave a crap if I was hungry or not.

"No," I replied.

"Water? Wine perhaps? Beer? Or are you more of a cosmopolitan drinker?"

My life was in its last few hours, at best. Staying silent was doing me no good. They weren't going to just let me walk out of here.

I met his gaze. "You have me tied up, waiting on a woman who hates me enough to order me dead, and you're asking me if I want a cocktail?" I asked him, not even trying to mask the annoyance in my tone.

Straight Fire

He grinned, and then he laughed. His eyes danced, as if he found me hilarious. Great, the man was a psychopath.

"I could untie your wrists and give you a cocktail if you prefer."

"You could untie my wrists because this rope is painful, but I don't need a cocktail. I'm not into taking drinks from strangers. I watch the news."

He laughed again.

Then, his laughter died, and he walked over to me, putting his hands on the armrests beside me again and lowering himself. "For a kiss." He said the words softly as he looked at my lips.

I considered spitting in his mouth. It was an appealing thought. However, he had a knife tucked in his right leg, and I could see the gun at his waist.

"I'll keep them tied."

His eyes shot back up to mine. "Because you find me repulsive or because you love someone else?"

Both, but I said nothing.

"The loyalty. Damn if I'm not jealous myself now. Who is he? Is this man worthy of your love? What has he done for you? He's not protecting you properly. That's something you should take into consideration." His hand moved to my face, and when he touched it, I flinched. "If you were mine, no one would have been able to get near you. Especially the dumbass shits I sent to pick you up. They did it so easily. Although I hear Dill hit you too hard in the head. I'm sorry about that." He sounded as if he cared, but the evil, deranged gleam in his eyes said something else.

I wasn't sure this man didn't eat the meat from those he killed.

"I've got a nice big dick. With four piercings. The pleasure I could give you would be earth-shattering."

I was going to throw up in my mouth.

Heels clicking down the hallway caught his attention.

His eyes lifted to the door, and he looked back at me and smiled. "Sounds like we have company."

I sat rigid, reminding myself that Destiny was out for revenge. But only on me. Not Gage. He was safe. She wouldn't throw his name out there.

The man straightened his stance, then turned to look at the door after giving me a wink. Destiny came striding in, wearing one of her signature, barely there dresses with stiletto heels and a furious look on her face.

She looked at the man, then swung her gaze to me. "WHY is she still alive, Jag?" She was close to shouting.

A tall man followed in behind her at a much slower, laid-back pace. He had the same dark hair and eyes that Destiny had. Except his few days of growth on his face and his wider lips made him the better-looking sibling. He looked at his sister, then swung his gaze to me.

"I needed more information," the man who she had identified as Jag said, sounding amused. "Once I got a look at that face"—he waved toward me—"I wasn't very keen on killing her."

Destiny clenched her teeth, glaring at me, as if this were my fault. "I'll do it then. Give me a fucking gun."

She held her hand out to Jag, who looked down at her hand, then back at her face. Then, he walked over toward me, ignoring her request.

I could still feel Acid's eyes on me. He hadn't stopped staring at me.

"Destiny, how do you know this woman?" he asked his sister.

I turned to look at her, then at him. It was clear they were related. The similarities really were strong.

"I told you, she tried to kill me," she spit.

I winced, but said nothing. If anything, I'd been horrified by what happened to her.

Her brother looked me over, then narrowed his gaze, turning back to his sister. "Her? She tried to kill you? How exactly? Because the *choking you out* description isn't working. She's shorter than you, smaller in size. She looks like a fucking fragile doll."

"Right!" Jag burst out. "That's what I said."

Destiny shifted her glare to Jag and then shook her head in disgust. "So, you're saying you don't believe me because of the fact that you think she's hot?"

Acid looked back at me. "I'm saying, she's never choked anyone out in her life."

"They'll find her. You need to kill her. Get rid of the body. Now. You're wasting time." Destiny sounded slightly frantic. "How long has she been here?"

Jag turned from me to look at Destiny. "Who will find her? Who would be looking for her?"

Destiny's face flushed as she looked at me.

NO! Don't tell them. Do not do this.

"How long have you been here?" she asked me.

I shrugged. "I don't know. A while."

But they wouldn't find me. I had no phone. There had been no witnesses. Nothing.

She looked at her brother. "You need to get this done fast."

"She's been here over six hours," Jag replied.

Destiny paled. Did she really think they would find me? And even if they could, in just six hours?

"Fuck," she muttered.

Jag grabbed Destiny's arm and shook her. "WHO?" he shouted.

She looked at me with panic in her eyes, and I knew she was going to tell them.

"NO ONE! No one will come looking for me. Just shoot me. Do what she says. Please," I begged, looking back at Destiny.

She was staring at me like I'd lost my mind.

Jag turned to me. "You want me to do what she said?"

I nodded. "Yes. Just get it over with. No one is coming. Kill me. Get rid of my body."

Acid walked over to me. "Who are you protecting?"

I shook my head. "No one."

"Yeah, sweetheart, you are. You're willing to die to keep them safe." He turned back to Destiny. "What is this about, D?"

She looked terrified. "She's as fucking psycho as he is," she muttered. "They know by now. He's not going to let her be gone this long. They'll be here."

Jag slapped her so hard across the face that she stumbled back. "TELL ME WHO, BITCH!" he roared.

It was nothing like the calm man who had talked to me earlier. That was the evil I'd seen in his eyes. I'd known it was there.

"Gage Presley. She's Gage—"

"NO!" I screamed to shut her up.

She turned to me. "You are fucking crazy! You are telling them to kill you to protect him? Are you that stupid?"

Jag turned to me. "Gage Presley, as in Blaise Hughes's soldier?"

I clenched my jaw tightly. "She wanted me. Not him. ME. Leave him out of this."

His eyes narrowed, and he walked toward me. "You're asking me to kill you to protect Gage Presley?"

"Please," I begged. "Just do it. Leave him out of it." My heart was hammering in my chest. I had to save him from this somehow.

He turned to look at Acid. "She's serious, isn't she?"

"I believe so," he replied.

"Listen, please, just forget about that. Gage had nothing to do with what happened to Destiny. She's right. It was me. I choked her out. I'm stronger than I look. It was all me. Just me. That's why she wanted me here. Just kill me and leave him alone. All of them. Blaise has a family. A wife and a kid. They had nothing to do with what I did to Destiny." Tears were rolling down my face as I pleaded. This was the last chance I was going to get. I had to make them believe me.

"Baby, that's the sweetest fucking thing I've ever heard." Gage's voice was both heaven and hell at the same time.

"No," I whispered as horror washed over me.

Destiny was right. He'd found me.

Jag spun around, and my eyes found Gage standing with his gun aimed at Jag's head. Huck had his gun pointed at Acid, and Blaise was standing beside Destiny with his gun against her forehead. There was a guy I'd never seen before standing in the back. He was younger, attractive, and amused. He winked at me as he stood there with his gun at the ready.

"Looks like it's just us," Gage drawled. "Seems you took what's mine. You'll understand why I killed the other motherfuckers in this building."

What?

"We weren't told she was yours," Jag replied. "Destiny never mentioned that. She said she wanted her dead because she tried to kill her. I'd have never touched her if I'd known."

Acid took a step, and Huck cocked his gun back.

"Don't move," he warned. "I don't want your blood sprayed on Shiloh, but if I have to, I will."

"Destiny is my sister. I should have checked into it before sending men out to get Shiloh. We assumed she was a former friend. Some bitch at the club. We didn't check into it."

"Yeah, you fucking should have," Gage replied, walking toward us. "You touch her?" he asked. "Either of you?"

They both shook their heads.

"They touch you, baby?" he asked me, not taking his eyes off Jag.

"No," I replied.

"They hurt you?" he asked me.

"No," I lied. I wasn't telling him about my head. That would worry him.

"Acid, untie my woman," he ordered without looking at the man. "Trev, get up close so you can see the bastard when he is bent down."

I stared up at him, completely in shock. He had his brace still on his leg. How had he barged in here and killed people? What was he thinking?

"Stop worrying about me, baby," he said, his jaw clenched, which was the only sign that he wasn't as calm as he was acting.

The younger guy I didn't know made his way over to where I sat.

Acid bent down and started untying my hands. "Fucking Christ," he muttered. "You were protecting him?"

I looked at Acid. "Yes," I clipped out.

"Don't talk to her." Gage's tone made the man untying me tremble.

He was terrified of Gage.

"He's a fucking lunatic," the young guy Gage had called Trev said. "Don't talk to her."

My wrists were free, and I let out a relieved moan. That felt so much better.

"Baby, you keep making those relieved sounds, and my finger's gonna slip. I don't want their blood spraying on you. Don't make me snap."

"Fucking hell," Acid said under his breath as he untied the ropes around my ankles.

Once I was free, I stretched my legs and feet in front of me. "Feel better?" Trev asked me.

I looked up at him and nodded. He looked completely out of place here. Why had they brought some college kid into this?

"Come here, Shiloh," Gage said to me.

Trev stepped back to give me a path to Gage.

I stood up and started toward him. Jag's hand reached out and grabbed my arm to stop me. It startled me, and for a moment, I was worried about the college kid on my other side, but just as quickly as he had grabbed me, he released me. Then, he fell backward. I stared down at him with a bleeding hole in his forehead. His eyes were wide with no sign of life staring up at me. I covered my mouth as I screamed.

The splatter of blood on my arms as I looked down at him had me frozen, unable to move. Arms came around me, and I tried to pull away when I realized it was Gage. He bent his head and kissed my face.

"I'll clean you up," he whispered. "Come on."

I looked back down at Jag bleeding on the floor at my feet. "You—you killed him," I said in disbelief.

"He asked for death the moment he grabbed your arm," Gage said, putting his arm around my shoulders, pulling me against him. "Let's go."

I swung my gaze to Acid, who was standing there, completely pale with eyes locked on Huck, who still held him at gunpoint.

"I didn't hear a gunshot," I said, looking up at Gage as we walked away from them.

"Silencer, baby," he replied.

"We killing the other two?" Huck asked Gage.

Gage turned to Blaise.

Blaise shrugged. "Your woman. Your call," he replied. "It would be good training for Trev."

I looked back at Acid, and his gaze was now locked on his sister. I could see the goodbye in his eyes. My chest hurt for them.

"Don't," I begged. "Please. Let them go."

Gage touched my chin and turned my face to him. "She tried to get you killed. He was helping her."

I shook my head. "He didn't know. He thought I'd tried to kill her. When he saw me, he said he didn't believe I'd tried to kill her. He called her out on her lie. He doesn't deserve to die, and he doesn't deserve to lose his sister."

Gage sighed. "Fuck, baby."

I turned back to Acid. "You weren't going to kill me, were you?"

He shook his head.

"He has a fucking gun pointed at him," Huck said dryly. "He's not gonna say yes, Shiloh."

"I swear, I couldn't have killed her. Jesus, look at her."

Gage moved so quickly that I hadn't seen him pull his gun out. But it was pointed at Acid.

"NO! Gage! NO!" I yelled. "What are you doing?"

"You heard him," Gage snarled.

"Yes, he said he wasn't going to kill me."

"He insinuated it was because of how you looked. Did he fucking touch you?"

"NO! He did not touch me. He was nice to me. Please, please do not kill him."

Gage's entire body was strung tight. He lowered his gun. "Don't look at her. Don't think about her. Don't say her name. Or I will know."

"I won't, I swear." Acid's voice cracked.

"Take her out. We'll be out next," Blaise said.

Gage didn't argue with him, but then the authority in Blaise's tone made me want to obey.

Pulling me close, Gage walked me out of the room. For a moment, I worried that I should stay. Make sure they didn't kill Acid or Destiny. But I wasn't sure if that would do more harm than good. Gage looked ready to combust. The fury was rolling off him in waves.

He led me out a back door and into a dark parking lot. A black SUV pulled up, and he opened the door and put me inside. The other three came walking out of the building next. Once we were all in the vehicle, I looked up at the driver, surprised to see Levi.

"Thank fuck," he said when his eyes met mine. "Glad you're okay. How'd little Hughes do?"

"Pro, baby," Trev said, climbing inside the back.

Levi chuckled and shook his head.

"Call Carmichael. Let him know she's safe," Blaise ordered someone. I didn't know who.

I was just thankful he was handling that. I hadn't thought about Uncle Neil.

I started to buckle up, but Gage stopped me and pulled me into his lap. He held me against him as we drove away. I could feel his heart pounding beneath my ear. I hadn't thought I would see him again. Touch him again. I'd thought we'd had our last moment together.

It was then I burst into tears.

Chapter Forty

SHILOH

Sunlight flooded Gage's bedroom when I woke up the next morning. It was bright, which meant I'd slept later than usual.

When we'd gotten here last night, Gage had taken off his brace and showered with me, taking his time to clean me thoroughly. He washed my hair carefully and placed kisses along my body. He dried me off, put balm on my wrists and ankles, then bandaged them before brushing my hair and putting me in bed. I'd fallen asleep almost immediately.

Stretching in the warmth of his big, soft bed, I had never been more content. I was alive. I was with Gage.

Turning, I found myself alone. Where he had slept was cool to the touch now. He'd been up for a while. I buried my face in his pillow and inhaled his scent.

"You smelling me, baby?" he asked, amused.

I lifted my head to see him walking toward me with a tray of food. He stopped, setting it down on the sofa.

I blushed, embarrassed to be caught smelling his pillow.

He went back and closed the door before getting the tray and joining me on the bed. "Trinity had a mini breakdown when she found out where we'd been. Huck didn't tell her that you'd been taken until we had you back safe. This is how she deals with her emotions. She cooks," Gage said as he set the massive amount of food in front of me.

"Wow. There is some of everything," I said in amazement.

"Yeah, there's a fucking buffet downstairs. You want more of something, let me know," he said, leaning in and pressing a kiss on my lips.

I reached for a strawberry and popped it in my mouth.

"Eat all you want. Your uncle will be here in an hour to check your head. I'll try not to fuck you so you have time to eat before he arrives."

I swallowed and looked up at him. "Why is he coming to check my head?" I asked because I hadn't said anything about being hit on my head.

Gage looked at me as if that was a dumb question. "I would think that was obvious."

Yes, but only if he'd known about the hit I'd taken to my head. I continued to look at him, trying to remember if I'd said something last night about it and not realized it.

"Baby, the security footage at the service station next door to Carmichael's office showed everything. I saw the son of a bitch hit you in the back of the head with a motherfucking board, then throw you over his shoulder and toss you in the back of a fucking van. He was the first one I killed last night when I walked into the shithole."

I blinked. I hadn't thought to ask him how they had found me. When they had shown up like the cavalry, I had been so shocked that I wasn't about to die that I didn't consider how they had known where I was. Destiny had been so sure they'd find me. She understood more about the family than I did.

Gage leaned over and pressed a kiss to my temple. "It's why I was so fucking gentle with your hair last night. There's a lump the size of an egg back there. Not sure I slept at all last night. I watched you breathe and woke you up several times just to see your eyes."

I didn't remember him waking me.

He smirked. "Keep looking at me with those blue eyes like I'm your hero, and you won't get to eat before Carmichael arrives."

Normally, that wouldn't be a threat. It would be a temptation, but my stomach growled, and I turned back to the food. I was starving.

Gage picked up a piece of bacon and held it to my lips. "Eat."

I obeyed and let him feed me. My thoughts went back to last night as I finished the bacon, and then he held up a fork to my mouth with a piece of cinnamon roll on it. I started to open, but stopped. I remembered something else about last night.

"The college kid there last night," I said, turning to Gage. "Levi called him little Hughes."

Gage nodded. "Blaise's younger brother."

"He's so young."

Gage chuckled. "Baby, he was born to the Mafia boss. It's in his blood. Blaise had already seen some bad shit by the time he was Trev's age. It's past time that Garrett put his youngest out to train."

This world was going to challenge me and shock me at every turn. I studied the food in front of me. Thinking about how the boys born into this family had no choice. It was what they did.

"You chose this life." I looked up at him.

He nodded. "I fought for it. Had to prove myself to Garrett. I wanted this."

I didn't understand why.

Gage looked at me for a moment, and I could see the turmoil in his eyes. "This is a story for another time. Just let me feed you," he replied.

I appeased him by letting him feed me the rest of the cinnamon roll. Then, he moved to an egg dish I didn't recognize, and I managed to eat a few bites of it before I shook my head. I couldn't eat any more.

He put the bite in his mouth instead and winked at me. As much as I wanted to crawl on top of him and forget everything but how good his body felt, I wanted to understand him and this life he was in more. I needed to understand it. After watching him kill a man, I had to know why Gage wanted to live this way.

"Please, tell me why you're a part of this. Why did you want this?"

For a moment, I thought he wasn't going to tell me. He seemed tense, almost angry that I'd asked. I hadn't meant to mess up our morning, but there were things I had to understand. I knew so little about him, about these people. We couldn't live in this room and fuck all the time. Facing the reality of our situation was important.

"The family I had been born into was one I didn't want to keep. My mother died from a drug overdose when I was four years old. My father was likely the cause of her addiction. He began beating me when I was six. The older I got, the worse the beatings were. When I was eleven years old, I hit a growth spurt. This fucking face I have now began to mature, and women noticed me. I came home from school one afternoon, and there was a woman with my father. She paid him for my virginity. It didn't end there. Others came, and I either took the beating or fucked the women."

I moved over and wrapped my arms around him, needing to comfort him and myself. He tensed under my touch, but I didn't back away. If he was going to share this with me, then I wasn't letting him suffer alone.

"I was fifteen when he brought home the first male. He held me by the throat and slammed me against the wall when I refused to let the man touch me. That day, something snapped inside of me. I hadn't known it was there. But I became someone else. I wasn't the boy who was afraid of his father or death anymore. I was someone else. My father was on the floor, unconscious, when the haze finally cleared, and I stood there, staring down at him. There was blood coming from his nose. For a moment, I thought he might be dead, and I didn't care. The man he'd brought in to fuck me was gone. I sat there, watching him breathe for over an hour. Trying to decide if I was going to let him live. If he hadn't opened his eyes when he did, I can't say I wouldn't have taken the gun he liked to threaten me with and used it on him."

I buried my face in his neck and inhaled deeply. His arms slipped around me and held me against him.

"I walked away that day after he stood up, wiping his bloody nose, threatening me. I packed a bag with the only things I needed and left that house. With nowhere to go, I slept at a park that night, and the next day, Blaise found out I was homeless. He talked to his dad, and I was moved into a man's house by the name of Waylon August. He was in his late sixties, but he'd been born into the family. He wasn't in great health, so he wasn't active within their ranks. He became the father my real one had never been. He liked you. Warned me you were too damn young, but he understood it. Two years ago, he died of a heart attack."

I pressed a kiss to his chest. He had lived through hell and survived. The family had saved him. They'd been there for an abused kid with no one. I could understand that. I wished I'd known earlier. I wouldn't have questioned so much. There was darkness in this life they chose, but it didn't have their souls.

"I love you," I whispered.

"I worship you," he replied.

Smiling, I tilted my head back and stared up into the eyes of the only man I could ever love. I didn't understand how I'd left him before. That haunted me—the cruelty of my behavior five years ago. I was thankful for the accident. Thankful that I hadn't woken up as that same selfish person who had been able to walk away from this man.

Chapter Forty-One

SHILOH

When Sunday finally arrived, I dreaded it. I knew the fight with Gage was coming about my returning to my apartment and job. We hadn't talked about the future or anything beyond the present. Gage hadn't wanted us to leave his room most of the time. My cheeks heated at the thought of how he'd taken me this morning in the shower. We had been in our own little world for two days.

Gage, Levi, and Huck had unexpectedly left on some business after breakfast. Trinity had said that happened rather regularly. We cleaned up the kitchen, and I went to get a shower, then pack up my things while Gage was gone. When he did get back, I'd be ready to leave. Not that I expected him to take that well.

Once I was finished, I made up his bed and straightened the room before heading back downstairs. When I reached the bottom step, the closed door that I had seen the guys coming and going from often opened, surprising me. None of them were here.

Blaise Hughes filled the doorway, and his eyes locked on me. "Shiloh, I need to speak with you," he said, stepping back and holding out his hand for me to enter the room I'd been told by Uncle Neil on day one not to ever go inside of.

I wasn't sure if I was more nervous or curious. Blaise wasn't someone I'd gotten to know, and although he wasn't as large as Huck, he intimidated the hell out of me. I glanced around, wondering where Trinity was but I didn't see her.

Stepping past Blaise, I saw what was clearly an office. I'd kinda suspected as much already.

"Please have a seat," Blaise told me, then walked over to sit in a leather chair across from a sofa.

I had expected him to take the chair behind the desk and for this to feel more formal.

I sat down on the sofa, feeling awkward. This was strange, and I didn't understand why he wanted to speak with me. Why couldn't he have done this when Gage was here? In fact, why was he here when the others were gone? My mind started going in several different directions, none of which made me feel good about this.

"The workings within this family are a dynamic that most wouldn't understand. With power comes difficult decisions, and in order to keep the balance, there are secrets. Lies are told, and things are done to protect our own. Even if that means hurting them to save them from themselves.

"I've had very little interaction with you since you arrived back into Gage's life. It was a choice I made because I was protecting my wife from any attachments that could hurt her later. You see, I did know you before. Gage didn't do many things without you by his side. I was the one who stepped in most times to keep him from ruining his fucking life over his jealousy where you were concerned.

"However, last night, when we walked into that room and you had no fucking idea we were there, I heard you. You were willing to give your life in order to protect Gage and me. But that isn't why we are having this conversation. You begged for my life to be spared because of my wife and child—the two people who are the reason I wake up in the mornings—so they wouldn't lose me. If there were magic words into my vault of secrets, you spoke them."

Blaise held out his hands, and then he smiled. Something I had never seen the man do. It was … surreal.

"I have a truth that you've earned. One about yourself. About your past. One that I was waiting to share with you until I felt like you were ready for it. This won't be easy to hear, but I believe, in some ways, it will also give you some peace." He paused and picked up a glass sitting beside him and took a long drink before turning back to me.

"You and Gage were fucking toxic. Not because of who you were, but because you were still a kid and he was obsessed with you. The level of his obsession with you was more than any teenage girl could handle. You didn't understand the depths of it. You weren't mature enough to see what you were doing to him. He was going to lose everything, and after the fucking hell he'd lived through, growing up, I couldn't let that happen.

"When he burned down the frat house, I knew that was it. Not only as his friend, but also as the future boss of this family, I had to save him from himself. I wanted Gage not only because he was one of the most lethal weapons we had, but he was also one of the best friends I had. Losing him because of his obsession with you wasn't something I could let happen.

"You were a wreck when you found out he'd been arrested. I waited for you in the parking lot of the jail where they

Straight Fire

were holding him, knowing you'd show up. When you did, I stopped you and led you to my car. Your eyes were swollen and red from crying. I told you I needed to speak with you about a way to help save Gage. That was all you needed to hear to leave with me.

"It was then I threatened to leave Gage behind bars, disengage him from the family, and turn my back on him if you didn't leave town. I explained that you had become a weakness for him and I couldn't allow that. If he chose you, then I was done with him. There would be no more saving him or stepping in. The years he'd spent proving his loyalty to the family would mean nothing. The only way for my father to step in and get him out of the mess he was in would be for you to leave, tell him it was over, that you didn't love him, and not return. No contact with him. Nothing."

Blaise paused, then sighed. "You wrote the letter to him while you sobbed." He leaned forward, resting his elbows on his knees. "You weren't a selfish bitch. You gave up the man you loved to save him. To protect him. The person who woke up in that hospital didn't have a change of personality. You were the same Shiloh; you were just grown up. The teenage girl who hadn't understood Gage or life in general was gone. She had existed before the accident. But without the memories to haunt you, to keep you living a life you didn't want, you had the courage to walk away from the things you didn't want."

I sat there, unable to speak. Form words. I just stared at him. My emotions were all over the place. What should I even feel right now?

"I kept tabs on you because you were important to Gage. Even if he thought he hated you. When I heard about your accident, I had you trailed. The moment I was told about the changes you were making—breaking off the engagement, no longer a part of the circle of friends you'd had—I knew it was time I gave you a chance. I contacted Carmichael and set your return in motion. It took six months of watching you, making sure you were mature enough to handle Gage, and, of course, figuring out the best way to put you in front of Gage again. When he chose to act like a fucking idiot and take on a group of men alone with no gun, he made that easy for me. He needed a nurse. You worked for our doctor.

"As for Wilder, he was never supposed to form an attachment to you. He stepped out of bounds when he stood up to Gage, trying to keep him from you. Gage could have killed him. I'd warned Wilder of that before, but he wanted you more, it would seem. He failed at his task in the end. He's been moved to continue his training back in Georgia, where his father is located."

I finally managed to find my voice. "Wilder?" I asked, thinking I might possibly be hallucinating from the trauma to my head.

"As for your apartment, the lease has now been terminated. Your things are being packed up and moved here today. Carmichael knows your job there has come to an end. He is aware it's not safe for you, and having you there will only cause your uncle undue stress. However, if you would like a job, Gage will help you find one that makes you happy within the safety of our properties."

I shook my head. Processing all this was too much at once. "My apartment lease isn't up for another seven months."

Blaise smirked. "That's no longer the case."

I knew he was waiting for me to say more, but I was almost afraid to ask. Could I take any more truths right now?

"Uncle Neil knew all of this?" That part was one of the most shocking details to me.

Blaise raised his eyebrows. "Do you really think your uncle, knowing Gage, would choose you to be his nurse? Doreen was the nurse Carmichael had lined up for Gage. When I called him to inform him I wanted you tending to Gage, it was the first time Carmichael had ever told me no. It took me promising him that I would make sure you were safe several times and that you wouldn't be there long before he agreed. And even then, he was not happy with me." Blaise was grinning, as if that was amusing to him.

"Why did you want me here if you knew Gage would send me away?"

Blaise chuckled. "Because I knew he just needed to see you once. No matter how much he thought he hated you, I knew he needed to see you one time. The rest would all fall into place."

He stood then and glanced at the clock on the wall. "They'll be back soon."

I stared up at him, trying to decide if he expected me to keep this to myself. Not to tell Gage. If I told Gage, would he do something stupid? Would I be ruining his life again?

Slowly, I stood up. "That's it? I'm supposed to just take all this and act as if nothing has changed? You want this to be kept a secret?"

Blaise lifted a shoulder. "I can't make that decision for you. I've done enough. If you love him, then you'll make the right choice."

I opened my mouth to ask him what the hell that meant when he turned and walked to the door. I thought he'd look back at me, but he opened it, then left me standing there with a mountain of truths that could change everything.

Chapter Forty-Two

SHILOH

I stood with my back to the door, looking out the window over the backyard, when Gage walked into the bedroom. It had been three hours since my talk with Blaise. When I had left the office, I had returned to Gage's bedroom and not left again.

The things Blaise had told me, I had thought about them while replaying my life from the moment I'd opened my eyes in the hospital. Small things I didn't think too much about, like my uncle Neil calling me to offer me a job when I had been wanting to find a life outside of the one I'd woken up in. The apartment being available the day I'd started looking when everything else in town had been unavailable. Wilder approaching me from the very first day, helping me, being there when I needed something. It had all been too easy, and I'd thought nothing of it.

Gage's arms came around me, and he held me to his chest. I closed my eyes and sank back against him, needing this more than anything else. When I was with him, I could deal with the rest of the world.

"What's wrong?" he asked, already sensing my mood.

I still had no idea if I was supposed to tell him or not. Was this a test? If I failed the loyalty test to Blaise, did that mean I would once again be sent away? The idea made me angry. If that was what this family was—loyalty proven by keeping secrets, lying to those you loved—I wanted no part of it.

My heart sank. I wanted Gage, and this was his life. Closing my eyes, I wished I'd never gone down those stairs. That I had never heard the truths Blaise thought I should know. I realized that a part of me was relieved. I hadn't been some awful person before my accident. It was a weight off my chest I hadn't even realized was there. Believing that I had the potential to be someone so careless, hateful, shallow, and cruel wasn't something that gave me the warm fuzzies. It had haunted me. Clung to me like a dark cloud over my head.

Was having that all lifted better than facing this? Telling Gage his best friend had lied to him, sent me away, let him believe I didn't love him, it would destroy this life he had fought so hard to have. He had a family—one that he wanted, that he would die for—and yet I had a secret that could ruin it for him.

I hated this. The hurt was so deep that it felt unbearable.

Gage took my arms and turned me to face him. He slipped his knuckle under my chin and forced me to meet his gaze. I knew he would see the unshed tears burning my eyes. I could either lie about why I was about to fall apart or tell him the truth. It was a no-win situation. If lying to someone kept them from being hurt, was it okay? Or did it add another layer of pain that would one day cause more destruction than if the truth had just been told to begin with?

"Baby, talk to me." The concern in his voice made me whimper.

How could I hurt this man? It was making me physically ill. Yet I couldn't *not* tell him the truth. I knew if I lied to him, it would eat me alive.

I let out a sob, then burst into tears, unable to hold back the agony inside of me. I wanted to make him happy. I wanted to protect him. To love him. To make up for all he'd been through. Yet I couldn't do those things because, to do them, I had to lie. And I couldn't lie to him. It was something I knew I'd never be able to do.

He held me against his chest, pressing kisses on my head, murmuring sweet things, reassuring me that everything would be okay. He promised that I didn't need to cry. I clung to him, wishing all those things were true. That he could fix it all by just holding me.

I didn't know how long I had been crying, but by the time I finished, he was holding me, cradled to his chest as he sat back on the bed. His lips were pressed against my temple, and his arms were wrapped tightly around me. I sniffled and took a deep breath, then looked up at him.

"I have to tell you something," I choked out.

The look on his face was so tender that it almost caused me to fall apart again.

"I'm listening," he said.

"Before I do, just know that I would do anything to protect you from hurt. Anything but lie to you. I've spent three hours in turmoil, and as much as I love you and as much as I can't stand to see you in pain, I can't keep things from you."

His arms tightened around me. "I'm glad," he said in a low voice thick with emotion.

I took a moment to pull myself together, then began to tell him word for word everything that Blaise had told me.

Straight Fire

I left out nothing. All the while, I should have been the one holding him to ease the pain, but he continued to hold on to me. When I finished, his eyes were still locked on me. He leaned down and covered my mouth with his.

This was not the reaction I had expected. However, my need to comfort him was stronger than my concern of how he was dealing with this emotionally. Gage laid me on the bed, then continued kissing me as he ran one hand down my body while holding himself up enough so that he didn't put all his weight on top of me.

I sank into the kiss, burying my fingers in his hair, loving the way he felt against me, his scent, the feel of his warm breath on my skin as he left my lips to trail kisses along my jaw, then down my neck. When his hand slid into the front of my leggings, then slipped underneath my panties, I lifted my hips to meet his touch. Needing it more than I needed oxygen right now.

Slowly, he worked his finger from my clit to my entrance, sinking into me, then back out again. Each time, he rubbed a little harder until I was panting and begging under his unhurried touch.

"Let it feel good, baby," he whispered against my ear as he licked at the tender skin beneath it. "You don't have to rush it. I want to watch you fall apart in my arms."

The frenzy was almost too much. I tried to rock against his fingers, needing him to go faster. He chuckled against my neck, slowing his pace even more.

"I fucking love the sounds you make. The way you say my name. Pleading with me."

Right now, I would do anything he asked if he'd just let me orgasm. The need for it was screaming inside of me.

"Please," I begged. "Please, oh God, harder, please."

Gage moved over me and pulled his hand away, making me cry out in panic. I had been so close. I started to reach for his hand and shove it back inside my pants when he took the sides of them and jerked them down to my ankles. I opened my legs, ready for him to finish me. Do something to get me there. The ache was pulsing so hard that it was painful.

He unzipped his jeans, then shoved them down his legs in one swift move before he lowered himself and thrust into me.

"FUCK!" he shouted as he filled me.

I bucked against him, crying out. This was what I needed. I clung to him as he lifted his hips just enough to almost slip free of me, then rocked back into me hard. It only took three more times before I was clawing at his back, screaming his name while my body shuddered with its release.

"Fuck yes," he groaned, watching me. He began to move faster, his breathing coming in pants. "Mine! This is mine! Tell me it's mine."

I looked up at him, watching his beautiful face stare down at me with a fierceness that made me tremble. "It's yours. All of me. I'm yours."

"GAH!" he roared, then exploded inside of me, filling me with a hard, warm rush that sent me spiraling into another euphoria.

When he rolled off me, he took me with him. My ear was pressed against his chest, and I could hear his racing heart. We lay there in silence while he ran his hands through my hair and our breathing returned to normal.

"Time to go downstairs," he finally said.

I moved so I could look at him. "What are you going to do?" I asked.

A small grin tugged at the corner of his lips. "Eat. I'm starving."

I frowned, but wasn't sure if I should ask more or let him digest this and deal with it in his own time. Had I underestimated Blaise's power over him? Did he forgive and accept Blaise on command?

He pressed a kiss to my forehead, then moved over me to pull my panties and leggings back up. "I want my cum leaking out of you," he said, then winked at me before getting off the bed and pulling his jeans back on.

I stood up, and he grabbed my chin to kiss me one more time, then threaded his fingers through mine before heading for the bedroom door. We went down to the kitchen in silence, but I heard the voices as we approached. Levi was laughing, and Trinity joined him.

We stepped into the kitchen, and the table was full. Levi at one end with Kye, Huck, Trinity on the far side. Trev, who I hadn't seen here before, was on the other side with Blaise, Maddy, and a high chair with an adorable blond boy shoving blueberries in his mouth.

"We started without you. Levi refused to wait," Trinity said apologetically.

"Yeah, because once they start fu—"

"Levi! Words," Maddy interrupted him, and then she smiled up at me.

Levi shrugged. "Once they *you know*, it could be hours before they come out of that room."

I looked up at Gage, unsure. Would he say anything? Or was this how it was done? Had this not been painful for him? He'd been lied to by someone he trusted. Even if it had been what Gage needed at the time.

"Well?" Blaise asked, turning to Gage.

"Like I said, she didn't need to be tested," Gage replied, then started to walk us toward the table.

I didn't move.

"What are you talking about?" I demanded.

Gage turned back to me and tugged on my hand hard enough to pull me to him. "Loyalty, baby. He had to test your loyalty. You're different now, but he needed to be positive."

"Yeah, because once, we couldn't trust you with shit," Levi said, causing Gage to scowl at him.

I shook my head, more confused than ever. "Wait … what? He told me all that to see if I'd be loyal to the family?"

Gage nodded.

"I'm, uh, stating the obvious here, but I wasn't loyal. I told you."

Gage smirked as he nodded his head. "Yeah, you did. About tore my heart out, seeing you so upset though. That part I hadn't been prepared for."

"I don't understand any of this," I said, getting annoyed. "And if all of that was some made-up story …" I stopped talking, feeling my temper start to stir.

"It was the truth. All of it," Gage assured me. "I wouldn't fuck with your head like that, baby."

"But you knew already, didn't you?"

He nodded.

"And I told Blaise's so-called secret, which means I was not loyal to him."

Blaise cleared his throat and stood up. "Not exactly the way I see it," he said. "Real loyalty requires love. We are bringing you in after a past that might make many members question our decision. You don't love me." He smirked. "Why would you be loyal to me? But if you loved Gage, then your loyalty would be strong enough. You proved it by being loyal to him, and Gage *is family*."

I hadn't looked at it that way. It was smart. A little complicated, but it made sense.

"I made the mistake once of lying to Madeline to protect her. In the end, I almost lost her. I wasn't loyal to her, and it could have destroyed us both. But I came clean. Suffered through watching her fall apart over something I never wanted her to know."

"And we lived happily ever after," Maddy finished for him.

Staring up at Gage, I frowned. "How long have you known?"

"A week," he replied.

"And you weren't upset?"

There was male laughter from the table.

Gage shot them a scowl, then turned back to me. "Yes, baby, I was upset."

"So was Ms. Jimmie when he smashed a lamp against the wall, and then he tried to take a swing at Blaise, which got him shoved into the bar by Huck and they ended up breaking an excellent bottle of scotch," Trev replied, grinning like the memory was funny.

Wide-eyed, I looked from Trev to Gage.

He shrugged. "I have a temper. Took me a bit to calm down."

"You were restrained for over an hour while Blaise talked to you," Huck said, sounding amused.

Suddenly, I was relieved he had known already and that the worst was over.

Levi stood up and clapped his hands together. "So, when are we going to load Shiloh's stuff and move her in?"

"They've still gotta eat," Huck said, scowling up at him.

Levi shrugged. "Fine, but I got a date tonight. Let's not push this too late."

"You don't date," Huck replied.

"Okay, then I got a fu—"

"LEVI!" Maddy interrupted him again.

"Uh, sorry."

Gage leaned down and brushed his lips against mine. "Are you okay?" he whispered.

I thought about all the reasons I shouldn't be okay, but looking up into Gage's eyes, I knew that as long as I had him, I would be fine. He was all I needed. I had experienced life without him, and I couldn't imagine going back to that.

"Yes," I replied.

His beautiful smile sent the flutters in my stomach free.

"I love you."

He cupped my face in his hands. "And I fucking worship you."

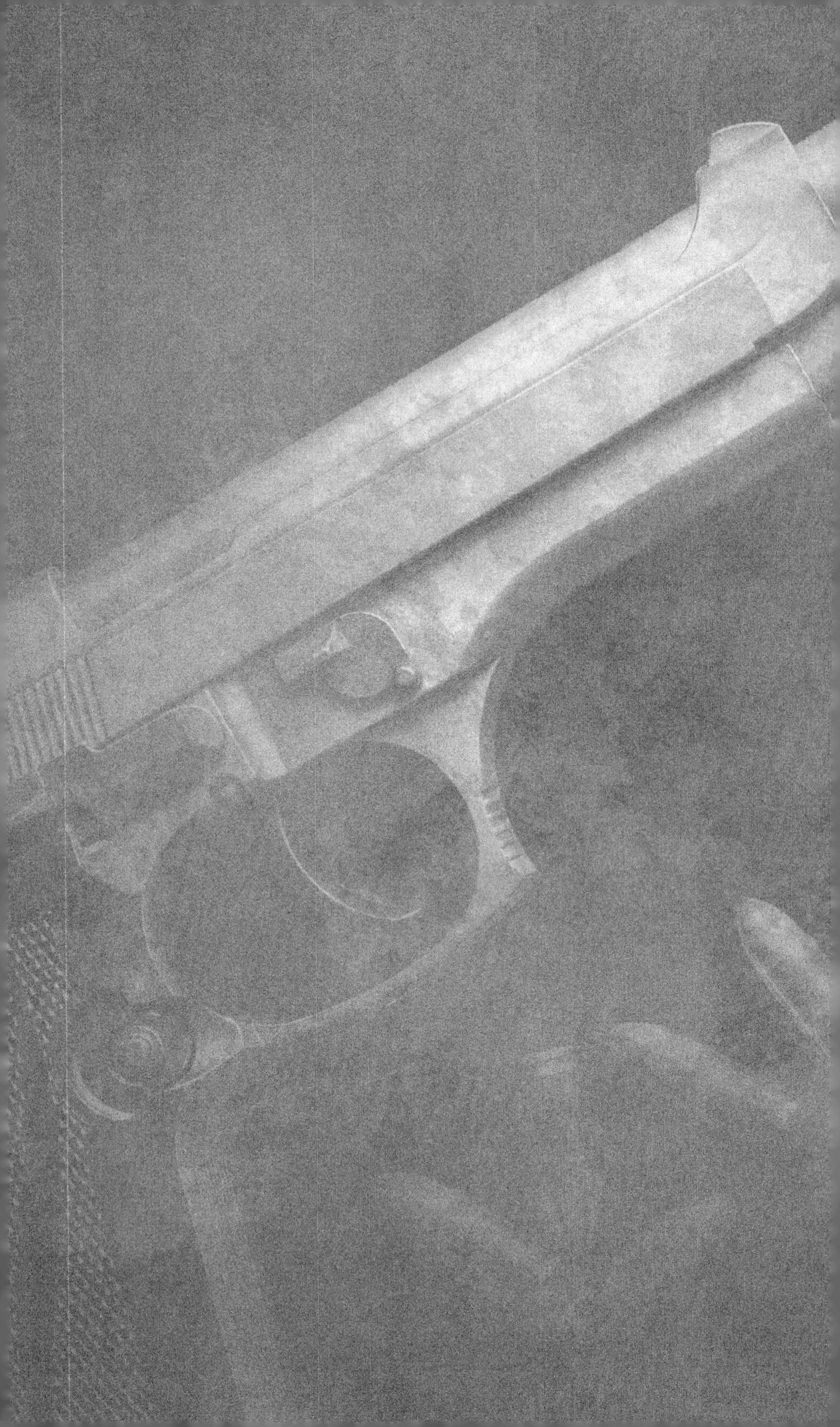

Firecracker Teaser...

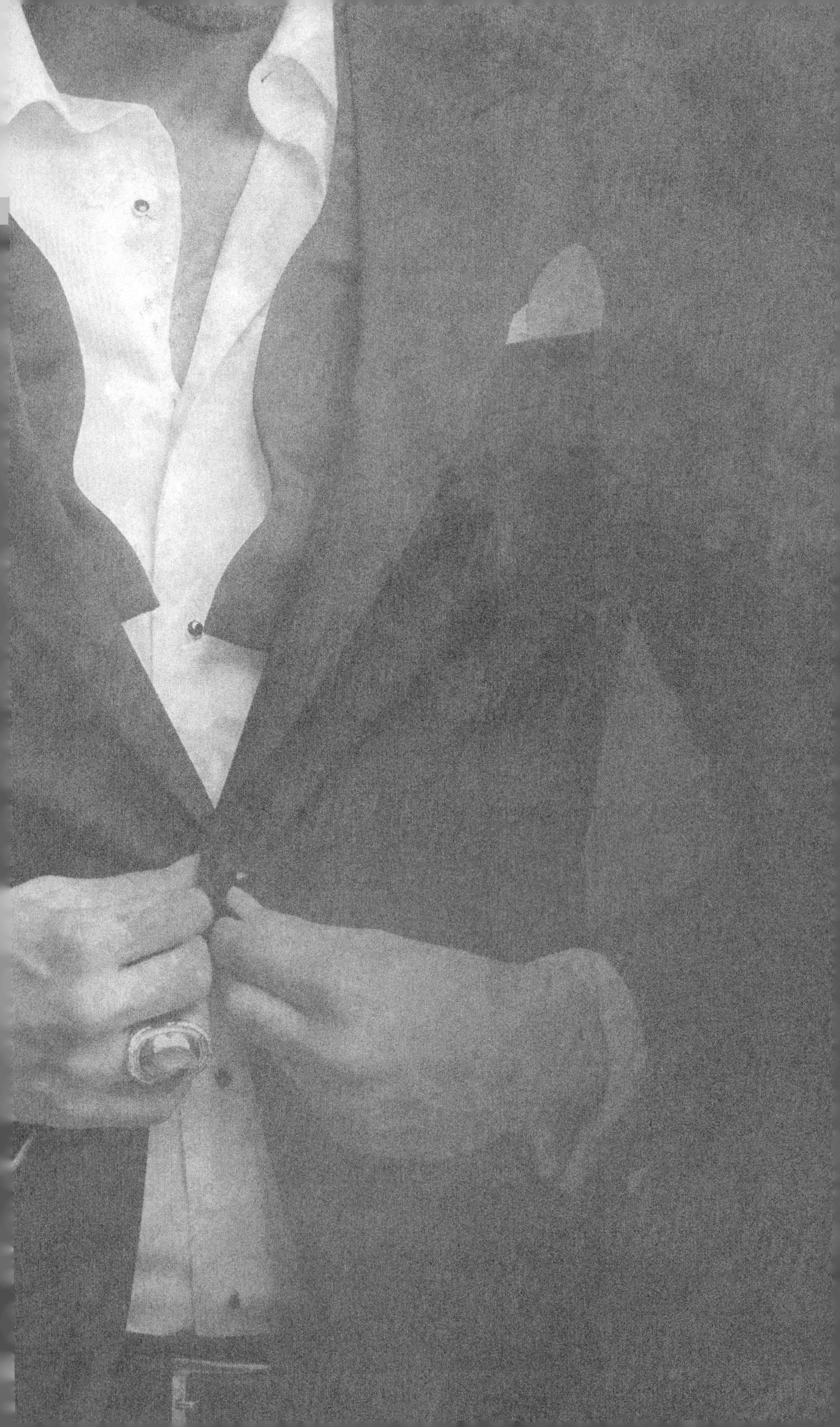

Chapter One

TREV

Horse racing was in my blood. It was the second-most important part of my family's legacy. However, if I was being brutally honest, this was my favorite part of the Kentucky Derby weekend—the Derby Eve galas. I typically hated fucking galas, but not these. I didn't even mind wearing a tux. My best friend didn't seem to share my sentiments. Saxon Houston looked annoyed. He was definitely here for the races. Horse racing *was* his first love.

Smirking, I turned toward him to lay one of my smart-ass comments that would get a smile out of the guy when my eyes found someone else instead. All other thoughts left me. The music being performed onstage by some old famous dude faded away. It was as if no one else was in the room. Just her.

Fucking hell, she was smokin'.

The lights caught the different shades of blonde in her long, curly hair. Bare, sun-kissed shoulders and—holy shit—that body in that formfitting hot-pink dress. She wasn't looking at me. Not directly. Her focus was on the old dude singing. From where I stood, her lips looked full. I wanted to see her eyes. I had a thing about eyes.

"I'll be back—maybe," I said, not taking my gaze off her when I spoke to Saxon.

"Where are you—oh," he replied, and I knew that he'd spotted my target.

He could keep his nice-guy bullshit right where it was. I had seen her first.

Moving through the crowd, I didn't even stop to speak to the Packers quarterback who had grown up in Ocala. Our families were friends. Even if Jon Bon Jovi stepped in front of me—and I was pretty sure he was here—I wasn't stopping.

She took a sip from the drink in her hand and finally let her gaze travel across the room.

Who was she with? Why the fuck was she alone?

Reaching her side, I pulled out all my Hughes charm and decided she was about to fall hard. I'd make sure of it.

"You owe me a drink," I said, leaning down close to her ear.

The tiniest jerk of her shoulders was followed by a slow turn of her body toward me. She lifted her eyes and … fuck me.

"I doubt it," she replied. Her thick Southern drawl was a smooth, smoky sound.

What color were her eyes? Honey? Could eyes be the color of honey? Because hers looked like warm honey with sunlight shining through. I struggled to get my head back in the game after she'd thrown me off with eyes I hadn't expected.

"Ah, but you do." I flashed her a smile that had been working for me since puberty.

She smirked. "Please continue. I can't wait to hear the rest of this cheesy pickup line."

Okay, fine, it was a pickup line, but, damn, it wasn't cheesy. It was fucking smooth.

"Because when I saw you, I dropped mine."

A grin tugged at those full pink lips, and then she laughed. Score. It'd worked.

"What color are your eyes?" I asked, fascinated.

"Hazel," she replied with another laugh.

I shook my head. "No, I've seen hazel eyes. That is something else. Sunshine and honey."

"Now, what would you have said if they'd been blue? What's your pickup line for that color?"

I shook my head. "That wasn't a line. I'm fucking serious."

"Mmhmm," she replied, taking a sip of her drink.

"You don't believe me?"

She raised her eyebrows. "Does it really matter? I don't even know you."

Ah, but we were gonna fix that.

I held out my hand. "Trev Hughes," I said.

The flicker of recognition in her eyes told me she must be connected to the horse racing world. Not just a guest or someone wanting to experience the Kentucky Derby. She knew the last name Hughes. Her eyes lowered to look at my hand as if she wasn't sure if touching me was something she wanted to do.

Fuck. What had Dad done to her family? He'd better not have fucked this up for me before it even had a chance.

I started to attempt damage control when she finally lifted her hand and slid it inside mine. Her skin was soft, and her hand was dainty with pink nails to match her dress. I liked how my hand seemed to swallow hers. A weird tightening in my chest that I wasn't familiar with struck me.

"Gypsi Parker," she replied.

I could see in her gaze that she was searching mine for any recognition. But I'd never met anyone named Gypsi in my life, and there was no fucking way I'd have forgotten her. Especially with those eyes.

Reluctantly, I released her hand but stepped closer to her, then bent my head to whisper in her ear. "I know you aren't here alone," I said. "Please tell me there isn't a guy somewhere who has a claim on you."

She laughed again. "That's a tricky question."

No, it wasn't. I needed her to answer me and then point him out so I could make him disappear.

"How so?"

She smirked again and turned to look out over the crowd. "A man did bring me." She paused and glanced back at me. There was a twinkle of mischief in her eyes. "He bought everything I'm wearing." Reaching up, she touched the simple diamond necklace around her neck. "Even the jewelry."

"I'm praying he's your father."

She laughed. "No. He is definitely not my father." This amused her. The humor in those honey-and-sunshine eyes was unmistakable.

"Fuck," I muttered.

She tilted her head to the side and reached out to touch my arm. I fought the urge to cover her hand with mine and keep it there. I'd dress her and buy her jewelry better than what she was wearing now, if that was what it would take. I started to say so, but she spoke first.

"You're not what I expected," she replied. "I think we might end up being good friends."

Oh, hell no. She was not friend-zoning me. When she started to move her hand away, I reached up and grasped it.

"I'm thinking something a little more exciting than friends."

Her eyes shifted away from me then, and I saw a change in her expression before she turned to look at me again.

"I need to be going."

"I'll go with you," I told her.

She wasn't running off like goddamn Cinderella.

She sighed, and I could see the battle in her eyes before she lifted them to me.

"Okay, fine. You lead the way."

Hell yes! I wrapped my arm around her waist and pulled her close to my side before walking toward an exit. The gala wasn't doing it for me anymore. Time to change locations.

Just as we reached an exit, my cell started ringing. The ringtone was my father's. Fucking hell, this'd better not be family shit he wants me in on tonight. I considered ignoring it, but I knew I'd regret it later. Glancing down at the girl beside me, I debated on it. She might just be worth my father's wrath.

"You gonna get that?" she asked once we were outside.

With a sigh, I reached into my pocket. "Yeah."

"Get Saxon. Meet Levi and Kye at their hotel suite. There's an issue that needs handled," Dad barked at me.

Motherfucker!

"Saxon?" I asked, making sure I'd heard him right.

"Yes. Kenneth agrees it's time," he replied.

Kenneth was Saxon's dad. He was also part of the family. Saxon hadn't been on any family business before. He never mentioned it, and I had thought he would just handle the horse racing part of our world. Hearing that Dad was bringing him into the other side surprised me. I wasn't sure Saxon had it in him.

"Okay." Irritated, I hung up and turned back to figure out how in the hell I was going to explain this to Gypsi and get her to hand over her phone number.

But I didn't get a chance to figure it out.
She was gone.

COMING JULY 30, 2023

ACKNOWLEDGMENTS

Those who I couldn't have done this without:

Britt is always the first I mention because he makes it possible for me to close myself away and write for endless hours a day. Without him, I wouldn't get any sleep, and I doubt I could finish a book.

Emerson, for dealing with the fact that I must write some days and she can't have my full attention. I'll admit, there were several times she did not understand, and I might have told my six-year-old, "You're not making it in my acknowledgments this time!" to which she did not care.

My older children, who live in other states, were great about me not being able to answer their calls most of the time and waiting until I could get back to them. They still love me and understand this part of Mom's world.

My editor, Jovana Shirley at Unforeseen Editing, for always working with my crazy schedules and making my stories the best they can be.

My formatter, Melissa Stevens at The Illustrated Author. She makes my books beautiful inside. It's hands down the best formatting I've ever had in my books.

Beta readers, who come through every time: Annabelle Glines, Jerilyn Martinez, and Vicci Kaighan. I love y'all!

Damonza, for my book cover. The book covers just seem to be getting better!

Abbi's Army, for being my support and cheering me on. I love y'all!

My readers, for allowing me to write books. Without you, this wouldn't be possible.

Printed in Great Britain
by Amazon